BETTER ENDINGS

THE TAMMY MELLOWS SERIES - BOOK TWO

TINA HOGAN GRANT

Edited by Pink Proof

Cover Design by T.E.Black Designs – http://www.teblackdesigns.com

Visit The Author's Website

www.tinahogangrant.com

❀ Created with Vellum

To my husband Gordon
& my son Mark
You are my Better Endings

PROLOGUE

At the tender age of seventeen, Tammy left England and moved to the States, leaving behind her mother and her other older sister Jenny. Her main objective was to find her older sister Donna—Jenny's twin—who, at the time, had been missing for three years. But Tammy's own poor choices led to a troubled life, full of turmoil and frustrations that kept getting in her way.

First, there was her secret affair with Raymond, a man twice her age and a good friend of her father's. After becoming pregnant by him, she revealed her affair to her father, shattering the friendship the two men shared and almost destroying her own. She ended up losing the baby and soon after, the relationship with Raymond dissolved.

She then went on to meet Steven, but it turned out he carried a dark secret. She discovered while pregnant with his child that he was a drug dealer and heroin addict. Determined to be a family and for her son to have a father, she remained with him, even while he continued to beat and steal from her. She tried relentlessly to change him, to give him a chance to be a father, but her efforts were to no avail. The drugs and his lifestyle consumed him.

After years of living in despair and fearing for the safety of herself and Matt, she finally plucked up the courage to leave him. But not without the help of many friends from work and by going into hiding for two months.

Her best friend Judy, whom she had met during this time, was also going through similar troubles with her husband. He too was a drug addict and was always in and out of jail, leaving Judy to raise their two young children, Kate and Christopher, alone. Kate was now eight and Christopher was close to Matt's age. Judy's relationship with her husband ended when he hit her for the first time, and Judy made sure it was the last time by leaving him.

Together, Tammy and Judy finally managed to rent a two-bedroom house in the outskirts of Los Angeles. It gave their children the home they deserved, but it also gave both women the support they needed.

Life was beginning to look good, until Steven somehow managed to find her—she has no idea how he did, even up to this day. Armed with a gun and high on heroin, he attempted to break into her home during the late hours of the evening, only to be confronted and knocked out by Judy.

The police were called and he spent eight years in jail for numerous charges, including armed robbery and being under the influence of a narcotic drug.

She doubted she would ever see him again.

During her troubled times, Tammy's sister Donna was found in an alley in Boston, beaten and left to die by her pimp. Once recovered from her injuries, their father bought her a plane ticket to California, where she lived with Tammy until she met Jason and eventually moved in with him. Jason was good for Donna and treated her like a queen, taking care of her every need. She never had to work. Jason owned his own business as a tree trimmer and provided enough for the both of them. For Donna, life was finally good. Not only had she found a good man but also her baby sister.

When Donna moved in with Jason, she didn't go far, just an hour away to Whittier. Jason had inherited his four-bedroom, three-bath house after his father's death and owned it free and clear. Bills were light and money was plentiful for the two of them.

After supporting each other through their troubled times, Tammy and Donna nourished their rekindled sisterhood and visited each other frequently. Donna had also bonded with her new-found nephew Matt and once in a while went over to babysit him.

Tammy's mother Rose remained in England close to Jenny, which comforted Tammy, knowing her mother was not alone. After the divorce from Tammy's father John, Rose dated other men for a while but never remarried. Her mother was content being on her own and in the comfort of her little flat, twenty minutes from Jenny.

John kept his promise and had flown Rose out to the States every year for the past four years to visit Tammy and Matt. Tammy wanted to make sure her mother got to do what every grandmother should do while visiting their grandson in California, including visits to Disneyland, Knottsberry Farm, LA Zoo and of course the beaches. She saved hard before her mother's visits by picking up extra shifts at work. But, sadly, her other older sister and Donna's twin Jenny were now estranged.

Because Jenny was on her honeymoon when Tammy left England, neither had gotten to say goodbye and it scarred their relationship beyond recovery. Tammy couldn't afford to buy plane tickets for her and Matt on her waitress salary or take any time off from work to go visit. Likewise, Jenny had no desire to visit the States, so they had grown apart. They kept in touch with the occasional letters, giving updates on their lives and sharing photos. Jenny was still married to her high school sweetheart and now had two children, a boy and a girl, but it seemed Tammy had gained one sister and lost another. Tammy had told herself since arriving in the States, one day she would make it back to England and rekindle her relationship with Jenny.

Even though it was hard being a single mother and raising Matt on her own, she wouldn't have it any other way. No one was going to dictate her life or put her and Matt's life in jeopardy ever again.

To make ends meet, she worked long hours at the restaurant, sometimes picking up extra shifts when others called in sick. She felt guilty leaving Matt in the care of Judy or the daycare center for many hours a day, but she justified it by reminding herself that the reason she worked so much was so she could be a good provider for Matt and give him a good home and maybe one day meet someone that could be a good father to him. Something he'd never had for the first four years of his life.

Thankfully, Tammy's future was beginning to look a little brighter. But this wouldn't be a story about Tammy without some more drama to cope with along the way.

CHAPTER 1

ammy tried to open her eyes, but the bright lights from above forced her to quickly close them again. She tried once more, allowing her eyes to adjust slowly to the piercing lights. She could only manage a squint. *Where am I?*

Then she felt the excruciating pain coming from her head. Wanting to rub it and relieve some of the discomfort she was experiencing, she tried to reach up with her right hand but discovered she couldn't move her arm. Something was holding it back. She only heard metal banging against metal every time she tried to move it. Without turning her head, she managed to look down in the direction of her hand and saw with disbelief that she was handcuffed to the rail of the bed.

"What the fuck?" she whispered out loud.

The repetitive beeping noise from her left distracted her thoughts. Even in pain, she managed to turn her head slowly in the direction of the annoying sound. With her eyes now fully adjusted to the lights, she saw she was hooked up to a monitor and an IV.

She scanned the room and saw an empty bed on her right, which was next to a large picture window with the shades drawn.

On the wall facing her was a television mounted up high. To the left of the TV was a door, which Tammy assumed led to a bathroom, and the other door in the room probably led to the way out.

I'm in a frigging hospital. What the hell happened? She scanned the room again. *How long have I been here?*

Confused and in a state of panic, she yelled, "Hello! Hello! Anyone hear me?"

Suddenly, the door opened, and an officer of the law appeared.

"Who are you? And where am I?" Tammy lifted her cuffed hand. "And why am I handcuffed?" she asked, still in a state of confusion.

The officer remained by the door. "You've been in a car accident. I need you to remain calm, until a nurse arrives to check you out," he said, using his tone of authority.

"But why the handcuffs? My head is killing me." She leaned her head back in the pillow, distraught. "What the hell happened?"

"I'll explain everything to you in just a moment." The officer peeked his head outside the door. "Here she comes now," he said, sounding relieved. "I'm going to leave you alone with her. I will be right outside the door."

Once he had left, Tammy's head went into a tailspin. *Car accident? Was anyone killed? God, why can't I remember?*

While deep in thought, the door opened again. This time it was the nurse with a clipboard in her hand. She was an older lady, skinny, and probably in her late forties. She had dark chestnut hair tied in a ponytail, and she gave Tammy a small smile as she approached the bed.

"Hi, welcome back. You've been out for a while." She stood by Tammy's side. "How are you feeling?"

"I am so confused. I remember nothing." Tammy strained to keep her head up. "My head is killing me, I'm handcuffed to this damn bed, and no one is telling me anything. How would you feel?" she replied sarcastically.

"All's I can tell you, is that you came in late last night with severe head injuries after being in a car accident." She turned to look at the monitor. "Your vitals look good." She looked down at the chart in her hand. "It says here that you had eleven stitches across your forehead, which is now bandaged. No broken bones and no internal injuries. I don't think you'll be here too much longer." She finished with another comforting smile.

Tammy tried her hardest to remember the night before. "Hey, what's today's date?" she asked.

"January first. Not exactly a great way to start out 1990 now, is it?" the nurse joked, followed by a chuckle.

"It was my birthday last night. New Year's Eve. Oh my god! That's right, I went out with some friends." Tammy closed her eyes, trying desperately to remember the night before. "We went to...oh, god, I don't remember. We went to a few places and drank all night." She cracked a laugh. "Well, I'll never forget my twenty-fifth birthday, that's for sure." Ignoring the pain in her neck, her body stiffened and her eyes grew wide. "Oh, shit! My son! I never went home." She looked over at the nurse, fear consuming her face. "My roommate Judy must be worried sick! I have to call her! She's watching my son."

The nurse tried to calm her. "I'm sure we can arrange for you to call her after the officer has spoken to you. I'm going to call him in now, and then I'll leave you two alone." She patted Tammy's free hand. "I'll see what we can do about that phone call, okay?" The nurse made her way to the door and opened it enough to call through, "Officer, you can come in now." Opening the door for the officer to enter, she stepped outside and closed the door behind her.

Tammy had a horrific thought and wasted no time asking, "Am I going to jail?" She didn't wait for his answer; she had to explain why she couldn't. "I can't. I have a son at home with my babysitter. He's only four," she pleaded.

The officer ignored her question and approached the bed with a stern look. Chilled by his presence, Tammy cowered back against her pillow.

He gave her a speech, in a manner like a father would give to a child. "You are a very lucky young lady. Do you realize you could have killed yourself?" Tammy nodded. "I'm surprised you don't have any more serious injuries," the officer added.

Tammy didn't want a lecture. She needed answers. "Can you please tell me what happened?" She paused and softened her tone. "Am I going to jail?" she asked again.

The officer continued in a stiff voice. "It seems you attempted to drive a vehicle last night while under the influence of alcohol. You apparently blacked out at the wheel and in the process hit five parked cars. When we received the call, you were found unconscious, stooped over the steering wheel with a large abrasion across your head. You were brought here by ambulance, where a blood sample was taken to measure your blood alcohol level. The results showed it to be 0.11, which is above the legal limit of 0.08. Therefore, you are in our custody for driving while intoxicated. Which is why you are handcuffed to the bed."

Tammy listened in disbelief. "Oh my god! I fucked up big time." She wanted the officer to believe her and tried to sound sincere when she spoke. "I honestly thought I was okay to drive, Officer."

He released a slight chuckle—the first facial expression since he had entered the room. "Everyone does, ma'am," the officer told her.

Tammy dreaded asking the next question, but she needed to know. "Can you tell me if anybody else was hurt?" She took in a deep breath. "I didn't kill anyone, did I? Oh, god, please tell me I didn't. I couldn't live with myself if I did."

The officer delayed his answer for a few seconds, letting her stew over the possibility. "Luckily, no one else was hurt. Just yourself."

Tammy held her hand up to her racing heart while briefly closing her eyes. "Oh, thank god," she gasped.

"And, like I said, you're very lucky to be here." He waited for Tammy to compose herself after hearing she hadn't killed anyone before continuing with his report. "Your car is totaled and has been impounded. They had to use the Jaws of Life to remove you from your vehicle, and I'm here to serve you a DUI." He paused for a moment and pulled out a yellow piece of paper from the top pocket of his shirt. "While you've been here, we ran a report on you. You have no priors or outstanding warrants. It seems this is your first offense."

Tammy spoke quickly. "Yes, it is. I've never been in trouble before."

"Because you've had no priors, we are releasing you on your own recognizance."

Tammy let out a huge sigh of relief, knowing she wasn't going to jail. "But," the officer stated, "you have to appear for your arraignment in two days at the court specified on this ticket I'm giving you to sign. If you don't appear, a warrant will be issued for your arrest."

"Oh, I'll be there. I promise," Tammy said eagerly.

"Okay then, before I remove the handcuffs, do you have any questions?"

"Will I be able to drive again?"

"The courts will explain everything to you. Being a first offense, they will probably suspend your license. But get another DUI and they won't be so lenient, and you will go to jail. I can promise you that."

"Oh, Officer, I've learnt my lesson. I'll never get behind the wheel drunk again. I promise."

"That's good to hear. Now I'm going to remove the cuffs and I'll need you to sign this citation."

"Okay."

Tammy watched as the officer walked to the right side of the bed and freed her wrist from the cuffs. Feeling relieved, she rubbed her now stiff, tired arm with her other hand.

"Thanks."

"No problem," he said while reaching into his top pocket for a pen. He turned and slid the bed tray in front of her and laid the ticket and pen down. "Here you go. Once this is signed, I'm all done here and the nurse will be in shortly to advise you on when they will be releasing you."

Tammy took the pen, and without reading the citation, signed her name. "Thank you, Officer. I promise you it won't happen again."

The officer took the pen, placed it back in his pocket, removed a copy of the citation and gave it to her while holding onto his copy. "I hope not. You have a good day now." He paused and smiled. "Oh, and happy new year."

Tammy chuckled. "Thanks. You too," she replied as she watched him walk out of the room, leaving her with her own thoughts.

She remembered nothing about the accident. She vaguely remembered getting in her car after saying good night to her friend Hailey, a friend from work. Judy, her roommate and best friend, had offered to babysit so she could enjoy her birthday. Hailey was also a single mother and wanted to take Tammy out after work.

Tammy thought of her son. What a terrible mother she was. Poor Matt must be wondering where Mommy was. Not to mention Judy. God, she fucked up this time. She needed to call home and apologize to Judy.

While deep in thought, the same nurse entered the room. "How are you feeling? I hear you've been released from custody. You're a very lucky lady you know."

"Yeah. I know. The cop told me the same thing."

The nurse walked to the side of the bed and checked the vital machine.

"I can't believe how stupid I've been. I'm a mother. I'm not supposed to be acting this way. I feel like such a failure to my son," Tammy confessed.

"I'm sure he's fine. You can use the phone next to the bed to call home. Just dial nine for an outside line then dial the number. I'll be back in a few minutes."

"Thank you! Oh, wait, what hospital am I in?"

"Huntington Memorial in Arcadia."

"Okay, thanks."

Before the nurse had left the room, Tammy already had the phone in her hand and was dialing home. After three rings, she heard Judy's voice on the other end.

"Hello?" she heard Judy say.

"Judy, it's Tammy."

"Tammy! I've been worried sick about you. Are you okay? Where are you?"

"I was in a car accident last night. I'm so sorry. I feel terrible."

"Oh my god! Are you okay?"

"Yeah, I'll be fine. I totaled my car though. I don't remember anything, and I woke up to find I was handcuffed to the bed."

"Handcuffed?"

"I'll tell you everything when I get home. Is Matt okay? God, I'm a terrible mother."

"No, you're not," Judy said in a harsh tone. "Don't you say that. He's fine. Do you need me to come get you?"

"I haven't been released yet. But I'm sure I will be soon. If you can, that would be great. I'm so sorry." Tammy paused to remember the name of the hospital. "I'm at Huntington Memorial. Thanks, Judy, I owe you one."

"Don't you worry about it. Matt loves going for car rides." Judy laughed. "I'll see you soon."

CHAPTER 2

*T*ammy was released from the hospital a few hours later. Not wanting to let go of her son, she opted to ride in the back seat with him for the journey home.

Having to explain to him why Mommy had a bandage on her head was difficult, but she explained as best she could. *"Mommy had a car accident, and they had to say goodbye to the car because, like Mommy, it got hurt and couldn't be fixed."*

Now, because of her stupidity, Tammy found herself without a car. Thank god Judy had one.

Over the next few days, remorse began to sink in. Tammy appeared for her arraignment before the judge and was ordered to attend twelve AA meetings. Her license was to be suspended for thirty days and she would have to pay a $1,500.00 fine.

Surprisingly, none of the owners of the cars that she'd hit threatened to sue her. They were all simply relieved she was going to be okay and told her their insurance would take care of any damage.

She could handle the court orders from the courts, but the $1500.00 fine worried her. She had no idea how she was going to come up with that kind of money. The judged gave her the option to do community service, but she couldn't afford to take the time off work so the judge gave her three months to pay the fine instead.

Feeling like a failure was taking its toll. She was a single mother and now, because she had chosen to be reckless and irresponsible, she found herself with no transportation for her and her son. She was back to taking the bus everywhere or hitching rides from Judy until she figured out how to buy another car, which probably wouldn't be until she got her tax refund in April—another four months away.

Tammy knew it was time to quit drinking. It was slowly destroying her life. Since Steven, the father of her child, had attempted to break into her home three years ago, alcohol had become her companion and her escape from the everyday stress of raising a child alone.

She knew she was sliding down a destructive path. She drank almost every night after work with Judy and was a regular at the British pub across the road from her job. She had been through a lot since arriving in the States from England over seven years ago, but that was no excuse to drink.

CHAPTER 3

Tammy had no desire to start dating anytime soon. She was enjoying every free moment she had with the only man she wanted in her life: her four-year-old son Matt.

For the next four months after the accident, Tammy struggled with not having a car. She couldn't rely on Judy all the time, and hustling with a child just to get groceries was taking its toll. What used to be an effortless chore with a vehicle, sometimes took hours. From waiting for the bus, walking to the store from the bus stop, doing the actual shopping and carting the groceries back to the bus stop and from there lugging them home with a child in tow, there was no longer any such thing as a quick run to the store. It was something she had to make time for and plan in her day.

Getting to work was also a hassle. She had to leave an hour earlier just to get there in time, and if Judy couldn't watch Matt, she had to leave at least two hours earlier to take Matt to the day care center and from there, take a bus to work. And, of course, she then had to do the same thing all over again on the way home.

. Finally, when April rolled around, Tammy filed her taxes as soon as the state allowed her to and used the entire $2,500 refund to buy a used car in the first week of May. With no other money saved, she returned to the court to ask for an extension on the fine from the accident. To her relief, the judge gave her an extension of eight weeks, telling her to return to court on May 25th.

Busy raising her son and trying to get her life back together, she wasn't looking for love or any kind or a serious relationship. When the time was right or when she felt she was ready, she knew it would find her.

And it did.

A few weeks after buying her car and with life now much less stressful, except for the huge fine hanging over her head, Tammy was working the dinner shift and had just taken an order for a party of five in a corner booth. Satisfied she had all their orders correct, she headed back to the kitchen station to pin the order to the chef's wheel. Halfway across the restaurant, she sensed some-body standing behind her and then felt a light tap on her shoulder.

"Excuse me, miss, may I give you my order?"

Tammy came to a sudden halt. The voice she heard made her knees almost buckle from beneath her. It was deep and assertive. It exuded power, strength and masculinity. As he spoke, she felt his warm breath on the back of her neck. She was afraid to turn around. How would she react if she turned and faced him? Would she be disappointed by what she saw, or would she just melt before him and act flustered and foolish like a high school teen?

"Miss?" she heard again.

She braced herself and slowly turned to face him. She was now staring at all six feet of him, and to her relief, she wasn't disap-pointed. She was greeted with the friendliest smile she had ever seen on a man. It warmed her and welcomed her into his space.

He had shoulder-length blond hair that feathered back away from his face, and she was immediately captivated when she stared into his ocean-blue eyes, finding herself lost in their gaze. And even though his blond moustache was tattered, it suited him. If it had been trimmed and groomed, it wouldn't have looked as good.

The skin on his arms and face was well tanned and rough, telling her that he liked the outdoors. He didn't over dress; in fact, he looked comfortable in his faded Levi jeans and white tee-shirt that enhanced his muscular arms.

Tammy returned the smile, but it was no ordinary smile. It was one of her cuter ones that revealed her dimples just above her cheeks. She wanted to get his attention. She wanted him to be attracted to her, just like she was to him. "Sure, I can take it for you," she said in a flirtatious manner, tossing her red hair back with a subtle swoop of her head.

Her flirting seemed to be working, as he was staring at her with his mouth slightly open. She wondered what he was thinking at that very moment. Did he like what he saw? She followed his eyes as he took in her whole being from her head to her toes, and when he smiled again, she sensed his approval.

"I'm sorry, what?" He had obviously forgotten his original question. "Oh, yes, my order." They both laughed at his forgetfulness, both knowing the reason why. "Yeah, I'm sitting at the counter over there." He pointed. "Can I get a Pepsi and a cheeseburger?"

"Sure, no problem, I'll bring it over when it's ready," she informed him while jotting down his order on her notepad.

But he wasn't ready to end the conversation. "I detect an accent. Where are you from?" he asked.

"England, and you? Where is your accent from?" Tammy said with a hint of sarcasm.

"Me, nah, I don't have an accent. Born and bred right here in California."

"You have an accent to me. It's not English," she replied with a smirk.

He chuckled at her sense of humor. "Got a point there, I must admit." He paused. "I love your accent. It makes you sound very posh."

"Ha! Trust me, I'm far from posh." She threw him a cheeky grin.

He chuckled again at her witty comment. He liked this girl. She had spunk.

As much as she wanted to continue talking to him, she had to get back to work before she got into trouble with the manager. "Well, if you want to eat, I'd best get your order in for you. It shouldn't take too long. Go ahead and have a seat and I'll bring your Pepsi over."

"Great, sounds good."

Tammy watched as he turned and walked toward the counter, admiring how well his jeans fit him. His body was well toned and muscular, and he walked with confidence, holding his head up high with his back straight. "Man is he cute," Tammy whispered to herself before scurrying off to the kitchen to fetch his drink.

She returned a few minutes later with Pepsi in hand and placed it in front of him on the counter. He looked up and smiled at her. "Thanks."

Tammy felt her cheeks blush. "You're welcome." There was a moment of awkward silence while they continued to stare at each other. *Should I stay and try to talk to him or should I go?* She chose to stay for just a moment. "So I've never seen you in here before. Do you live around here?" she asked.

"Nah, I just dropped off my son at his mother's."

"Oh, you have a son?" She couldn't hide the hint of disappointment, assuming this also meant he was married.

"I do. His name is Justin. He lives with his mother, and I visit him on weekends or he comes and stays with me on my boat."

He's separated...yes! "Wow! You have a boat! Impressive. I have a son too," she confessed. And quickly added, "His dad isn't around. It's just me and my boy."

"Really? How old is he?"

"He'll be five in a few months. His name is Matt. How old is your son?" Tammy asked.

"He's seven."

The chef from the kitchen interrupted their conversation.

"Number twenty-six. Order up!"

"Oh, that's mine. I gotta go. I'll bring your food out shortly," Tammy said, even though she wanted to stay and chit-chat with him some more.

"That's fine. I'm not going anywhere." He gave her a suggestive wink as she walked away.

Since being on her own, she hadn't met anyone that she truly wanted to get to know. Yes, she had dated the occasional guy, but they were meaningless relationships and for her just physical. Since her horrific relationship with Steven, she was afraid to let anyone into her world. She had been hurt and lied to and had issues with trust.

But this guy was different. The physical attraction was definitely there, but unlike other guys that had crossed her path, she had a desire to get to know him more. Deep in thought while picking up her order, she turned her head discreetly in his direction and was shocked to find him glancing her way. She blushed and gave him a quick subtle smile before picking up the rest of her order and scurrying off to deliver the meals to a party of four across the restaurant.

Five minutes later, the cute guy's order was up. Feeling a little flustered, she managed to pick up the single plate and headed to the end of the counter where he was sitting. She felt his eyes on her as she approached. Standing before him on the other side of the counter, she gave him one of her best smiles. "Here you go," she said as she placed the plate in front him. "Can I get you anything else?"

He glanced at his plate and then back at her, ignoring her question. "You know, it just occurred to me that I don't even know your name."

"It's Tammy. And you are?"

"I'm Dwayne, and it's a pleasure to meet you, Tammy," he said with an alluring smile.

Tammy tried hard to suppress the butterflies fluttering in her stomach. "Likewise, Dwayne." Feeling more at ease, she rested a hand on the counter, inches from his, and leaned in a little closer. "So, Dwayne, you know what I do for a living. What do you do?"

"I'm a commercial fisherman. I fish for lobsters," he said with a hint of pride.

Tammy was intrigued. She had never met a commercial fisherman before. The thought excited her. "Really? Well, that's something you don't hear in LA every day. I would love to know more." She paused for a moment, not wanting to seem too forward. "I've never been on a boat before. How exciting that must be."

Dwayne threw her a flirtatious smile, catching Tammy off guard. "I think we'll have to do something about that. When's your next day off?" He didn't wait for her to answer. "Come on down and check it out and I'll buy you lunch."

Tammy couldn't hide her enthusiasm. "Wow, that would be awesome. I would love to."

Dwayne chuckled at her excitement before surprising her again. "Hey, when do you get off? I can give you directions to the boat and my phone number. I don't mind sticking around. Maybe we can go play a game of pool or something."

Caught in his web, Tammy beamed a radiant smile. "I would love that." She checked her watch. "I get off in about an hour. That's not too long, is it?" She held her breath, nervously waiting for his answer.

"That's just fine with me. After I've eaten, I'll go grab a paper while I'm waiting."

"Great!" Tammy replied, her feet frozen to the floor. Not wanting to tear herself away, she realized she felt at ease with Dwayne. Something she hadn't felt in a long time, and it felt good. "Well, I guess I should get back to work," she said, disappointment lingering in her voice. "Let me know if I can get you anything."

"I'm good," Dwayne replied, followed by his alluring smile.

Oh, I know you're good. Tammy headed back to the kitchen, thinking this was going to be the longest last hour of work ever.

CHAPTER 4

*T*ammy lost count of the amount of times she checked her watch during the final hour of her shift. Eight o'clock couldn't come fast enough. Sometimes, only five minutes had passed in between checking her watch.

For the rest of her shift, Tammy failed miserably at trying to concentrate on the tasks at hand and put herself on auto pilot as she went about doing what she'd done for years without putting a lot of thought into it—filling the ketchups and condiments, folding napkins, replenishing the salad bar and making fresh coffee.

Periodically, she'd glance over at Dwayne and admire him from afar. Hunched over the counter while reading the paper on the counter, his blond hair cascaded down to his shoulders and his biceps bulged slightly over his bent elbows. She had to quickly look away a few times when he slowly raised his head and looked over in her direction, but she didn't miss him throwing her a warm, sensual smile. Caught off guard and embarrassed that he'd seen her staring, she could only give him a nervous smile before returning to her duties.

When her shift finally came to an end, she pulled off her apron and skipped over to Dwayne. "Hey, I'm all done. I just need to go in the back really quick, grab my things and call my roommate to let her know I'll be home a little later. She's watching my son."

Dwayne raised his head and met her eyes. "No problem. Go right ahead. I'll wait here for you."

"Thanks. I won't be long."

With her heart racing, Tammy scurried off and disappeared behind the swinging kitchen doors. Before retrieving her things from her locker, she decided to call Judy first and headed to the payphone in the lunchroom.

After two rings, Judy came on the line. "Hello?"

"Hey, Judy, it's Tammy. How's my little man?"

"Oh hi, Tammy. He's fine. He just got out of the tub and is now watching a movie with Kate and Christopher. What's up? Are you on your way home?"

Tammy ignored her question. "You're not going to believe this. I've met this amazing guy. He's absolutely gorgeous."

"What! Tell me more. I'm all ears."

"He came in the restaurant a few hours ago and he's still here, waiting to take me out for a game of pool." An excited giggle burst from Tammy's lips. "I can't believe he's waited here this long."

"Wow. Well, you must go. Don't worry about Matt. He's fine. Go have a good time. You can tell me all about it when you come home. Oh, by the way, I'm off tomorrow, so you can tell me about it tomorrow if you end up spending the night with him."

Tammy shrieked into the phone, "Judy! I'll be home tonight. Yes, it might be hard to pull myself away, but I can promise you I'll be home."

"Hmm, I'm not so sure. I've not heard you sound this excited over a guy before. Now go on, don't keep the guy waiting any longer. Love ya."

"Love you too. Hugs to the kids. Bye."

"Bye."

With the night now hers, Tammy hung up the phone and

skipped over to her locker to retrieve her things. After applying a fresh coat of lipstick, a splash of perfume and a quick brush of her hair, she did a quick check in the mirror on her locker door before closing it and throwing her purse over her shoulder. After taking a deep breath, she smiled to herself and headed back out to the restaurant to meet Dwayne.

With butterflies still stirring in her stomach, Tammy approached Dwayne from his side of the counter. The scent of his masculine musk cologne captured her attention as she stood beside him, her arms folded nervously in front of her. "Hey, I'm all set. Ready to go?"

Dwayne looked up from where he sat and beamed her a smile that melted her heart. "I sure am. Now where's there a good place to play pool?"

"Actually, there's an English pub right across the street. They have a couple of pool tables. We can walk there."

Dwayne nodded his approval and slid himself off his stool. "Sounds good. Lead the way."

Tammy led him through the restaurant toward the main entrance, staying a couple of footsteps ahead of him. As she passed the hostess station, Paul, her manager who had helped her through the dark times with Steven and was now somewhat protective of her, raised his head from the cash register. "Night, Tammy. See you tomorrow. Where are you off to?"

When Tammy paused at the station where Paul stood, Dwayne came to a standstill next to her. "Oh, I'm off to play some pool with Dwayne." Tammy turned and rested her hand on Dwayne's shoulder. "Paul, this is Dwayne." Tammy swayed her arm between them while introducing them. "Dwayne, this is my boss Paul."

Both men nodded their heads and shook hands before Tammy scurried Dwayne out of the restaurant. "See you tomorrow, Paul."

Once outside, Tammy checked her watch. "It's only a little after eight and a week day. The pub shouldn't be too crowded. Sometimes on weekends you have to wait over an hour for a pool table to open up."

"I guess you're a regular." Dwayne chuckled.

"It's the closest place from work. I sometimes come here with my co-workers after my shift." Tammy turned to face Dwayne. "Not every night, I might add," she said with a cocky grin, not wanting to reveal that she was a regular.

Dwayne raised his hands in a joking manner. "Hey, I'm not judging. So where's this pub? I don't think I've ever been inside an English pub before."

"Oh, you're in for a treat." In a mad dash before any cars came around the corner, Tammy grabbed his hand. "Come on, follow me." Halfway across the road, it hit her that she had made the first move by taking his hand. His strong fingers felt good wrapped around hers; his palms felt rough and his grip was strong. Tammy squeezed his hand a little tighter as they approached the other side of the road, and to her delight, he tightened his hold in return. Tammy pointed to the left. "It's right over here."

Dwayne followed her finger and saw the green and black sign of "The Tudor Pub" illuminated by two floodlights.

Still holding hands, with Tammy leading the way through the heavy black door, they entered the pub.

They were immediately greeted by a middle-aged man wearing a long white bar apron and rolled up green shirt sleeves. "Hi ya, Tammy," he said with a thick British accent.

Feeling embarrassed that the bartender knew her name, Tammy shied away from his stare. "Oh hi, Mike," she replied while quickly scanning the bar for a table across the room.

As she had predicted, the pub wasn't busy. Better yet, she didn't see any of her regular drinking buddies present. Tammy glanced around the room and led them over to a quiet table in the corner next to the two empty pool tables.

"Not a regular, eh?" Dwayne said with a hint of sarcasm.

"I told you I come here sometimes," Tammy replied in a defensive tone.

When they reached the table, she was surprised when Dwayne pulled out a chair for her. "Wow, a gentleman too," she said with a pleasing smile while taking a seat.

Dwayne laughed. "Must be one of my good days."

Tammy chuckled at his joke and then scanned the bar again. A couple sat across the room, holding hands and whispering to each other; three single guys stood at the bar, and over at the juke box stood a young lady, holding a glass of wine while debating which tune she should play next.

Still standing, Dwayne looked down and met Tammy's eyes. "I should get us a
couple of drinks. What are you having?"

"You know, if you've never been in an English pub, I bet you've never had Guinness. Want to try one?"

"Oh, I don't drink. I'm going to have a Pepsi."

Tammy's jaw dropped. "You don't drink? Wow! That's a first. I don't think I've ever met anyone that didn't drink before."

Dwayne let out another chuckle. "Yeah, I tend to get the same reaction whenever I mention it. What shall I get you?"

Feeling somewhat flabbergasted, along with a tinge of uneasiness, Tammy felt she had to ask. "Do you mind if I have a beer?"

"No not all. Draft okay?"

"Sure, that's fine. Thanks."

As he headed to the bar, Tammy's eyes followed him, admiring his rear end that fit so well in his jeans. Then she watched as he perched one foot up on the brass foot rail and rested his elbows on the surface of the bar. Tammy moistened her lips with her tongue, watching his jeans grow tighter as he leaned in to give the bartender his order. "Damn, he's cute," Tammy mumbled to herself. Feeling her attraction intensifying by the minute, she shook her head to compose herself and fumbled in her purse for a cigarette.

She had managed to quit smoking while pregnant with her son and for a year after his birth. But she fell into the nicotine trap again three years ago.

After pulling almost everything out of her purse and setting the contents on the table, she finally located her pack of Marlboro lights at the bottom. With a sigh of relief, she pulled out a lighter and hastily took a cigarette out of the pack and lit it. She took a long drag and enjoyed the instant satisfaction it provided. Still holding the cigarette in her mouth, Tammy quickly tossed the contents of her purse back into her bag before Dwayne returned.

With just a few seconds to spare, she took another hit of her cigarette and sat back to enjoy watching Dwayne striding back to the table with their drinks.

"Here you go," Dwayne said while setting their drinks in the center of the table and taking a seat.

"Thanks. Do you want a cigarette?" Tammy asked while picking up the pack.

Dwayne picked up his can of Pepsi and took a sip. "No thanks. I don't smoke."

For the first time, Tammy became self-conscious and slightly embarrassed by her habits and hastily slid the pack of cigarettes back to her side of the table. "Oh, I'm sorry. Will it bother you if I smoke?"

"No, not all at. Go right ahead. I used to smoke, but I quit about two years ago. Hardest thing I've ever done."

"I know what you mean. I quit a few years back when I was pregnant with my son. Now look at me. I'm back at it." Tammy laughed before taking another hit. "So why'd you quit drinking?"

"Oh. I'd had enough to last me a lifetime by the time I was twenty-four," he said. "Can't believe I lived through it. That was almost eleven years ago."

"You're thirty-five?"

"Yep. Does that bother you?"

Tammy shook her head. "No, no," she quickly replied, realizing he was ten years older than her.

"So tell me about the fishing. I've never met a fisherman before. In fact, I've never been on a boat." She laughed. "What a way to make a living. It must be awesome."

"It can be at times, but it's a lot of hard work. Labor intensive. I grew up around boats. My dad sold yachts for a living and owned a couple of boats himself. It's in my blood."

Tammy wanted to know more. She found herself fascinated by the whole fishing thing. "I want to see it all," she said with a huge grin, her eyes beaming with enthusiasm. "I want to see your boat, the ocean, and I want to know everything there is to know about fishing. Will you show me?"

"Sure, but it's not as glamorous as it sounds." He leaned in closer, his elbows resting on the table. "How about you come down this weekend? You and your son. I'll take you both for a boat ride."

"Really? That would be awesome! I can't wait." Tammy reached over and squeezed his knee. "Thank you!"

"Don't thank me yet. You might hate it."

Suddenly, the song *Every Breath You Take* by The Police blasted from the jukebox. It seemed the woman had finally made her choice. Tammy began to tap her fingers on the table to the beat of the music. To make sure he was heard, Dwayne leaned in closer, his lips almost brushing Tammy's ear. This caused Tammy to flush as she felt his warm breath tickling the side of her face.

"So how good of a pool player are you?" he asked.

"Oh, you have nothing to worry about. I'm sure I won't be much of a challenge for you."

Dwayne scooted his chair back, stood up, squeezed his hand into his front pocket and pulled out a handful of change. "Let's find out," he said, retrieving two quarters and returning the rest of the change to his pocket.

"Okay." Tammy smiled and followed him over to the pool table.

She watched with admiration as Dwayne picked out two cues and handed her one. "Thanks."

Standing off to the side, Tammy allowed Dwayne to set up the table. While holding her cue and swaying her body to the beat of the music, she watched and admired him as he slowly took one hand and ran it through his long blond hair before bending down to insert the change into the coin slots. Tammy took a deep breath; she liked what she saw. Dwayne excited her.

The sudden clatter of the balls dropping snapped Tammy out of her thoughts, but she continued to watch closely as she waited for Dwayne to set up the game.

During what turned out to be four games, two of which Tammy won but with suspicions that Dwayne let her, Tammy found herself milking her beer. Having never been around someone that didn't drink before, she suddenly found herself conscious of how much she was drinking. After playing pool for a few hours, she realized she could have easily had five beers instead of just the one. Even at this early stage, she could tell Dwayne was good for her. It was the same with the cigarettes. She found herself not wanting to smoke in front of him and dismissed the urge each time it crept up.

The chemistry between them couldn't be denied. Her heart often skipped a beat when he brushed against her, and he always smiled before taking his position for his next shot. She returned the favor by sliding by him, allowing her breasts to gently glide across his chest, and she noticed he didn't move back. As their bodies touched for that slight moment, Tammy paused and met his eyes. She felt at such ease with Dwayne.

When they returned to their seats, Tammy glanced at her watch and was saddened to see it was almost midnight. Not wanting the night to end, she frowned and turned to Dwayne, who she noticed had slid his chair next to hers.

"I'm really sorry, but I have to go."

Dwayne reached over and squeezed her thigh. "I was afraid you were going to say that."

She grabbed his hand and added, "I don't want to. But I must."

He leaned in to meet her gaze, leaving just inches between their lips. "I know. I feel the same way. I'm having such a good time with you."

"Me too." She attempted a cute smile.

Mesmerized by his eyes, she found herself lost in his stare and welcomed the flushes of heat she was feeling. While still holding her hand, he lifted his other hand and gently brushed the side of her cheek. Tammy closed her eyes and breathed in heavily. She felt his warm breath on her lips, telling her he was close. Seconds later, he placed his lips softly upon hers. With the warm sensation from his kiss, followed by the tickling of his blond moustache, Tammy could do nothing but surrender and kiss him back.

While still locked in a kiss, Dwayne cupped his hands around Tammy's neck and pulled her in close. As the passion of the kiss intensified, both became oblivious to the rest of the world. The kiss was everything Tammy had hoped for—passionate and sensual. When they finally broke free, she was left with the desire of wanting more.

"Wow!" was all she managed to say while catching her breath.

"My sentiments exactly," Dwayne said while rubbing her thigh. "Come on, I'll walk you to your car."

Reluctantly, Tammy rose from her seat, grabbed her purse and took Dwayne's hand.

They walked back to her car arm in arm, their bodies close, holding each other tight, neither wanting to let go. Tammy felt safe with him and more importantly, she felt she could trust him. Something she'd not been able to do since breaking up with Steven.

When they reached her car, Tammy stalled before opening the door. Instead, she leaned her back against it and pulled Dwayne in closer. Dwayne smiled and pressed his body against hers, pinning her to the car with his hands wrapped around her waist. Tammy let her purse fall to the ground from her shoulder and locked her hands around his neck. She pulled his lips to hers, where they met in another passionate kiss

This time, the kiss was longer and harder as they explored each other's mouths with their tongues. While savoring the taste of her lips and his heart now beating like a hammer, Dwayne slid his hand down over Tammy's shirt until it rested over one of her breasts. Tammy had to break away from the kiss for a second, gasping from his touch. When she returned to the kiss, Dwayne cupped her breasts and squeezed her now protruding nipples before massaging them deeply with his palms.

Panting, Tammy had to break away from the kiss again. As turned on as she was, and as much as she wanted Dwayne, she didn't want to have sex in her car, especially not with it sitting in the middle of the parking lot. "Fuck! What are you doing to me? I'd better go," she said, her chest still heaving with desire.

Dwayne rearranged the pronounced bulge in his jeans and let out a cocky laugh. "What are you doing to me, more like? I stop in a restaurant for a bite to eat, and yet I'm still here hours later."

Tammy tossed her head back and laughed. "And I was supposed to be home hours ago." She gave her hair a good shake and tried to run her fingers through it. "Will I see you again?" she asked.

"Only if you'll let me," he replied. "Besides, you want to see my boat, don't you?"

"I do, yes."

Dwayne reached into his back pocket and pulled out a black wallet, from which he took a business card and handed it to her. "Here's my pager number. I don't have a phone on the boat. You can call and leave a message when you want to come down and I'll call you right back and give you directions."

"Great. I can't wait. Is this weekend good?" Tammy asked, not wasting any time.

Dwayne laughed at her enthusiasm. "Yes, it is. Now, before I have my way with you, I best let you go."

"If we weren't in a parking lot, I'd probably let you." She failed to hide her devilish grin.

Dwayne smacked her playfully on the butt. "Come on, get in the car. You're killing me here. I'll see you this weekend."

Tammy turned and opened the driver's door. "Okay. I'm going, I'm going." She giggled as she jumped in and started up the engine. Winding down the window, she leaned her head out to meet Dwayne in another kiss. In a failed attempt to release herself from him, she squeezed out her words with his lips still on hers. "Okay, I'm backing up now."

She put the car in reverse and eased onto the gas.

Dwayne didn't let go and instead walked with the car, still kissing her as Tammy slowly backed out of her parking space. Tammy muffled a giggle and with force, unlocked her lips from his. "Okay. I'm gone." She beamed him a bright smile. "I'll see you this weekend!"

Dwayne patted the top of her car. "I can't wait. Drive safe."

"I will. Bye for now."

As she put the car in drive and began to inch forward, she blew him a kiss and waved to him in the rearview mirror. Her head had been in a tailspin since their first kiss, and her heart was beating like a drum so much she couldn't calm it down. She'd forgotten how it felt to be totally smitten. It had been a long time, and now she couldn't wait to get home and tell Judy all about it over a glass of wine.

CHAPTER 5

*J*udy was anxious to hear all about the new guy Tammy
had met. She didn't want to wait until the morning to
hear all the juicy details so had decided to stay up and
wait for her. She knew she'd be sorry in the morning, having to
work the breakfast shift, but this was big news. It would be
worth it.

It reminded Judy of the time she'd met her boyfriend Joel, just
over a year ago. She too had met Joel at work and, like Tammy, she
couldn't wait to get home and tell her best friend the news. They
shared everything, and she knew how excited Tammy was feeling.
It was the first time Judy had heard Tammy being overly excited
about a guy since they had decided to join forces over three year
ago and raise their kids together. Judy knew Tammy deserved this.

After Steven, Tammy had become gun-shy about settling down
with anyone, but from the moment Tammy burst back through the
door to their home, Judy could tell Dwayne was different. There
was a sparkle in Tammy's eyes that she hadn't seen before.

Tammy sat next to her on the couch while nursing a glass of

white wine. "I'm falling for him really fast," Tammy said before even taking a sip of her drink. "I need to slow down. I've just met him. But he seems so perfect." Tammy turned to face Judy with wide eyes. "You know he doesn't drink or smoke?"

Judy's jaw dropped. "What! You're kidding me."

"Nope, I'm not kidding. I've never met anyone that didn't drink. Non-smoker, yes, but not non-drinker. What are we supposed to do for fun?" Tammy allowed her body to flop back against the couch. "Every time I've gone out with a guy, we've always gone to the bar for drinks. I honestly have no idea what else to do."

"Damn, Tammy. Me neither. It's what Joel and I always do unless we're here at the house with the kids. Even then, we have a bottle of wine going." She snickered while nudging Tammy's elbow.

"This is all new to me. You know, when we were at the pub tonight, I was so self-conscious of my drinking and smoking. I didn't really notice before Dwayne came along how much I would normally drink. I could easily have had four or five beers, but tonight I had just the one. The same with the cigarettes. Maybe I should think about quitting?"

Judy let out a loud, cocky laugh. "Yeah, right. You, quit drinking? Who are you kidding? You almost killed yourself in a car accident from being drunk and you're still drinking. I don't think some guy who happens not to drink is going to make you quit anytime soon."

Tammy listened to Judy's words carefully. Even though she said them in a friendly manner, she knew she was right. She HAD almost killed herself and was still drinking. But before meeting Dwayne, she really hadn't thought about it. Maybe Dwayne was what she needed in her life.

Her court date was coming up the following week and Tammy already knew she wouldn't have the money for the fine. Yet again, she was going to have to plead with the judge for another extension. But Tammy didn't want to think about that right now so brushed it aside. Her thoughts were all about the upcoming weekend, when she would finally see Dwayne again and he would get to meet Matt for the first time.

The next three days couldn't go by fast enough. Consumed daily with thoughts of Dwayne, Tammy desperately wanted the week to end. There were many times she wanted to call him, but she refused the urge because she didn't want to seem like she was coming on too strong.

Finally, when Friday rolled around, she waited until she was home in the afternoon and had fed Matt before dialing his beeper number. After hearing the two beeps, Tammy entered her phone number and hung up. Clasping her hands together, she stared at the phone, waiting anxiously for it to ring. After what began to feel like an eternity of silence, Tammy started having terrifying thoughts. *What if he doesn't call me back? What if I never see him again?*

As the minutes ticked by, Tammy started to convince herself that there was a possibility he may never call back.

A pain-staking two hours passed by with no call. Tammy tried to stay positive and keep busy by entertaining Matt outside. Of course, she left the front door open so she could hear the phone if it were to ring. With her ears and mind focused elsewhere, she halfheartedly played catch with Matt.

And then she heard that joyous sound—the ring tone of the phone. In a rush to reach it in time, Tammy grabbed Matt's hand and pulled him along behind her. "Come on, buddy, let's go inside. The phone's ringing."

She slammed the door closed and raced across the room to get to the phone.

She took a second to catch her breath before picking up the receiver. "Hello?"

"Hey, Tammy, it's Dwayne. Sorry I didn't get back to you right away. I was out working on a boat and there wasn't a phone booth close by."

Tammy closed her eyes and heaved a huge sigh of relief, warmed by the sound of his voice. "That's okay," she said, trying to calm the butterflies churning in her stomach. "I just called to see about coming down tomorrow."

"Oh, you bet," Dwayne almost screeched. "I've been looking forward to it all week. I've missed you."

"Really?" His confession took her by surprise.

"Yes. Really. What, you haven't missed me?"

Tammy hugged the phone. "Yes, I have actually."

With their feelings clearly mutual, Dwayne gave Tammy directions to the boat yard where his boat was docked, and they made plans to meet at ten the next morning. After ending the call, Tammy carefully folded the piece of paper and tucked it securely in her purse.

~

Having already packed everything for her weekend getaway the night before, she was up bright and early the following morning. She'd picked out a denim mini-skirt and a blue tank-top to wear. After hugging Judy goodbye and giving Kate and Christopher a peck on the cheek, she headed out the door to put Matt in his car seat.

Heading south, she took the 110 freeway to the 10 freeway, west onto the 405-freeway and finally the 90 freeway, which took her into the heart of the marina. Being a weekend, the traffic was light and the drive took just over an hour. In less than a couple of minutes of pulling off the freeway, she turned into the parking lot of the Anchors Boatyard.

She smiled to herself when she saw Dwayne standing by the main gate, dressed casually in tanned shorts, a white tee-shirt and loafers. His perfectly tanned arms and legs glowed against the light colors of his clothes.

"Damn, he's fine," Tammy mumbled under her breath.

Dwayne, upon seeing Tammy pull in, beamed her a smile and waved, and then he wasted no time in rushing over to the car to open her door and greet her.

"You made it," he said with another heart-warming smile as he reached out his hand.

Tammy took his hand and stepped out of the car. "I did." She smiled when she noticed a slight ocean breeze combing through her hair.

Still holding her hand, Dwayne gazed into her eyes, leaned in and kissed her. With his warm breath coating her mouth, Tammy closed her eyes and kissed him back with greater force, using her tongue to explore beyond his lips. Dwayne let out a little moan and cupped his arm around her waist.

"Damn, I've missed you," he muffled through the kiss.

"I've missed you too," she said before reluctantly breaking away. "I have to get Matt out of the car," she said between panted breaths.

Dwayne licked his lips, savoring her taste. "That's right, I get to meet your son."

"Yes, you do." She straightened out her mini skirt before walking around the car to let Matt out of his car seat. She held his hand as they walked over to Dwayne and then knelt beside him with her arm around his waist. "Hey, sweetie, this is mommy's friend, Dwayne."

Dwayne knelt down to Matt's level and took his hand. "Hi buddy. It's good to meet you."

Matt had never been a shy child and beamed Dwayne a big smile as he replied, "Hi."

Dwayne leaned in a little closer. "So do you want to see some boats, Matt?"

Matt's smile got even bigger. Letting go of Tammy, he jumped up and down with his arms flying in the air. "Yes!"

Tammy and Dwayne laughed.

"I guess that's a yes," Dwayne said while taking Matt's hand. "I'll get your bags." he added.

Tammy took Matt's other hand and together they walked over to the main gate. After entering a code on a number pad, Dwayne swung open the gate and led them into the boatyard.

Not only was this the first time for Matt to be around boats, it was also Tammy's first time. In all her twenty-six years, she had never stepped foot on a boat. She scanned the huge and busy yard as they walked toward the docks. For as far as she could see, boats of all shapes and sizes stood in neat rows on metal stands. Sail-boats, power boats and fishing boats. Each one had a set of large metal ladders next to it so the boat could be accessed while it was being worked on.

It was a noisy place with radios blasting from the various workstations, crews sanding the bottom of some boats, some were drilling, others were hammering. To her left, cranes lifted boats in and out of the water. Throughout the entire yard, chatter was loud, but the laughs were even louder. Fascinated by her new surroundings, Tammy took her time walking down to the docks. She wanted to take it all in, this world that she never knew existed, and for reasons she didn't quite understand, she knew right away she wanted to be a part of it.

Tammy was impressed by the friendly atmosphere. She couldn't help but notice the skew of waves and smiles Dwayne received as they walked through the yard. It was a gesture she never saw in the city, a place where everyone kept to themselves and no one ever smiled or said hello.

Dwayne led them down a ramp onto the floating docks. Tammy paused for a moment to steady her feet, but the wobbling of the dock took her by surprise and caused her to let out a giggle.

Dwayne turned to face her. "Are you okay?"

"Yeah, I've never walked on a dock before. It moves!" She laughed and tried to balance herself with an outstretched arm. " Even Matt is walking better than me."

"Oh, you'll get used to it. Hang around with me and you'll have your sea legs in no time."

Wobbling her way down the dock, Tammy marveled at the rows of boats, most of which were white, all of which were squeaky clean and glistened in the sun. The rigging on the masts of sailboats rattled in the breeze. She looked out at the inviting sparkles dancing on the surface of the ocean to her left. Beyond the water on the other side of the channel, she noticed a park with more boats hugging the docks. The cheerful sounds of kids playing and adults laughing could be heard, even from where Tammy stood. She was surprised how clear the sounds could be heard from so far away.

Tammy looked out beyond the dock on which they were standing and saw several large boats cruising the marina at a slow speed. Most had music blasting from them, and quite a few boasted beautiful, bikini-clad women with perfectly slim bodies dancing and sunbathing across the deck and bow of the boat. Everywhere Tammy looked, she saw people were having fun, living life to the fullest. She couldn't help but think what a great place it would be to live.

Dwayne led them down to the third slip, where a medium sized power boat with a large deck was docked. "Welcome to my humble abode," he said, motioning his hand toward the vessel.

Unable to hide his enthusiasm, Matt pulled away from Tammy's hand and raced to Dwayne's side. "A boat! Can we go on it?" he asked with wide eyes.

Tammy and Dwayne chuckled at his excitement, but Dwayne wasted no time in sweeping Matt off his feet and lifting him up onto the boat. As fast as his little legs could run, Matt disappeared down into the cabin. "Mommy, come see. There's a bed in here."

"I'm coming." Tammy was promptly escorted onto the boat by Dwayne's

extended hand. The rocking on board was even more intense than on the dock and took her by surprise. Afraid of losing her balance, Tammy reached for the rail and held on until her feet steadied.

Dwayne laughed at her uneasiness, and was equally amused that little Matt wasn't fazed at all by the experience and was still in awe down in the cabin.

It was a simple boat with a large, spacious deck, which Dwayne explained was ideal for stacking and hauling gear. The helm, where the steering wheel and radio equipment were positioned, were on the starboard side of the boat, which Tammy soon learned meant the right-hand side. Three wooden steps to the left led down to the small cabin below, which had all the amenities one would need while out at sea. A bed, a table with two benches, a small sink and the smallest bathroom Tammy had ever seen. The sight of it ignited a flashback to the horrible trailer she had lived in with Steven when they moved to Seattle. Even though the boat's cabin was small, it was still far better than the trailer.

Tammy peeked into the tiny cabin and giggled when Matt waved from the bed, where he appeared to be testing its bounciness.

"You live in here?" Tammy asked Dwayne.

"Yep, I sure do. I don't need much, and you can't beat the view."

Tammy had to agree with him. People would pay thousands for an ocean view like this.

He went on to tell her the history of the boat, and Tammy listened intently. It was an old wooden 1959 Drake Baywatch lifeguard boat with twin 440 Chrysler gas engines. Dwayne told her with an added snarky laugh that they were gas guzzlers and not ideal for fishing. Most commercial vessels had diesel engines, which were a lot more efficient to run. But he loved the size of the deck for hauling gear, so when the boat was retired from service in

1988, he bought it and converted it into a fishing boat. The boat was already called *Baywatch*, so he simply changed one letter and named her *Baywitch* instead.

Dwayne had what was called a double-wide slip, which allowed tow boats to be docked in it. While he was telling Tammy the story about the *Baywitch*, he pointed to a small gray boat next to them. "That's mine too," he said proudly.

"You have two boats?"

"I do. That one over there, I built myself. I found the hull in a field behind a boat repair shop. It was being used as a dumpster. I liked the shape of it and asked the owner if he'd sell it to me. To my surprise, he said yes, as long as I took all the trash away that was piled in it. Of course, I jumped on it and hauled it away." He looked over at it with pride shining from his eyes. "It took me about three years to build. She's a nineteen- foot outboard skiff. I added the little cabin. It has just enough room to camp down for the night if I need to."

"What did you name that boat?" Tammy asked.

"Little Boat," Dwayne replied with a smirk.

"Well, that's original." Tammy laughed. "Why do you need two boats?"

Before Dwayne could answer, Matt raced out of the cabin. "Mom, this is so cool!" he squealed with excitement.

Tammy held out her arms and stopped him in mid-stride. "No running on the boat, honey."

Dwayne approached Matt and just like in the parking lot, he knelt to Matt's level. Dwayne's way of handling her son really impressed Tammy. He took Matt's hand. "Hey, buddy, how would you like to go for a boat ride?"

"Really!" He looked up at Tammy with the eyes of a child left alone in a candy store. "Mom, can we?" he pleaded.

Tammy was just as excited as her son. "Dwayne, that would be amazing. We would love to."

Dwayne clapped his hands together. "Okay then. Consider this your first boating lesson. And I'll tell you why I need two boats while we're cruising the marina. I don't think Matt wants to wait any longer."

Having no clue what to do on a boat, Tammy stood aside, held Matt's hand and watched Dwayne's every move, taking everything in. After putting a life jacket on Matt, Dwayne went to the helm and fired up the boat. The roar of the motors took Tammy by surprise, and she soon discovered that yelling was the only way to be heard over the noise.

While still at the helm, Dwayne glanced over at Tammy and shouted, "I'll let you untie the boat."

"Me?" Tammy hollered back, shocked.

"Yes, just untie the two ropes around the cleats. Jump off the boat and do the front one first. Then come back on the boat and untie the one on the stern."

Tammy was slowly making sense of all the boating terms Dwayne was throwing at her. *Cleat, bow, stern, helm, hull.* She soon realized she had a lot to learn. She let go of Matt's hand and told him in a stern voice to stay put. She then stepped off the boat and instantly found she needed to brace herself for a few seconds while the dock rocked beneath her feet. After regaining her balance, she walked to the front of the boat to find the rope.

While fumbling with the rope tied around the cleat, she was thinking there must be a simpler way to do it and struggled for some time before finally untying it and throwing it on the boat.

Once she was back on the deck, Dwayne instructed her to take the rope from the front and lay it on the edge of the deck alongside the cabin so it didn't fly out. Tammy followed his instructions and then headed to the stern—the back—of the boat, where she made eye contact with him and waited for the signal that he was ready.

Dwayne nodded, giving her the sign she was waiting for. The second time around, the rope was easier to untie from the cleat and without being told, she tucked it safely on the deck of the boat.

"See, the two rubber fenders hanging over the sides?" Dwayne hollered while pointing in their direction with his finger. "Those stop the boat from rubbing on the dock. Go ahead and flip them over into the boat. No need to untie them."

Tammy located the fenders and followed Dwayne's orders precisely.

Dwayne smiled and gave her a thumbs up.

Feeling pleased with herself, she took Matt's hand and joined Dwayne at the helm.

She watched as Dwayne put the boat in reverse, using a throttle on his right, and the boat began to putter and release smoke from the stern. With ease, he maneuvered the boat out of the slip and turned it around so it was facing the main channel. Being her first time on a boat, Tammy braced herself by holding on to the dash while her legs found their balance. Again, Tammy watched Dwayne's every move and was impressed how easily he drove the boat, although she had no idea how he did any of it with no brakes.

Puttering at five knots, they headed out to the main channel. Matt was placed in the captain's chair between where Dwayne and Tammy stood, holding hands, while Dwayne steered the boat one-handed.

As they cruised down the channel, Tammy took it all in. Sail boats tacked in front of them caught the wind in their sails as they zigzagged toward the open ocean, the heavy material flapping in the breeze. Power boats chugged through the water, abundant with fishermen, families and partiers. Some seemed to be returning to their slips after a morning on the ocean, while others were leaving to see what the open waters had to offer. Scattered throughout the channel were kayakers and little dinghies, some with motors and others being rowed.

Tammy was in a new world. She had no idea that such a lifestyle existed just an hour away from home. To her, the place smelt like money.

As they cruised closer to the open waters, they passed high-rise condominiums overlooking the water's edge. Mega yachts were docked on the end ties, and large party boats with disco music blasting were beginning to meander into the channel. Tammy pointed all the things out to Matt who, like her, was also taking it all in. Only he was being much more vocal with high-pitched squeals of excitement.

"I could get use to this," Tammy said over the sound of the motors into Dwayne's ear.

Dwayne nodded. "Yeah, it's not a bad way to live. I have no complaints."

As they passed the break wall, which was the entrance to the marina, Dwayne sped the boat up to a comfortable fourteen knots, causing Tammy to force herself up against the captain's chair for support. More squeals came from Matt as he too clung on to the chair.

Fearing she may lose her balance, Dwayne locked his arm around her waist and gave her a smile. Thankful for the extra support, Tammy looked up and smiled back.

The spray of sea water kicked up by the boat felt cool and refreshing against

the exposed skin of her arms and legs. She loved the feeling of the wind rushing through her hair and across her face. The city quickly felt like a distant memory, one she was in no rush to return to.

As they headed out to sea, Tammy listened to the sound of the water crashing

against the boat as the vessel plowed its way through the water. She watched the seagulls flying above, following the trail of the boat in hunt of a free meal or a place to land. She spotted boats far away on the horizon and in the other direction, people frolicking in the waves on the beach.

Dwayne leaned in close to her ear so he could be heard above the motors. "How are your sea legs? Are they getting any better?"

"Yes. I'm still standing." Tammy laughed.

Suddenly, he let go of the wheel and stood back. "Come on, you drive," he said with a devious grin.

Tammy gasped. "What! I don't know how to drive a bloody boat. Are you insane? What if I hit something?"

CHAPTER 6

*D*wayne scanned the ocean, wearing a sarcastic grin. "What are you going to hit? The nearest boat is five miles away." He returned to the wheel and pulled the throttle toward him to slow it down to a comfortable eight knots. "Out here is the best place to learn to drive a boat. Come on, give it a try," he said, standing away from the wheel again.

Enjoying Dwayne's new game, it didn't take long for Matt to take sides. "Come on, Mommy, you can do it," he squealed while banging the arms of the chair with his palms.

With no one at the wheel, Dwayne threw Tammy another playful smile. "Better hurry up, the boat isn't going to drive itself."

Obviously having no say in the debate, Tammy shook her head, released a nervous smile and approached the wheel. "So what do I do?"

"Well, for starters, you can take a hold of the wheel." Dwayne looked to be trying to suppress a chuckle.

With apprehension and feeling somewhat intimidated by the cold metal wheel, she grasped it with both hands and locked her fingers securely around it until her knuckles turned white.

A squeal of delight roared from Matt's lungs. "Yeah, Mommy is driving the boat!"

Afraid to take her eyes of the ocean, Tammy threw Matt a quick smile.

"Easy now," Dwayne said. "You don't have to hold it so tight. It's not going

anywhere." Dwayne stood next to her and pointed dead ahead. "See that island way out there on the horizon?"

"Yes."

"That's Catalina Island. Aim the bow of the boat for that."

Seeing it was slightly to her left, Tammy steered the wheel toward it, but nothing happened so she tried again. This time, the boat turned too much, so she steered in the other direction to try and correct the problem. Instantly, the boat began to zigzag.

Tammy let out a nervous laugh. "I don't know what I'm doing. I'm steering but it's not working."

Dwayne rolled his eyes. "What you're doing is over-steering. Don't worry; it's a common mistake for first-time boaters. The key is that you have to remember a boat doesn't steer like a car. A car steers from the front, whereas a boat steers from the back. It takes a while for the boat to recognize the wheel has been turned. When you turn the wheel, it takes a few seconds for the boat to begin turning. If you try and correct it then you get the zigzags. Does that make sense?"

Tammy smiled. "It actually does."

"Okay. Good. Now, aim for Catalina again." Dwayne turned, picked up Matt and sat him on the ledge next to the wheel where he could hold him steady. "Matt and I will watch," he said with a wink.

Tammy was beginning to understand the steering part of a boat a little better, and she adjusted the wheel to point the bow in the direction of the island. Dwayne stood in silence next to her, letting her get the feel of the boat. He was impressed with her eagerness to learn, but he could still see the frustration on her face as the boat continued to sway from side to side across the water.

"It takes time to get a feel for it and know when not to over-steer. You'll get it. You're off to a good start." He didn't want her to feel discouraged.

"It's a lot harder than it looks," Tammy announced, her eyes still fixed straight ahead.

"Do you want to try speeding up the boat a little?" Dwayne asked.

"Yes! I want to go fast," Matt screeched in delight.

Tammy laughed at her son's enthusiasm. "When Dwayne is driving, we will go fast. Okay?" She turned to Dwayne. "We can go a little faster but not much. How do I do that?" She looked down at the controls while waiting for an answer.

"See that silver throttle next to you on your right, the one with the red knob on the end?"

Tammy looked across. "Yes."

"If you push it forward, it speeds up the boat; put it in the middle, you'll be in neutral, and all the way back toward you is reverse. So, to go a little faster, push the throttle forward —SLOWLY."

Tammy listened to his instructions and with a gentle touch, just like he had instructed, she pushed the throttle forward. The boat instantly picked up power and speed and as the noise from the motors increased, Tammy couldn't help but feel pleased with herself.

"Well done. Now you can cruise at that speed for a while. Let yourself get comfortable and just concentrate on keeping the boat straight," Dwayne instructed her.

Tammy nodded.

Dwayne lifted Matt off the ledge. "Come on, big fella, let's go to the back of the boat and see if we can see any dolphins."

Tammy felt a rush of panic. "Don't leave me! What if I crash? Where are the brakes?"

Dwayne laughed. "Crash into what? And there are no brakes on a boat."

"What?" Tammy said with a look of horror. "Then how do I stop the bloody thing?"

"You use the throttle to slow it down. Give it a go. Pull the throttle back easy until you are in neutral."

Tammy followed his instructions and smiled when the boat slowed down and began to idle. "Oh, okay. Can I speed it up again?"

"Sure! You're in control of the boat right now. Come on, Matt," Dwayne replied before leading Matt to the stern.

Tammy had discovered a new lifestyle. Never in her wildest dreams did she ever think she'd be driving a boat. The freedom she was experiencing out on the open ocean was exhilarating. She looked at the coastline of Santa Monica and beyond, at all the other cities clustered together. Where people lived liked ants, all on top of each other in concrete cities while dealing with the chaos and stress that ran their lives. There was none of that out here. For the first time, she felt disconnected from all her worries as a single mother and trying to make ends meet. Out here, she felt completely free.

She glanced over at Matt and Dwayne, and what she saw warmed her heart. The smile on her son's face said it all. Curled over in a protective manner, Dwayne was pointing to a school of dolphins following the boat. This is what her son needed, a male figure in his life.

Since leaving Steven, it'd always been just her and Matt. She'd done her best to provide for him and had give him a good home, but she could never give him that male influence that a young boy needed. Being on the boat, watching Dwayne with her son, just felt right. She hated to admit it so soon, but she felt like a real family. Was she setting herself up to have her heart crushed?

They spent the whole day on the boat. Dwayne had obviously planned ahead and surprised them with an ice-chest full of sodas and lunch. In one afternoon, Tammy and Matt had experienced so many new things, and so many new doors had been opened. For the first time, she got to see her son fish, and the excitement that masked his face when he caught his first mackerel would be forever planted in her mind. Like herself, he was eager to learn and was a natural on the boat.

Tammy also gave fishing a go. It was another first for her. She admired Dwayne's patience as he showed her how to bait the hook with live anchovies that he pulled out of a bait tank. Tammy soon discovered that there was an art to grabbing one of the slippery creatures from the tank and keeping hold of it so it didn't slip through her hand. After a few attempts and giggles from Matt and Dwayne, she succeeded. She cringed a little when she hooked the anchovy to the line, but that soon passed when she caught her first sea bass. After that, she was eager to get the line back in the water in the hopes of catching another.

They stayed out until the sun began to set over the horizon. Before heading in, Dwayne turned off the boat, leaving just the calming sound of the sea splashing against the hull. "Hey, guys, I want to show you something," he said while holding out his hand.

Not questioning him, Tammy had Matt take Dwayne's hand and followed them both to the bow of the boat. "Here, have a seat," Dwayne said while pointing to the bow.

Wrapping an arm around Matt, Tammy followed his directions and then looked out to sea. She gasped at the breathtaking view of the sunset in front of her. The sky was now a brilliant shade of orange, entangled with streaks of red and yellow. The surface of the water danced and shimmered from the glow, and a feeling of peace engulfed her as she watched the ocean and the night sky slowly going to sleep in its own magical way.

"Oh my god, that is absolutely amazing. I've never seen anything like it," Tammy said, her hand held to her chest in awe.

Dwayne took a seat next to her and curled his arm around her shoulder. Tammy welcomed his embrace and nuzzled her head into the crook of his neck.

"You don't see that in the city, now, do you?" he said in a soft voice.

"No, you don't."

Mesmerized by the beauty that surrounded her, Tammy had never felt such calmness in her life. Back home, she was always on the go, chasing the almighty dollar, struggling to make ends meet and focusing entirely on providing for Matt.

She looked down at her son. Worn out from the day's events, he had fallen asleep nestled in her arms. "Look, he's sleeping," Tammy whispered.

Dwayne leaned in and peeked at Matt. "I guess he had a good day."

"He did, thanks to you. You showed him so much today." She let out a light chuckle. "And me too." She paused and gave him a sweet smile. "I had a good time. Thanks."

Dwayne returned the smile while brushing her hair away from her face with his hand. "You're welcome."

Moved by the gesture, Tammy held his palm close to her cheek before kissing it tenderly. Embracing his masculine scent, she leaned in and met him in a kiss.

As she sat back and watched the sun set, she realized she didn't want the day to end. Everything was perfect and felt so right. She had a strange sense of belonging. This was the life she wanted. But did Dwayne want the same? She knew she was thinking too fast and needed to slow down. She'd made so many hasty mistakes in the past. First, there was Raymond, who almost cost her her relationship with her father, and then there was Steven the drug addict. Just thinking about him made Tammy cringe. She had only just met Dwayne and knew absolutely nothing about him, except for the wonderful life he led.

Dwayne stirred her from her thoughts. "Hey, what are you thinking about?"

"Oh, just how beautiful it is out here. It's so peaceful. You're so lucky to wake up to this every day. I envy you."

Dwayne gave her shoulder a light squeeze and pulled her in closer. "You and Matt can come down here anytime you want."

"Don't say that, you'll never get rid of me." Tammy laughed.

"I have no objections."

Hearing him say that warmed Tammy's heart. She knew she was falling for him fast, but she didn't know how to put on the brakes. Much like the boat, it appeared she didn't have any.

Although Dwayne seemed perfect in every way possible, because of her wrecked relationships in the past, she was expecting the inevitable bomb to land in the middle of her happiness at any moment. So far, it had not. But the past she had lived reminded her to tread carefully.

They lay in each other's arms for the next half hour, cuddling and sharing kisses while Matt slept soundly in Tammy's arms. For her, life couldn't get any better. She didn't want it to end but knew she should get her son home and into bed at a reasonable hour. Plus, she had to work in the morning. Tammy let out a big sigh. "I guess we should get going."

Dwayne ran his fingers through her hair, stroking it over her shoulders. "I was afraid you were going to say that soon."

Tammy strained her neck and looked up at him. "Believe me when I say I don't want to. But this little guy needs to be in his bed, and unfortunately I have to go work tomorrow. It's been an amazing day and I honestly hate to see it end."

Dwayne squeezed her tight while kissing the top of her head. "It's been an amazing day for me too. But as they say, all good things must come to an end." While releasing his hold on Tammy, he shifted his body to allow himself to stand up. "I'll fire up the boat and take us back to the dock. You can stay here with Matt, I'll drive slow. We are only a few minutes out of the marina's main channel."

After a few minutes with the engines idling, Dwayne returned with a blanket. "Here, you can cover Matt with this. There might be a chill when the boat starts moving."

Tammy looked up and smiled as she took the blanket. "Thanks."

Within ten minutes, they were tied up to the dock and the night returned to a tranquil silence after Dwayne shut off the motors. Amazingly, Matt didn't stir during the ride back to the dock.

Once the boat was secured, Dwayne returned to the bow of the boat and held out his hand to Tammy. "Come on, let's get you to your car. I'll carry Matt for you."

Being careful not to disturb Matt from his sound sleep, Tammy rose slowly and stood precariously on her feet as she handed Matt to Dwayne. Once he was safely in Dwayne's arms and thankfully still asleep, Tammy headed to the deck of the boat while guiding herself with the rail. After searching for her purse, which she found on the table in the cabin, she threw it over her shoulder and took Dwayne's free hand. With Dwayne already on the dock, she stepped off the boat into his arms.

A few minutes later, they had Matt secured in his car seat and covered with his favorite blanket. Tammy stood next to her car, wrapped in Dwayne's arms and not wanting to leave. "Thank you for a fantastic day. I'll never forget it," she said while gazing up into his eyes.

"Hey, you say it like we're never going to see each other again." He brushed his lips against hers, lingering for a moment as his breathing became deeper.

Feeling his warm breath close to hers, Tammy pulled him in to her lips and saturated her mouth with his as they locked in a sensual kiss. Tammy latched her hands around his neck and gave way to the subtle moans escaping her throat. She suddenly gasped when she felt his hand slide up under her shirt and gently massage her breast.

"Oh god, I want you," Tammy panted between breaths.

"I want you too," Dwayne whispered as he broke away from the kiss and slid his tongue delicately across her neck, smothering her with kisses.

With a heaving chest, Tammy closed her eyes and leaned back against the car while holding Dwayne's head close to her breast. Rotating his hips, he pushed his body hard against hers as he worked his lips down to the V between her breasts.

"Stop..." Tammy reluctantly moaned between baited breaths. "Matt's in the car. I really should go."

Still breathing heavily, Dwayne lifted his head and stood before her, his hand still cupping her breast. "I know." He kissed her gently on the lips and released a slight chuckle. "We need a weekend alone."

Tammy placed her hand on his and squeezed it before pulling it away from her breast. She smiled and kissed him back. "I agree. I can't wait. When do you suggest?"

With the passion between them now subsided, Dwayne retrieved his hand from under her shirt and wrapped his arms around her waist while staring into her eyes. An inquisitive smile appeared across his face. "Well, I'm entered in a shark tournament this weekend. Want to join me? Can always use an extra hand on the boat."

Tammy's jaw dropped. "A shark tournament? As in, you catch sharks?"

Dwayne laughed out loud, amused by the look of horror that had invaded her face. "Yes, I catch sharks," he said with a smirk.

"And you're not afraid they will attack you?" She shook her head in disbelief. "Are you insane? I've never heard of such a thing."

Even though he was enjoying Tammy's reaction, Dwayne felt he needed to explain a little further. "It's a competition I enter every year. In fact, I've won for the past two years," he said with a hint of pride. "The prize money is twenty five hundred bucks."

"Wow!" Tammy shrieked.

"We can only catch Mako sharks—which, by the way, are delicious—and all others are thrown back. The shark isn't wasted; it's caught for consumption. The tournament lasts two days, with the biggest fish winning the prize money." He folded his arms and grinned at Tammy. "So do you wanna go?"

"Wow! This I gotta see," Tammy said, her eyes beaming with enthusiasm. "I've never seen a shark up close before. Only on the TV and even then, they look too damn scary. To see one up close on a boat, well, that's just too crazy to miss." Tammy raised her voice and added, "Hell yeah I want to go. I can't wait! Let me talk to Judy and see if she can watch Matt this weekend."

Dwayne loved her spirit. "Great! Page me this week. Okay?"

Tammy planted another kiss on his lips before stepping in her car and firing it up. "I will." She leaned back into her seat and stared up at Dwayne. "Oh, I really hope Judy has the weekend off. Wait till I tell her I'm going shark fishing." Her eyes became wide again. "I can't wait to see the look on her face!"

Dwayne tossed his head back and let out another laugh. "You'll have to tell me all about it. I hope you can make it." He leaned through the window and gave her one last kiss before stepping away so she could back up.

"One way or another, I will make it," she said with a beaming smile. "There's no way I'm going to miss shark fishing."

$\mathcal{T}$ammy didn't pull into her driveway until close to eleven and was thrilled to see the lights were still on. After putting the car in park and shutting off the engine, she turned to check on Matt and found he was still sound asleep. She quickly grabbed her purse and other bags off the front seat and after exiting her car, she skipped across the grass to the front door and burst into the house. She found Judy stretched out on the couch, dressed in her usual evening attire of blue pajamas and fuzzy black slippers. With her kids in bed, she was doing her favorite things— watching black and white movies and sipping on a glass of white wine.

"You're up!" Tammy squealed while tossing her bags on the foot of the couch next to Judy's feet.

"Of course I'm up," she said with a sarcastic roll of her eyes. "Joel just left and I want to hear all about your day on the boat. How was it?" Judy swung her legs onto the floor and sat up. "I'm dying to hear."

A huge smile blanketed Tammy's face. "Oh, Judy, I can't wait to tell you." Tammy glanced quickly at the open front door. "I have to get Matt out of the car and put him in bed, and then I'll be right back to tell you everything."

"Oh, this sounds like it's going to be good." Judy laughed while making her way across the room to turn off the TV. "I'll go pour you a glass of wine. Then I'll be waiting right here."

"Great. I'll be right back. I've not had a drink all day."

After Matt was tucked into his bed, Tammy did a quick change of clothes into her favorite comfortable white pajamas and joined Judy on the couch. "Come on. Have a seat," Judy pleaded while handing Tammy a glass of chilled wine.

Before spilling the events of her day, Tammy inhaled a huge gulp of wine and smacked her lips. "Damn, that tastes good."

"I can tell you had a great time. You can't stop smiling." Judy patted Tammy's knee. "Come on, tell me. I want to hear all the juicy details."

Tammy lit a cigarette, took a long drag and threw her head back into the pillows of the couch. "Oh god! It was amazing. I don't know where to start. Dwayne just seems so perfect, and he was totally awesome with Matt." Tammy took another sip of wine. "He has a son too, so it makes senses he'd be good with kids, right?"

Judy nodded and gave Tammy's arm a nudge. "Go on. Tell me more."

"Matt had so much fun; he really likes Dwayne," she said while putting her feet up on the coffee table. "Do you want to know something?"

"What?" Judy asked.

"Today was the first time I saw my son fish, and the look on his face when he reeled in his first catch was absolutely breathtaking. It brought tears to my eyes." Tammy let her head fall back against the cushions. "Oh, Judy, what am I going to do?"

Judy creased her brow. "What do you mean? What are you going to do?"

Tammy sat up and stubbed out her cigarette while she spoke. "I really like him, and yet I'm scared. I don't know if I'm ready for a serious relationship. What if I get hurt again?"

Judy understood where Tammy was coming from. They had both made poor decisions in the past when it came to men, which is how they ended up living and raising their kids together.

Judy tried to give Tammy some advice. "Who says it has to be serious? Just have some fun, girl. After all, you deserve it." Tammy listened and nodded. "You've been working so hard, raising Matt and giving him everything he needs. And doing a damn good job, I might add. It's time you started thinking about yourself. Maybe this guy is just what you need."

Tammy let out a sigh. "Oh, Judy, I don't know. Why am I so petrified? I've gone on the odd date or two in the past, but Dwayne is different. I feel so comfortable when I'm with him, and the life-style he lives, well, I want it. It's like a different world down there. Everyone waves and talks to you. There's no traffic like there is here. And people are actually nice to each other." Tammy shifted her body, unable to hide her excitement. "And, get this, I drove the boat! All by myself."

"What!" Judy almost choked on her wine with the shock. "Wow!"

Tammy couldn't contain herself. Rising from the couch, she began walking in circles around the room. "Judy, I loved every-thing about the boat and found myself wanting to learn everything Dwayne showed me. I want to learn more. I'm fascinated by it all." A devious smile grew across her face. "In fact, he's invited me to go shark fishing this weekend and I really want to go."

Judy almost fell off the couch. "Shark fishing! Are you fucking nuts?"

"That's what I said to Dwayne. But I can't explain it. I'm honestly excited by this whole fishing and boating thing. I've never been exposed to such a lifestyle before and I'm totally intrigued by it. I want to learn everything about it. Please say you'll watch Matt this weekend. It will be the first time I've ever been away from him overnight, but I really want this and I know he'll be safe with you."

Judy's eyes lit up. "Oooh, so you'll be spending the night, will you? And we all know what that means!"

Tammy reached over and slapped Judy's shoulder. "Stop! Tell me you can watch Matt. Please?"

"Of course I'll watch him. I have the weekend off and I'll have Joel spend the night here." She laughed and added, "Which means we'll both be getting some nookie."

Tammy slapped her again. "You're terrible."

"Nah. Just honest. Don't worry about Matt. He'll be fine. Just go have some fun, okay?"

Tammy embraced her friend, who had always been her rock in the past. "Thank you so much!"

After finishing her wine, Tammy set down her glass on the coffee table and looked at Judy with a frown.

"What's up?" Judy asked, looking puzzled. "Everything okay? You suddenly went from bloom to gloom."

"Yeah, I'm okay. I just realized I have to go back to court this week and ask the stupid judge for another extension to pay my fine. What if he says no? Will they take me to jail right then while I'm in court?"

Seeing the worried look on her friend's face, Judy tried to ease her mind. "I don't think so, hon. I think you're entitled to three extensions."

"But you're not sure, are you?"

"Well, no, I'm not."

Wearing a worried look, Tammy leaned in closer to Judy and placed her hand or Judy's knee. "Judy, I need to know, if they take me to jail, that Matt will be okay with you." She gave Judy's knee another squeeze. "Can you promise me that? I know it's a lot to ask but I have no one else to turn to."

Judy took Tammy's hand, followed by a warm smile. "Don't you worry about Matt. He will be just fine. Now come on, let's have another glass of wine and get back to talking about Dwayne. Enough of this legal bullshit crap." Judy paused before adding, "Hey, does Dwayne know about your accident and the courts?"

"Oh, god no! I don't want to scare him off." She laughed. "I'll try and hide it from him as long as I can. By then, he'll hopefully like me enough to forgive me."

Judy nodded. "I like your way of thinking, girl. Now, off I go to get us some more wine," she said, pulling herself up off the couch.

CHAPTER 8

*D*ressed in the best outfit Tammy could find, which consisted of a beige knee-length skirt and a white shirt, she returned to court on May 25th to face the judge one more time.

Once her name was called, Tammy made her way to the front of the court room. She nervously rubbed her sweaty palms on the sides of her legs while she waited for the judge to speak, and the piercing stare he gave her over his glasses caused her to shudder.

"Miss Mellows, do you have the one thousand five hundred dollar fine?" the judge asked in a stern voice.

Tammy swallowed the lump that was now invading her throat and tried to calm her racing heart. "No, Your Honor, I do not."

The judge was silent while he picked up her case file and began to read. Again, he looked up and gave Tammy a cold stare. Tammy clenched her hands in front of her, trying to control their shaking.

"Well, Miss Mellows, the fine was due today."

Trembling, Tammy struggled to speak. "I know, Your Honor, and I apologize. I...um...would like to know if I could get an extension."

The judge pursed his lips and again looked at her file. "You've had two extensions already, Miss Mellows."

"I know, Your Honor. I have a young son and I had to buy a car."

"I don't want to hear your excuses," the judge snarled.

Tammy cowered before him, her knees feeling like they were about to buckle. "Sorry, Your Honor," she replied in a timid voice.

Before speaking, the judge removed his glasses and squinted his eyes over at Tammy. "Miss Mellows, I will give you one final extension."

Tammy released a huge sigh of relief as all the worries of going to jail began to subside. "Thank you, Your Honor."

"I'm not done yet," the judge quickly added. "I'm giving you until August fifteenth to pay the fine. On your next court appearance, you must pay the fine or do jail time. This is your final extension. Do I make myself clear, Miss Mellows?"

"Yes, Your Honor. I understand," Tammy replied. She was unable to hide her smile but at the same time, she was counting in her head that she had roughly ten weeks to come up with the money.

The judge closed her file and put it to the side. "Miss Mellows, you are dismissed. We will see you back here in court on August fifteenth."

"Thank you, Your Honor," Tammy answered before quickly exiting the court room.

or Tammy, the following weekend couldn't come fast enough. She paged Dwayne earlier in the week to tell him she would be able to make it for the shark tournament. He had called her back within five minutes and sounded beyond excited when he spoke to her over the phone. "That's fantastic! I can't wait to see you. I hope I get a shark this year so you can see one up close and personal," he had said.

When Friday finally rolled around, Tammy was ready. She had packed her bag the night before and couldn't wait to rush home from work, take a shower and grab her things.

Saying goodbye to Matt wasn't easy. Trying to hold it together for her son, she held back her tears and swallowed the lump in her throat. But Matt didn't seem fazed at all. When she knelt to his level in the driveway to say goodbye, he simply locked his arms around her neck and gave her a quick peck on the cheek before rushing off back to the game he was playing with Judy's kids. Left alone, Tammy remained on her knees and watched him for a moment as she brushed away the few tears that had escaped and rolled down her cheeks.

"Don't you worry. He'll be fine," Judy said from her spot on the front porch.

Tammy approached her friend and gave her a firm embrace. "I know. I love you, girlfriend, and thank you."

"You're welcome. Now go on, get out of here." She shooed Tammy away.

By four o'clock, Tammy was on the road heading to Dwayne's.

With the infamous LA traffic, it took her two hours to reach the boatyard. Once the car was in park, she grabbed her bags from the back seat and checked her car was all locked up. She let herself through the gate with the code Dwayne had given her over the phone and headed toward his boat. While walking through the yard, she was greeted with smiles and waves from people she recognized from the previous week. God, she loved this place and how friendly the people were.

When she reached Dwayne's boat, she was stunned to see all the stuff packed on the deck and the hatches to the motors lying open. Dwayne was nowhere in sight. She scanned the docks in search of him but had no luck.

"Dwayne?"

Tammy almost fell backwards when she heard a voice coming from down by the engines. "Hey, Tammy! Hold on, I'll be right there," Dwayne hollered from beneath the deck.

A few minutes later, his head popped up from the open hatch in the deck. "Hi. You made it," he said with a smile that creased the motor oil stains on his cheeks. "Just making a few last-minute checks before we head out in the morning. Making sure the motors are okay."

His droopy eyes were a dead giveaway, not to mention the huge yawn. "You look tired," she said, sounding concerned.

"Yeah, I've been up since five getting the boat ready. There's always a ton of things to do when you want to go fishing. It's never an easy task."

Tammy scanned the boat. "I can see that. What's all this stuff?"

Dwayne pulled himself out of the engine hatch and wiped his hands with a towel before pointing to various objects on the deck.

"Well, over there, we have our six fishing poles rigged with heavy test line and shark hooks. We have boxes of mackerel for bait. Over on that side, we have white buckets of chum." He looked over at Tammy and beamed her a smile. "And we have two chairs and an ice-chest full of food." He pointed to the back of the boat. "That large gray box is full of ice to keep any sharks we may catch cold until we get back into port, and this pile of stuff next to me is mainly tools and replacement parts in case we have mechanical issues with the boat. I still need to put them away."

"I had no idea so much went into fishing," Tammy said, still looking at the gear stacked neatly around her.

Dwayne laughed. "This is nothing. Wait until I go lobster fishing in a couple of months. Then you will really see what fishing involves." A warm smile blanketed his face as he held out his arms. "Come here. I've missed you."

That's all it took for Tammy's heart to melt. She returned the warm smile and stepped on the boat. After dropping her bags on the deck, she welcomed Dwayne's open arms and met him in a warm sensual kiss.

"Man, you taste good," he said before giving her a devious smile. "You know, I could take a break. Do you want to join me?"

Tammy looked around where they stood. "And where do you take a shower? I've never seen one on the boat."

Dwayne pointed to a gray building just off to the left at the top of the ramp. "Over there. It's a community shower." He gave her a smirk. "Don't worry, it has a lock on it."

Tammy playfully slapped his chest and gave him a peck on the cheek. "I'd love to join you."

"Great! Let me grab my shower bag and a couple of towels and some clean clothes."

"Okay. I'll wait right here," Tammy replied, feeling a twinge of excitement.

Once Dwayne had gathered their stuff, he took Tammy's hand and led her up the ramp to the gray building he had pointed at. She stood behind him, holding his hand while he used a key to open the door.

After entering, Dwayne had a quick look around. "Good, it's empty," Dwayne whispered before locking the door behind them.

Tammy took in their surroundings while she waited for Dwayne to put their things on a wooden bench and run the shower. There wasn't much to the place. The walls flaked with dull gray paint, large white tiles covered most of the floor, and there was just one shower stall and one sink. Tammy held her hands up to her mouth and began shivering.

"It's cold in here," she muffled while blowing warm breath into her hands.

Dwayne turned to face her, his arm stretched out. "Come here. I'll take care of that."

Tammy didn't hesitate and nestled herself into his embrace, allowing the warmth of his body to overshadow the chill lingering in the air. She snuggled against his chest, feeling the faint beat of his heart against her ear.

Dwayne squeezed her tight, lowered his head and gazed into her eyes before kissing her passionately, exploring her mouth deep with his tongue. He had an unexpected fresh salty taste from the ocean air that Tammy found refreshing, and she soon found herself melting beneath him. With force, she pushed her body into his while locking her hands around his neck and gripping the ends of his blond hair.

This was the first time they had been alone, and both felt the long anticipated hunger building once again between them. Dwayne ran his hands up and down her body, squeezing her skin between his fingers and kneading her curves with the palms of his hands. Untamed and consumed by lust, he ravished her voluptuous breast through her shirt and moaned at the touch of her perked nipple.

Feeling his masculine strength take control, Tammy gasped as her chest heaved from his touch. She pulled away from his mouth, sucking in a lungful of much-needed air. Dwayne continued to kiss her on the neck, sucking her flesh with his lips and tracing her jaw line with his tongue. Tammy let out another gasp as she tossed back her head and stretched her neck, welcoming the moist touch of his heated breath.

Pressed hard against each other, their bodies merging as one, Dwayne reached up and entwined his fingers in Tammy's hair before engulfing her mouth once more.

"Let's get in the shower," he panted between short gasps of air.

Tammy could only manage a short "Yes!" before being smothered by his lips once more. Her body became invaded by his heavy caresses.

Dwayne struggled to unbutton his jeans while keeping his lips locked on hers. With fumbled fingers, he managed to unsnap the button and pull down the zipper. He released a satisfying moan as his now erect manhood revealed itself from his pants. Craving to be inside of her, he reached down and began stroking his aching member.

With his heart now pounding, Dwayne reluctantly pulled himself away from Tammy, leaving her panting for air. "Come on, let's get undressed. I want you." He wasted no time in tearing his jeans away from his body.

In a passionate frenzy, Tammy pulled her t-shirt over her head and threw it on the ground.

Dwayne paused for just a second while he admired her full breasts peeking out of her sheer white bra. "God! You are beautiful. Hurry up. Take off your pants," he urged while freeing himself from his shirt. Tammy met him in his rushed state and peeled her jeans off her body.

Intoxicated by her standing before him, wearing only a bra and white lace panties, Dwayne couldn't resist and pulled her in to his chest once more. He devoured her mouth while smothering her breasts with his hands.

Overwhelmed by his scent and the jabbing of his manhood between her legs, Tammy wrapped her arms around his neck and latched on to his lips with fury, exploring every inch of the inside of his mouth with her lips and tongue.

Dwayne reached down between her legs and grasped the sheer material of her panties. Charged by his touch, Tammy released a high-pitched shriek while taking in a deep breath and gasping for air. In one swift movement, Dwayne had her underwear at her feet. Tammy hastily stepped out of them without breaking away from his lips. Still latched together, their breathing intense, Dwayne reached around and unsnapped her bra, freeing her breasts from the sheer material. Tammy inched back, allowing the last piece of clothing to fall to the floor.

Still locked in a heated kiss, unable to break away, Dwayne used his strength to guide Tammy to the shower while stumbling over their clothes scattered across the floor. They clumsily stepped inside the now steamy stall and, still using his body, Dwayne pushed Tammy against the cold tile of the shower wall and pressed her back against it. The chill stunned her for a moment and she let out a shrill squeal before closing her eyes to the shower of warm water drenching her face.

Pressed against the wall, Tammy clasped onto Dwayne's now wet body, digging her nails into his shoulders as he deeply massaged her buttocks, pulling her closer to him and thrusting his hips. The anticipation of this moment was finally here and neither wanted to waste any more time. Feeling him thrust into her, Tammy wiggled her body to welcome him inside of her and both released loud simultaneous moans of pleasure and satisfaction as they devoured every moment of pleasure they were sharing.

After the heated sweat of an intense orgasm and no longer feeling the cold, Tammy clung to Dwayne's limp body with loose arms, trying to catch her breath after their shared climax. A satisfied smile spread across her face.

Dwayne raised his head from her chest, cupped her face in his palms and smooched her lips. "Damn, girl. What did you do to me? I can't feel my legs." He shuffled his feet helplessly around the stall floor, trying to regain his balance.

Tammy laughed and shook her head before breaking away from the wall and loosening her hold on him. "Come on. I need a cigarette after that," she replied before squeezing past Dwayne to exit the shower and get dressed.

"Hang on a sec. I'll join you."

Tammy froze while putting her jeans on. "What! You quit smoking."

"Well, that was until I met you."

A look of guilt invaded Tammy's face. "That's not funny, Dwayne. You've not smoked in over two years. I don't want to be the person that made you start up again. Do you know how awful that would make me feel?"

Dwayne reached for a towel on the counter and swabbed his body before picking up his jeans from the floor. "It's not your fault. It's the sex. Sex hasn't been that good in a long time. I'm blaming the sex, not you, silly." He shuffled his body into his jeans before grabbing his t-shirt.

Tammy frowned. "I don't care. I still feel bad."

Amused by her guilt, Dwayne chuckled. "Well, I haven't had one yet. I may change my mind by the time we get back to the boat." He gave her a loving hug and a peck on the cheek. "Now come on, let's go. You're craving a smoke and I want a Pepsi."

A few minutes later, they were back at the boat with their hair still damp and their bodies slightly chilled from the cool evening air. Dwayne went down into the cabin and grabbed himself a Pepsi from the compact fridge buried under one of the counters. Tammy stayed on the deck and lit a cigarette.

"Let me have one," Dwayne said as he approached her, breathing in the smoke that she exhaled.

"No!" Tammy shrieked, turning her body away from him in an attempt to keep the cigarette she was holding out of his reach.

Dwayne looked around the boat and spotted her pack sticking out of the top of her purse.

"Ahh ha!" he bellowed in triumph while heading toward it. "Would it make you feel better if I got my own instead of you giving me one?" he asked with a devious smile.

"No, it doesn't. No matter how you look at it, Dwayne, if I wasn't here, the thought of smoking would never have crossed your mind. I'll feel awful if you have one." She was trying her best to convince him not to do it, but he ignored her requests.

With apprehension, hoping he would change his mind, Tammy watched him reach into her purse and take out a cigarette and her red lighter.

"Don't do it, Dwayne," she pleaded.

He paused for a moment and turned to look at her. A cheeky smile covered his face as he held the cigarette up to his nose and breathed in heavily. "Been a long time since I held one of these," he said.

Tammy closed her eyes, praying he wouldn't light it. But the sound of the flicker from the lighter and the sudden bout of coughing told her he did. "Damn it, Dwayne! Why did you do that?"

After releasing a few more coughs, he laughed and said, "Will you stop feeling so guilty? This isn't your fault. I've missed these for a long time and it feels damn good." He took in another long hit, this time with no coughs. "I've forgotten how good this feels. I've not had one in so long that I'm getting dizzy."

Tammy approached him and gave him a light slap on the chest. "Oh, stop it. I still feel terrible."

Dwayne rolled his eyes before giving her a playful squeeze.

"Well, I can't help that. Tell you what. Why don't I take you out for dinner before we head out?"

Tammy was shocked. "We're leaving tonight?"

"We sure are. We gotta claim our spot and get some chum in the water."

Tammy creased her brow. "Chum? What's that?"

"Well, if you must know, it's buckets of fish waste and guts to attract the sharks."

"Yuk! That's just gross."

Dwayne laughed at Tammy's expression and couldn't help thinking about what an interesting trip lay ahead. He stubbed out his cigarette and downed the last swig of Pepsi in his can. "Come on, let's go eat. I know a good seafood restaurant across the marina."

Tammy curled her upper lip in disgust. "Yuk. I don't like seafood."

Dwayne started coughing again at her reaction. "What! You're dating a fisherman and you don't eat seafood? Well, we're going to have to do something about that. You're English. You like fish and chips, right?"

"I do," Tammy replied.

"Great! Well, they have that. Come on, let's go. I'm starving." He grabbed Tammy's hand and led her away for a seafood supper.

CHAPTER 10

They returned to the boat shortly after ten, with their bellies full and Tammy slightly tipsy from the three glasses of wine she had over dinner. Dwayne did one last check on his gear and supplies before announcing to Tammy they were ready to head out. Remembering their last trip and wanting to help as much as she could, Tammy saluted Dwayne, followed by a cute smile. "Aye, aye, Captain. I'll untie the boat."

Amused and impressed, Dwayne played along while she got into position at the front of the boat and stood to attention, ready to untie the rope on the bow. Dwayne fired up the engine. "Go ahead, First Mate!" he yelled.

Tammy remembered the routine like clockwork and repeated the same process at the stern, and without being told, she flipped the fenders into the boat before joining Dwayne at the helm as they drove out of the harbor under the night skies.

When he noticed Tammy rubbing her shoulders from the chill of the cool air, Dwayne reached for his jacket hanging on the back of his captain's chair and wrapped it around her. With a smile, she leaned in close to his chest and snuggled against his warm body. Life couldn't get any better than this. That was until they pulled out of the harbor into the dark open water of the Pacific Ocean.

Mesmerized by the beauty of the full moon reflecting off the calm water, Tammy pulled away from the comfort of Dwayne's chest to take it all in. She breathed in deeply, moved by the tranquility and peacefulness that surrounded them. "Wow! It's absolutely gorgeous out here." Tammy looked up at the dark sky. "Look at all the stars above us. I've never seen so many."

"It's one of the reasons why I love being on boats. You don't get this in the city."

"Oh, Dwayne. You don't know how lucky you are." Tammy did a three sixty. "I mean, look at this. We are the only ones out here for miles. I've never experienced such freedom. If I wanted to, I could strip off all my clothes and run around the boat naked."

Dwayne laughed. "Be my guest."

"Ha! You would love that, I'm sure."

Dwayne pulled her back into his arms. "I'm so glad you like boats. They take some getting used to."

"Like them?" Tammy's eyes widened. "I love them. I'm hooked, trust me."

For the next hour, they putted along at a comfortable eight knots. Tammy stayed close to Dwayne's side, even taking the wheel a few times. Her zigzags were becoming fewer and further between, but they were still there. Dwayne was impressed by how she managed to stay on course by following the dim light of the compass on the dash.

When they finally reached their spot, just outside the shipping lanes, Dwayne brought the boat to a stop and turned off the motors.

"Do you hear that?" Tammy whispered.

Dwayne pinned his ears. "I don't hear anything."

A large grin appeared across Tammy's face. "Exactly! Absolute silence, and it sounds friggin' wonderful. All's I hear is the water softly splashing up against the hull." She looked up at the sky one more time. "It's just you, me, the moon and the stars, and I love it."

"You really do like it out here, don't you?"

Tammy beamed. "I do!"

Dwayne went on to explain to her that they were in five thousand feet of water, and because it was too deep to set anchor, they would be drifting through the night. He continued to explain to her what he was doing as he prepped the boat for shark fishing. Tammy watched intently, following his every move. After turning on the flood lights on the deck, she paid close attention when he tied the chum buckets to the back of the boat and let them hang in the water. A few minutes later, she saw the blood ooze out of the holes from the buckets into the water, making a trail around the boat.

"See, they are making a scent that will attract the sharks. It's called a chum line," Dwayne explained.

"Aren't they going to come a little too close to the boat though?" Tammy asked, wearing a worried look.

"Well, we can't catch them way out there," Dwayne said, laughing.

Not sure how to react to the thought of sharks being next to the boat, Tammy simply nodded.

After completing the necessary tasks before they could actually put their poles in the water and start fishing in the morning, Dwayne let out a loud yawn while stretching his body.

"You look tired," Tammy said.

He yawned again. "I am. I was up most of the night and now I'm running on fumes. I haven't got much sleep in the last few nights. Would you mind if I went and lay down for an hour?"

"No, not at all. Go get some rest. Is there anything I need to do?" Tammy asked.

"Not really. Just keep watch. We're drifting, so keep a look out for other boats, especially large ones. We're close to the shipping lanes so wake me up if you see anything."

Tammy took a seat on the deck chair, and before Dwayne headed down to the cabin, he reached inside and grabbed a blanket off the bench and covered Tammy's legs. "Here you go," he said, planting a soft kiss on her lips.

Tammy looked up and smiled. "Thanks."

She watched him as he made his way down into the cabin, leaving the door open and crawling onto the bed. Within a few minutes, she heard the faint sound of snoring.

She chuckled and made herself comfortable in the chair, snuggling into the blanket and gazing up at the stars. The view took her breath away and for the first time in her life, she saw a shooting star and wished Matt was with her to witness it.

Tammy hadn't realized it, but she must have dozed off and was woken by a flapping sound in the water. Upset with herself for not doing the one thing Dwayne had asked her do and keep watch, she jumped up from her chair in a state of panic, letting the blanket fall to her feet.

In a frenzy, she quickly scanned the horizon for any other boats and let out a huge sigh of relief when she saw there were none. She glanced at her watch. It was 2:00 a.m. She'd nodded off for at least an hour. Peering down into the cabin, she heard snoring, telling her Dwayne was still asleep. Figuring there was no need to wake him just yet, she decided to let him sleep a while longer. He needed all the rest he could get.

The flapping sound continued from the stern and sparked Tammy's curiosity. With apprehension and feeling somewhat fearful of the unknown, she picked up the blanket and wrapped herself in it before slowly tiptoeing to the back of the boat. She peered into the dark water, illuminated only by the flood lights on the deck, and gasped.

"Holy shit!" Leaping back, she couldn't believe what she had just seen. Consumed with adrenaline and her nerves piqued, she inched her way over to the stern to take one more look. "Fuck! Look at them all," she whispered out loud, afraid they might see her. She'd never seen even a single shark up close, and now she found herself peering over the stern at a dozen of them splashing in the water, swimming in circles around the boat.

"Holy fuck!" She watched with horror as they swam in a frenzy, their tails hitting and splashing the surface of the water. Their bodies moved in circles as they fed off the scraps of fish and guts oozing out of the chum buckets. Finding a little more courage, although still stunned by what she was seeing, she strained her neck to get a closer view while still holding her body back. On the swim step, she noticed there were eight cardboard boxes. The bottom ones were now crushed and soaked from the weight of the top ones and were also seeping blood into the water.

Tammy watched with a dropped jaw as the sharks bit on the swim step, trying to get to the boxes of bait. She was horrified and stepped back away from the stern, afraid they might jump on the boat. Having no clue what to do, she yelled out to no one in particular, "I've gotta wake up Dwayne!"

In a mad dash, she headed down in to the cabin where she found Dwayne in a deep sleep, his face covered with the blankets. Tammy nudged his shoulder. "Dwayne! Dwayne! Wake up!"

His body stirred. "Huh? Is the boat okay?" he asked in a delirious mumble.

"Yes, it's fine. But there are sharks all around the boat. Wake up." She shook him again, using more force. "Come on, Dwayne! Wake up."

He hadn't heard the part about sharks. He only heard her say the boat was fine so, exhausted from a lack of sleep in the past twenty-four hours, he rolled his body away from her. "I'll be right there," he said before starting to snore again.

Realizing her attempts to wake him had failed, she stopped shaking him and decided to let him rest. She knew the boat was in no danger and she was certain the sharks wouldn't jump on board. With her decision made, she covered Dwayne's bare shoulders with the blanket. He moaned and curled his body to the welcome warmth. Tammy stroked his shoulder, which was now covered with the blanket, and smiled. "Get some rest. Everything's fine," she whispered before heading back out onto the deck.

Still hearing the commotion and splashing in the water, she tip-toed her way to the stern and again strained her neck to glance over the side. The scene was just how she had left it. The out-of-control school of sharks were still feasting on the chum in a mad feeding frenzy. Tammy whispered out loud, "Wow!"

For a few minutes, she stood motionless, watching the scene before her. The sharks were unaware of her presence as they continued to feed on the blood-infested waters, snapping their jaws at the pieces of chum floating on the surface while exposing their razor-sharp teeth. Their smooth, wet bodies glistened in the glow of the floodlights, and their tails slapped on the surface in excitement.

Tammy turned her head while shading her eyes from the glare of the floodlights and stared into the cabin. From where she stood, she could tell Dwayne had not moved and had returned to a deep sleep. Tammy knew there was nothing she could do about the situation so inched her chair away from the stern, grabbed her blanket and cigarettes and took a seat.

After inhaling a long, much-needed smoke, she heard the splashing sounds becoming quieter and less frantic. To confirm, she pulled herself up and while still wrapped in her blanket, peeked over the side. Yes, there were fewer sharks and less chum in the water. Relieved, she returned to her seat and after a few minutes began to drift off to sleep.

CHAPTER 11

*U*nsure how long she had been asleep, Tammy was woken by the soft whisper of Dwayne's voice in her ear and a slight shaking of her shoulder. "Hey, kiddo, wake up. The sun's about to come up. It's time to go fishing."

Still haunted by the night's events, Tammy jumped up from her seat, startling Dwayne. "You're up!" she shrieked.

Puzzled by her outburst, Dwayne cautiously answered, "Yes. Are you okay?"

"Shit, Dwayne! I tried to wake you. There were a ton of sharks right next to the boat last night, feeding on that chum stuff. It was crazy! I've never seen anything like it."

"What! Holy shit! You're kidding me? And I slept through the whole thing?" He raced to the back of the boat and peered over the side. "Oh, damn. They did a number on the paintwork of the swim step." He looked at the few remaining boxes. "I left the boxes of bait back there too. They were feeding on the soaked boxes. I was so tired I forgot to bring them onto the boat. Here, give me a hand with these."

Tammy walked over and helped him bring the remaining four boxes onto the deck.

Standing with the boxes between them, Dwayne took count. "Wow, we lost four boxes of bait, but we still have enough to fish with. I can't believe I missed all the excitement. I must have been really tired."

"I tried to wake you but it was impossible. It was amazing. I watched them for a while. There were some big ones too."

Dwayne laughed. "I don't need to hear that. That may have been the winning fish that got away. Let's hope they come back for more chum." He chuckled while scanning the horizon and saw there were a few other fishing boats in the distance. He glanced at his watch. It was just before 6:00 a.m. and the sun was almost up.

"How are you feeling? Did you get any sleep?" he asked.

"Oh, I feel fine. Just thirsty, that's all."

Dwayne turned around, opened the lid of the ice chest behind him and pulled out an orange juice. "Here you go."

Tammy swiped it from his hand and quenched her thirst.

"So are you ready to go shark fishing?" Dwayne said with a smirk.

Tammy beamed him a smile. "I sure am. After seeing all those sharks up close, I can't wait to see you catch one."

Dwayne rubbed his hands together, eager to get started. "Okay then. Let's get the gear ready and try to catch the winning shark."

Not having a clue how he might go about catching a shark, Tammy watched Dwayne's every move with intrigue and listened carefully as he explained what he was doing. First, he tied off two more buckets of chum to the back of the boat and hung them in the water.

"We need another chum line. Why don't you open one of those boxes of bait and see if the mackerels are defrosted?"

"Okay," Tammy replied, anxious to help. When she had the box open, she pulled out one of the top fish from the uniformed stack and gave it a gentle squeeze."Yep, it's defiantly defrosted. It feels kind of squishy between my fingers."

"Great, hand it to me." Dwayne couldn't help but chuckle at Tammy's look of disgust.

Trying not to let the fish slip between her fingers, Tammy used both hands to pass it to him. When she looked up, she saw he was now holding a large fishing pole equipped with a huge reel and a hook that glistened in the sun. She watched as he pierced the mouth of the dead mackerel with the hook and secured it into place.

"Eww. That's disgusting," Tammy squealed.

"No, that's fishing." Dwayne laughed. "You'll get us to it. People always get grossed out the first time they see it."

Tammy continued to hand Dwayne four more fish for the remaining poles, each one getting easier to handle. She watched with fascination as he took each pole, baited it and let the line out into the water before placing each pole in a holder around the boat.

After the last pole had been rigged, Tammy leaned over the side of the boat, rinsed her hands in the cool water and dried them off with a rag.

"What's next?" she asked with enthusiasm and a big smile.

After washing his hands, Dwayne grabbed one of Tammy's cigarettes from the pack sitting on the deck, lit it and took a long drag. "We wait."

"Wait for what?"

"For a shark to take the bait." He rolled his eyes at her innocence.

But Tammy was still confused. "How do we know when that happens? We can't see anything."

"Oh, trust me, you will know."

Tammy walked over to the dash and joined Dwayne in a smoke. After taking his last hit, he had an idea.

"While we're waiting, let's chop up some of the mackerel and throw the bits in the water. That should attract the sharks."

"Okay!" Tammy agreed, thrilled there was more to do. Sitting idle was not her thing.

Dwayne walked to the other side of the deck, grabbed a large plastic chopping board and a knife and handed them to her.

"Here, set these up on the back of the deck and I'll pass you the fish to chop up. You just need to cut them up into small chunks and I'll throw them overboard."

Eager to get started, Tammy claimed her spot and began chopping while Dwayne scooped the pieces into a bucket and began tossing them into the ocean. Within a few minutes, a flock of seagulls appeared, squawking and hovering above the boat while diving into the water after the chunks of fish.

"Damn seagulls," Dwayne hollered.

"Where did they come from?" Tammy laughed. "They weren't here a minute ago and we're in the middle of nowhere."

"I swear they can spot a fish a mile away. Just keep cutting. The sharks will eventually smell it."

"Okay, Captain," she said with a salute before returning to the task.

After improving the chum line and having cereal for breakfast, Dwayne had Tammy help him clear a space on the deck in the hopes of bringing a shark on board.

"It's been two hours. Maybe they're full from their feeding frenzy last night," Tammy said while pushing a box of bait off to the side with her foot.

"Oh, they'll be back. I promise."

Another hour passed and Tammy had just about had enough of the idle time when suddenly, one of the poles began to make a loud buzzing sound and the line was being pulled out from the reel at high speed. In a flash, Dwayne was on his feet yelling, "Fish on!"

"Really?" Tammy squealed, leaping to her feet.

In one quick movement, Dwayne grabbed the pole and pointed

to a fishing harness off to his side. "Quick, grab that, put it around my waist and snap the buckle into place."

Fueled by adrenaline, Tammy asked no questions and followed his directions. Once the harness was in place, Dwayne lifted the pole and set it in the holder on the front of the harness. Unable to contain the sudden rush of excitement, Dwayne's voice was loud as he explained the process to Tammy.

"This is what's called a fighting harness. It gives me support while I'm fighting the shark. Right now, I'm letting the shark take the bait. I want it to be completely in his mouth before I set the hook. See how the line is still going out? He's running with the bait. I'll give him a little more time before I set the hook."

Tammy watched from his side, not wanting to get in his way. It seemed the sudden commotion had left her lost for words, as only a murmur of agreement left her lips.

Dwayne continued to holler instructions. "I want you to go around and reel in the other lines. Last thing I need is another shark to get hooked." He let out a sarcastic laugh. "Unless you want to reel it in?"

"Ha! If I knew what I was bloody doing, I might consider it. But I've never handled a fishing pole. What do I do?"

Suddenly, Dwayne yanked the rod he was holding and began reeling. "Hold on!" he yelled. "I just set the hook. Now I need to wear him out."

Tammy watched with her eyes wide as Dwayne began to work the line, reeling it in a little at a time, using his back and knees for support. "This feels like a big fish!" he said with a huge smile. "Okay, take each rod and reel the line in with the handle. Once the mackerel is out of the water, push the button on the side to lock the line and just let the mackerel dangle. Place the rod back in the holder."

Tammy understood his instructions and proceeded to reel each line in while Dwayne continued to work on tiring out the shark. Once done, she stood to the side and watched in amazement as

Dwayne's pole almost doubled over with the weight of the catch. Dwayne used all his strength to reel in the line a little at a time, but the shark was clearly putting up a tremendous fight beneath the water.

"How do you know it's a shark? We can't see anything."

"Only a shark will take the whole mackerel. Hopefully, it's not a blue shark. We can't eat those," Dwayne yelled, still driven by adrenaline.

Tammy watched with admiration as each well-defined muscles flexed under his tight skin. She moistened her lips, stood back and enjoyed the view. *Now that's a real man.*

"I want you to go grab me that blue rope at the back of the boat and that long gaff lying along the side. It's the wooden pole with the large hook at the end," Dwayne yelled while still fighting the shark.

Tammy scanned the boat and quickly spotted the items he needed. She dashed over to retrieve them and brought them to his side. "Here you go."

Dwayne held on to the fishing pole tight with both hands and looked to be struggling to reel in the line. He didn't take his eyes off the water while he spoke. "Hold on to them. I'll tell you when I'm ready."

"Okay."

For the next thirty minutes, Tammy watched with fascination as Dwayne continued to work the line to wear down the fish. At times, she though the pole was going to snap because of the way it was bent over, but Dwayne told her they were made to handle such tension and weight. Suddenly, Tammy squealed.

"Oh my god! I see its fin! It's right there!" she yelled while jumping up and down, full of excitement and pointing in the direction of the huge fish circling and splashing in the water.

Dwayne began to work the reel harder. "This feels like a big one."

"I've never seen anything like it. That is un-fucking believable."

After twenty more minutes of fighting the shark, Dwayne finally managed to tie off the tail, gaff it and bring it on the boat.

While still flapping around on the deck in a frenzy, exposing its razor-sharp teeth as it snapped its jaws repeatedly, Tammy took a step back and couldn't help but wonder how they were going to get the huge creature back to shore without it doing them or the boat some serious damage. Her question was soon answered when she saw Dwayne pulling a large knife from a leather sheath hanging by the helm. She knew what was about to happen. It was one of the realities of shark fishing, a necessary evil, but it was one she wasn't ready to stand and watch first hand—not yet, possibly not ever. As Dwayne approached the shark and lifted the knife, Tammy turned her head and walked as far away as she could within the confines of the boat.

After the dreaded task was done, the shark laid lifeless, no longer a threat. Still panting and out of breath but wearing a huge smile, he removed the harness and bent over to catch his breath. "That's a good size fish. We may just have the winning shark," he said, beaming.

No longer feeling threatened by the beast, Tammy's mood lightened and she soon realized this was probably a chance in a lifetime photo opportunity. No one was going to believe her without a picture as proof. "Where's my camera? I need to take a picture. Judy is never going to believe me, and I want to show Matt too."

While Dwayne dealt with securing the shark, Tammy dashed down to the cabin in search of something to capture this momentous occasion with. A few minutes later, she returned waving her disposable camera in her hand. "Found it!" she yelled from a distance as she started to snap a few pictures.

"I bet you this is a hundred-fifty-pound mako," Dwayne said with pride. "I heard on the radio that the biggest fish weighed in so far is a hundred twenty pounds."

"Really? You mean you may win this thing?"

"Yeah. If I'm right about the weight and no bigger fish is caught by tomorrow afternoon then yep, I win the two thousand five hundred dollar prize money."

"Wow! That's awesome."

Dwayne checked the shark one more time. Satisfied it was secured, he began clearing off the deck. "Only way to find out, is to head back in and get this puppy weighed. Let's clean up the deck and head back to the marina. We're done fishing in the tournament." He couldn't hide his contented smile.

"Okay!" Tammy beamed.

CHAPTER 12

*A*n hour later, they were pulling into a slip back at the marina and were greeted by dozens of spectators standing on the docks. A couple of guys helped tie off the boat to the cleats. Within minutes of Dwayne turning off the motors, they were surrounded by a crowd of people who had spotted the shark from a distance and hurried over to get a closer look.

Conversations were loud and eyes were wide, and everyone congratulated them on their successful catch, patting Dwayne on the back as he stepped off the boat wearing a huge grin. It took three guys plus Dwayne to get the shark over to the scale.

With anticipation, Dwayne stood with his arm around Tammy's waist, circled by the many onlookers waiting for the official weigh-in. Everyone fell silent while the officials of the tournament hoisted the huge shark up onto the scale and took notes. After what felt like hours, the announcement was made. "One hundred and fifty seven pounds!"

No sooner had the weight been announced, loud cheers erupted all around them and the crowd swarmed in closer, all wanting to congratulate them personally. Tammy squealed and planted a big kiss on Dwayne's lips while others reached out and patted whatever part of his body they could reach. Tammy felt like they had just won the super bowl.

While the crowd continued in a frenzy of cheers, snapping pictures of each other standing next to the giant catch, the officials clarified that Dwayne currently had the biggest fish. Now all they had to do was wait out the tournament until it ended at 5:00 p.m. tomorrow and hope that no other boat caught a larger one. Tammy and Dwayne both agreed it was going to be a long weekend.

Once the shark was returned to Dwayne's boat and put on ice, Tammy left the crowd in the hunt for a phone booth. Being away from Matt was taking its toll and she desperately wanted to hear his voice. As she walked up the ramp, she chuckled to herself when she overheard Dwayne telling the crowd the events of the catch. She never knew fishing could be so much fun.

After a long chat with Matt, who sounded his usual happy self, Tammy realized she was probably having a much harder time being separated from him than he was. Judy came on the phone and confirmed her suspicions, assuring Tammy that Matt was fine. After going over the fish story and telling Judy she had photos to prove it, Tammy hung up the phone in better spirits.

When she returned to the boat, she found Dwayne still surrounded by an excited mass of people, all wanting to hear how and where he caught the shark. Tammy watched from a safe distance, feeling proud to be his girlfriend.

His face glowed with joy as he repeated the story of the catch to any new people that approached the boat. It was a fishing tale that would stay with him for years. With wide eyes and gaping mouths, the spectators listened. The other fisherman, however, merely scowled with envy, giving him only a cordial congratulation.

For the rest of the day, they hung out on the docks of the tournament, where Tammy mingled with the crowds and made new friends. She could get used to this lifestyle of chatting with friendly boaters, sipping on cocktails and walking barefoot wherever she pleased.

By five o'clock, no larger shark had been caught and Dwayne was still in the lead. With fingers crossed that he would still hold the record by tomorrow evening, they drove *The Baywitch* back to the boatyard and tied it up in Dwayne's slip. Shortly after, friends from the tournament joined them for a mako feast, barbecued by Dwayne. It took a lot of coaxing from the group to get Tammy to try the fish, but when she eventually did, she loved it and wanted more.

The next morning after having breakfast in a nearby restaurant, they headed back to the docks of the tournament where they planned on hanging out all day to witness other catches being weighed in. At noon, a fishing vessel radioed in that they had a big shark and were bringing it in. As the news spread that the fish may be bigger than Dwayne's, anticipation filled the air and Dwayne, who spent his time pacing the dock, was unable to hide the worried look on his face.

An hour later, the vessel pulled into a slip and like yesterday with Dwayne's boat, it was met by a crowd of people eager to see the shark. Tammy and Dwayne held hands while looking on from a distance. There was no doubt it was a good size fish. Dwayne knew it was going to be close. With clenched fists, they followed the crowd to the scale and waited for the weight to be announced. The crowd became silent as they watched the officials compare notes and nod their heads in agreement. Finally, the weight was announced. "One hundred and thirty-three pounds."

The crowd turned to Dwayne and Tammy and cheered.

"You're still in the lead," Tammy squealed in excitement.

Dwayne let out a loud "Yes!" while picking up Tammy off her feet and spinning her around in his arms. Tammy screamed a joyous cry of relief as the crowd circled them, leaving the disappointed fisherman alone with their catch.

Tammy checked her watch. It was almost two o'clock. They still had another three antagonizing hours to wait until the tournament was officially closed. There was still time for another large shark to be caught. And Tammy learned if someone calls in a catch at five minutes to five and they are an hour out, that shark can still be brought in to be weighed and would still be entered because they called it in before the deadline.

For the next three hours, they hung around the docks mingling with others to pass the time. Dwayne constantly checked his radio for the latest fish report updates, each time feeling relieved when nothing was reported. But Dwayne knew from past experiences that could easily change.

By four thirty, Dwayne was already receiving congratulating hand-shakes by those that already believed he had won the contest. But Dwayne refused to acknowledge it until it was officially five o'clock. For the next thirty minutes, he and Tammy held each other's hands tight while counting down the minutes and pacing the docks. It was the longest thirty minutes Tammy had ever known.

At the five o'clock hour, the sound of a loud horn quieted the noise of the crowd and echoed throughout the marina, closely followed by one of the official's voices booming over the loud speaker. "We have a winner! With a magnificent weight of one hundred fifty-seven pounds, Dwayne Carson is this year's winner of the annual mako shark tournament. Congratulations! Come on up here, Dwayne."

In a buzzing frenzy, Dwayne and Tammy were swarmed by the crowd with hugs and pats as they made their way up to the podium. Tammy had never felt so proud of anyone other than her son, and at that very moment, she felt honored to be by Dwayne's side.

Wearing a huge grin, Dwayne walked up to the announcer, still holding Tammy's hand, and the crowd cheered them on when he was handed a blue ribbon and twenty five hundred dollars in cash. In triumph, Dwayne waved the cash above his head while being swarmed by photographers. It truly was a momentous occasion.

As much as Tammy didn't want the weekend to end, she knew she had to get back to her life in Pasadena. The thought depressed her. She wished she could give Matt Dwayne's lifestyle. He would learn so much about boats, fishing, the ocean and so much more from living in the marina. After procrastinating leaving as long as she could, she couldn't avoid it anymore when seven o'clock came around. Reluctantly, she pulled Dwayne away from the crowd, where he was still telling the great fishing story, and with a solemn look told him she had to go.

"Already?" he asked, glancing at his watch.

"Yes. I have to watch the kids tomorrow morning and take Judy's daughter to school. She's working the breakfast and lunch shift. I work tomorrow night. I'm really sorry. I would love to stay."

Dwayne took her in his arms. "It's okay. You don't have to apologize. I'll take you back to your car at the boatyard. Let me tell these guys I'll be back shortly and we'll get going. Okay?"

"Sure, that's fine. I'll come say goodnight too."

Fifteen minutes later, after retrieving her things from Dwayne's boat, they were standing by her car ready to say good night.

Embraced in his arms, her arms wrapped around his waist, Tammy gave Dwayne a loving smile. "Thank you for an amazing weekend. It was incredible. I can't wait to tell Matt and show him the pictures I took. I'm going to take the film in tomorrow to get it developed."

"Cool! Get a couple of copies. I'd love to have a set."

"Sure. I hope they turned out good." She paused for a moment and gave him a tender kiss. "I gotta go. Call me?"

"Better yet, I may be up your way this week. I didn't see my son because of the tournament, so I may go up one night this week after he gets out of school. If I do, I'll definitely give you a call."

"That would be great!" she said with a huge smile. Before entering her car, she met him in another sensual kiss. "Bye," she whispered, leaving his arms.

"Bye," he echoed.

CHAPTER 13

Tammy returned home to the welcome sight of her son running out the front door as fast as his little legs could carry him, dressed in his blue pajamas with his arms wide open. After smothering him with motherly kisses in the driveway, she scurried him inside to tell him all about the shark stories. They were going to be so much better than any children's book she had ever read to him.

Over the next few days, Tammy's mind was flooded with thoughts of Dwayne. She constantly talked about him to Judy and anyone else who was willing to listen to her at work. Judy never got tired of listening. The sparkle that shone in Tammy's eyes said it all and lit up the entire room. She had never seen Tammy so happy. Since she had returned from her getaway with Dwayne, she hadn't complained about her job, the long hours she worked or the stress of raising a child alone. Then it occurred to Judy that she too had quit complaining about her woes in life when she had met Joel. Somehow, life just seemed much easier when you had a good guy by your side.

Miraculously, Tammy and Judy both had the following Friday

off. Judy took advantage of Tammy being home and disappeared into the bathroom to dye her hair, something she had wanted to do for weeks. Finally, she had worked up the courage to go blond after letting her hair grow back to its natural light auburn color a few years ago.

Tammy had only heard from Dwayne once since seeing him last week. With him only having a pager, she couldn't pick up the phone whenever she felt like it and call him. She pretty much had to wait for him to call her. To her disappointment, he never made it up in the middle of the week to see his son. He had a big job on a boat to finish and just couldn't get away. But he made up for it by calling her unexpectedly that Friday afternoon.

"Hey Dwayne," she said with an accelerated heart rate.

"Hey Tammy. How's it going? Sorry I've not called. I've wanted to but by the time I get done with work, I always think it's too late to call."

"It's fine, Dwayne. You're calling now." She paused before adding, "I've missed you."

"I've missed you too. Which is why I'm coming up."

"What? You mean now?" Tammy asked, unable to hide the sudden panic in her voice.

"Yeah. I'm leaving here in ten minutes. It's okay, isn't it?"

Tammy scanned the living room, seeing the kids' toys scattered across the floor, the empty beer cans on the coffee table and the laundry piled high on the couch waiting to be folded. It was a real mess. "Um, yeah, sure, that's fine. I can't wait to see you."

"Well, I had an idea. I'm picking up my son and having him for the entire weekend. How would you and Matt like to join us?"

"Really? That would be fantastic! I can't wait to meet Justin. I'll be ready by the time you get here."

"Wonderful. We can all ride in my truck. There's enough room on the front seat. I'll swing by and get Justin first and then come by and pick you guys up." He suddenly laughed.

"What's funny?" Tammy asked.

"It just dawned on me, I've never been to your house. I need to know where you live."

Tammy joined him in the laughter before giving him her address.

As soon as the call ended, panic set in and in a frenzy, she began dashing around the house yelling, "Judy! Judy!" There was no answer. Only the sound of the radio blasting from the bathroom. "Damn it!" she said to herself, realizing it was probably going to be left to her to clean the house before Dwayne's arrival.

Tammy quickly popped her head outside the back door to check on the kids before making a start on the house. Engulfed in a game of tag, they hadn't even noticed her so, satisfied they were fine, Tammy returned inside and began yelling for Judy again. This time, she heard a reply, closely followed by Judy appearing from the bathroom with her hair now wet and blond. "Everything okay?"

Seeing her hair for the first time, Tammy came to a sudden halt. "Wow, that looks good. I love the color on you."

"Thanks. What's up?"

Tammy shook her head, remembering her predicament. "Oh, shit, yeah. Dwayne is on his way here. I've got to get this place cleaned up. Can you help me? The kids are playing in the back. They're fine."

"Fuck! You mean now? Um, yeah, sure, but let me get dressed first." She quickly scurried past Tammy to her room.

Tammy first tackled the dishes in the sink while still holding a conversation with Judy who was hollering from her room, "I can't wait to finally meet him."

"I'm sure you'll like him."

A few minutes later, Judy appeared wearing jeans, a red-t-shirt and a new hair color. "Okay, what do you want me to do?"

We gotta get rid of all these beer cans and empty wine bottles. I don't want Dwayne to see how much we've been drinking. He knows I drink but damn, Judy, when you start looking around, there's quite a few empties. It looks pretty bad."

"What am I supposed to do with them?"

"I don't know. Put them in the neighbor's trash can? I'll help you. They aren't home."

Judy threw her a devious smile as she began scooping up empty cans. "Good idea!"

It took a few minutes to fill up the trash bags and during the process, a concerned look appeared on Tammy's face.

"Are you okay?" Judy asked.

"I really need to quit drinking, Judy. Look at this. I never realized how much I drank until I started dating Dwayne. I can't keep hiding this from him. It's not a good way to begin a relationship." Tammy threw a few cans in the trash bag. "I've gotta tell him about my accident and my upcoming court date in August."

Judy approached Tammy and placed the last can in the open bag. "Whoa, girl, slow down. Don't be so hard on yourself. I drink too you know. This isn't all you. If you want to come clean with Dwayne, I suggest you do it when you're alone and not with the kids."

Tammy thought for a moment. "Yeah, you're right. I'm gonna go sneak over to the neighbor's yard with this trash and check on the kids. Can you help me fold the laundry and pick up the toys? He's going to be here soon."

"Sure, I'm on it."

After bathing Matt, Tammy was just putting the last pieces of clothing in her bags when she heard the rumbling of a truck pulling up in front of the house.

"They're here!" she hollered from the bedroom.

Judy shouted back, "Okay! I'll be out back with my kids so you can be alone for a while. But make sure you come out and introduce me before you leave."

"I will," Tammy replied while rushing to the front door with Matt by her side.

Before opening the door, she took one quick glance around the room. Satisfied with how it looked, she took a deep breath and headed outside.

Dwayne was already out of his truck and standing next to him was a young boy. He too had blond hair and was the splitting image of his father.

"Hey, Tammy, I want you to meet my son, Justin."

Tammy approached him slowly. He seemed shy. "Hi Justin." She turned to Matt. "This is my son, Matt."

He spoke only one word in a soft voice, his eyes focusing on the ground. "Hi…"

Matt came to the rescue. After saying hi to him, he took his hand and led him into the house saying, "Come on, let me show you my toys."

Now in each other's arms, both Tammy and Dwayne laughed as they watched the two boys scurry off into the house.

"How sweet is that?" Tammy chuckled. "I'm all ready to go. I just need to grab our bags from the bedroom. Oh, and my room-mate is dying to meet you."

"Uh-oh. Is this the moment where you're seeking her approval?"

Tammy gave him a playful slap on the chest. "No, silly. She's heard so much about you. It's about time she met you." She grabbed Dwayne's hand. "Come on. She's in the back yard."

Tammy proceeded to lead him through the house and out the back door, where they found Judy sitting in a lounge chair smoking a cigarette. Tammy had known her for a long time and had gotten to know her body language pretty well. From her smiles and subtle nods, Tammy knew after just a few minutes that Judy liked Dwayne.

∽

That weekend, Tammy couldn't help but feel like a real family. Something she had never experienced before. Matt looked up to Justin like an older brother and followed his every move, and Justin protected him like a younger sibling. The whole weekend was all about the boys and making sure they had a good time. Matt experienced so many first-time events that Tammy had never been able to give him before.

After a successful Saturday morning fishing trip, they all headed to the rocks of the main channel, where they spent the afternoon searching for mussels and digging for small sand crabs. The evening was spent on the boat, barbequing steak and mako, and Dwayne gave everyone rowing lessons around his boat in his dinghy.

Sunday was spent at the nearby Venice Beach, where the boys frolicked in the surf with boogie boards and played with frisbees on the sand and before heading home, Dwayne took everyone out on the dinghy again.

Like previous times, Tammy didn't want her stay to end and had a hard time leaving him, especially when she didn't know when she would see him again. Living an hour away and leading separate lives was becoming increasingly difficult as time went on. She wanted to be with him all the time, but his lifestyle of fishing and her job in Pasadena prevented that.

Before packing up her car, Dwayne told her that lobster season was only four months away and every spare minute he had would be spent preparing for the season. He explained to her that this was the busiest time of the year for him. After working on boats all day, he would be working late into the night getting the gear ready for fishing lobsters. It was intense and it wouldn't leave much time for them. He didn't know when he would make it up to Pasadena again to see his son. During this time of year, it wasn't as often as it had been, maybe once a month if he was lucky.

Tammy's heart sank. She couldn't bear the thought of seeing

him only once a month and surprised him when she eagerly squealed, "I want to help!"

A puzzled look spanned Dwayne's face. "You want to help? With getting the gear ready?" he asked.

Tammy couldn't contain her excitement. She had loved every minute of being with him shark fishing and being on the boat. She was fascinated that he was going to be fishing for lobsters next.

"Yes! I want to know everything there is to know about lobster fishing. I would love to come down here when I'm not working and help you. I won't be in your way, I promise."

Dwayne was surprised by her eagerness and her genuine interest in the industry, but he was also thrilled that she wanted to learn about it. "Really? I would love to have you come down. But I have to warn you, it's a lot of hard work and long hours. It's hard on the body. You'll go to bed with aching bones and tired muscles. Are you really up to it?" he asked with a soft smile.

"Yes. I'm up to it. I've never been afraid of hard work." But there was one thing that would prevent her from getting on board, and she needed Dwayne to know. "I have to ask though. Would I be able to bring Matt sometimes? I can't leave him with Judy all the time. And not only that, I don't want to be away from him. I'd make sure he wouldn't interrupt your tight schedule."

"Of course, that's fine."

Tammy suddenly had an idea. "Hey, I could pick up Justin too. He's only a short distance from my house."

Dwayne shook his head. "Nah. I don't think his mother would go with the idea of my current girlfriend being at her house. She's one of those jealous kinds. But thanks for the offer. I'll make time to see him."

Tammy jumped in the air like a little school girl before running into Dwayne's arms. "Oooh, I'm so excited. I'll page you this week and let you know when I can come down."

That weekend, Tammy left the marina with a feeling that she was leaving a part of her behind. She had gotten to know

Dwayne's son and everyone had bonded. She had a sense of belonging. It was a lifestyle that Tammy wanted her son to have. He had grown and learnt so much over the past few days because of Dwayne's influence. She also realized that Dwayne was good for her too. She hadn't drunk any alcohol over the entire weekend. There were a few times where she craved a beer or two, but with all the fun they were having, the cravings soon subsided.

But Tammy knew she'd have to come clean with Dwayne soon and tell him about her upcoming court date. She didn't want to jeopardize what they had by keeping secrets from him.

CHAPTER 14

A painful two weeks went by before Tammy could finally plan another trip to Dwayne's boat. She and Judy relied on each other to rotate watching the kids and working, and Judy hadn't had the last two weekends off so Tammy was stuck at home babysitting. But since spending time in the marina, home didn't feel the same.

As soon as she had returned, all the stresses of living in the city and the constant pressure of bills and being a single mother haunted her. For the first time, she had a sense of not belonging. She was living her life in auto-mode, doing what she needed to do just to get by. Day in, day out, the routine was the same. There were no waves of excitement or breathtaking views to lose yourself in. She missed the clean air of the ocean and being able to look up and see the stars. She no longer wanted the life she was living. Dwayne's lifestyle offered so much more, not only for her but also for Matt.

But Tammy had to keep reminding herself there might be a possibility that Dwayne wouldn't want anything to do with her once he found out about her accident and the upcoming court date. She feared his reaction when he discovered how long she had been keeping it from him. He would have every right to be angry with her; after all, you don't begin a new relationship with secrets. She had prepared herself for the worst—the fact that Dwayne may just break up with her over this. If he did, she was willing to accept it and would have to make the best of her life in the city, just like she always had before meeting him. She simply hadn't realized up until now that it wasn't the life she wanted.

Tired of not being completely honest with Dwayne, Tammy was anxious to tell him and come clean. She had arranged to leave Matt with Judy the next weekend so she could talk to Dwayne alone. As much as she was dreading it, she couldn't postpone it any longer. Her court date was just two months away and she no idea when she could get another weekend alone with him.

After packing her bags and saying goodbye to Matt, she left feeling hesitant about her trip for the first time. Not knowing what the outcome would be after telling Dwayne, she couldn't help but wonder if it was going to be her last trip to the marina.

She arrived at the boatyard around noon, but Dwayne was nowhere to be found. She checked his boat, the office, and his truck that was parked in the lot before finally asking one of the guys working in the yard. They had all become familiar faces, giving her a wave and a smile whenever they saw her. This man she knew as Jose. He directed her to one of the far corners of the yard away from all the boats and told her Dwayne was working over there. Tammy thanked him and headed in the direction he was pointing.

She found Dwayne, shirtless, wearing just a pair of Levis. His tanned back was facing her as he stood in front of a large work bench cutting a humungous roll of wire. Admiring the view, Tammy moistened her lips with her tongue. A radio perched on a wooden stool was blasting a Rolling Stones song and Dwayne was unaware of her presence. Tammy stopped for a moment to enjoy the sight of him working while he was oblivious to his surroundings.

She noticed beads of sweat forming on his back from the intense heat of the sun, and she watched as they began to trickle slowly down over his parched skin. His blond hair shimmered and rested on his shoulders, gently blowing from the subtle ocean breeze. As he cut the wire, she was drawn to his muscular arms, flexed and well toned. God, she was a lucky woman. She only hoped he would still feel the same way by the end of the weekend.

Not wanting to startle him while he was using sharp cutting shears, she approached the bench slowly to make her presence known. As soon as Dwayne spotted her, he threw down the shears and greeted her with a bear hug and a passionate kiss.

"Hey gorgeous! I've missed you."

Tammy squeezed him tight. "I've missed you too." While still in his arms, she scanned the area and saw five more rolls of wire stacked away from the bench and a mound of white buoys lying on the ground along with five large reels of rope. More piles of various supplies and an array of tools were also stored haphazardly around his bench. "What's all this stuff?" she asked.

"This stuff, as you call it," Dwayne said with a chuckle, "is all the material needed to make lobster traps. I need to make a hundred fifty of them within the next month. And that's on my spare time when I'm not out hustling and working on boats. Wanna help?" he said while tickling her side.

Tammy darted away from his invasive fingers. "Wow! That's a lot of traps you've got to make." She threw her purse off to the side and placed her hands on her hips. "You bet I want to help! Put me to work."

Tammy never failed to impress Dwayne with her dedication and enthusiasm. "Tell you what, I'll start you off with something easy. You know how to paint, right?"

"Yes," Tammy replied, her voice dripping with sarcasm.

Dwayne pointed to the pile of white buoys. "Good! All those

buoys over there need to be branded with my numbers and then painted with my colors, which are a red and black stripe. The numbers are so Fish and Game know who the traps belong to if they ever decide to pull it up and check it, and the colors help fisherman identify their traps while out pulling their gear."

"I never realized so much went into fishing." She tilted her head inquisitively. "And normally you would do all this by yourself?"

Dwayne nodded. "Yep."

"Wow. That's a lot of work."

"Well, this year I'm going to San Clemente Island. I've never been there but I hear the fishing is really good. In the past, I've only fished locally, and I came home every night. But San Clemente is much farther away, so I'll be spending at least a week out there and to make the trip worth-while, I'll need a lot more traps. In fact, I'm doubling the amount I normally fish with, so technically, I've doubled my work."

"And you'll be out there all by yourself?" She shuddered at the thought. "For a week?"

"Yep." Dwayne pulled her in close and whispered in a husky voice, "It will get lonely out there you know."

Tammy's heart skipped a beat. Thoughts of being alone with Dwayne, miles away from civilization, on a boat in the middle of the Pacific Ocean for an entire week sounded appealing. She couldn't believe she was actually considering going with him. She didn't reveal her thoughts to Dwayne. It was too soon. Plus, she had Matt to think about, and her job. Who could take care of Matt for a whole week? And how could she ever afford to take a week off from work to go fishing?

Tammy knew she tended to act on impulse and not follow things through with any kind of consideration. She could feel herself doing it again. But this was the chance of a lifetime, and she honestly didn't want to pass it up. Even though Dwayne hadn't officially asked her to go with him, he just dropped the biggest hint by telling her how lonely he was going to be. There had to be a way to go with him. She was going to somehow figure it out and surprise him. She couldn't wait to see his reaction when she told him.

But the daydream didn't last long. It suddenly occurred to her that she still needed to tell Dwayne about her court date and that she might possibly have a drinking problem. It's funny how just the thought of telling him ignited her cravings for a drink.

It suddenly occurred to her that she got a lot of her courage from liquor. Whenever something was bothering her, or life was too stressful, she'd open a beer or have a shot of whisky to numb her feelings. For the first time, Tammy was looking at her drinking habits in a different light. No longer did she believe it was a fun social habit; instead, she realized she depended on alcohol to get her through most of the struggles she faced in life. Yet the problems she was trying to avoid by drinking never went away and were never resolved. Alcohol just temporarily numbed them.

When she left Steven, she turned to alcohol for comfort. Ironically, unbeknown to her until she met Dwayne, she was still depending on it. Tammy was finally understanding herself but needed to gather her thoughts some more before explaining her new discovery to Dwayne.

She didn't know how long she had been self-absorbed in her thoughts, but it must have been a while because she heard Dwayne's voice calling through the fog of her reverie.

"Tammy? Tammy, are you okay? You look like you're miles away."

Tammy shook her head to clear it. "Yeah. Sorry. I was just thinking about Matt. I miss him already."

Dwayne took her hand and led her over to the buoys. "Well, let's put you to work. That will take your mind off him."

Tammy followed him and together they hung a length of rope up across the back of the workspace, and after Dwayne branded each buoy with his fishing numbers, Tammy threaded them onto the rope and spent the next two hours painting them.

Her previous thoughts were soon forgotten and her craving for alcohol quickly subsided. She was enjoying doing something other than waiting on tables and tolerating rude and impatient customers. Instead, she was working outside next to the ocean and learning so much with a fantastic guy. They were a team, working together, side by side. There was no clock to pay attention to, no boss to answer to, and she was working in shorts and flip flops. It couldn't get any better. She began to wonder if she could actually make money from doing this like Dwayne.

They continued to work until the sun went down. Tammy was eager to learn and quickly picked up on all the tasks Dwayne threw at her, from cutting the wire, clipping the traps together, and making funnels to go inside the traps. To Dwayne, she was a natural. Impressed by the amount of work they had accomplished between them, Dwayne told her he was going to treat her to a fancy dinner in the marina. Tammy loved the idea, but in reality, she knew it would also be a good time to tell him about the accident and her upcoming day in court.

CHAPTER 15

*A*fter another heated session of lovemaking in the shower, Dwayne took Tammy to a high-end steak and seafood restaurant that overlooked the main channel of the marina. The male host led them to a secluded window table with spectacular views over the water. From their table, they could see the entire marina, where endless rows of powerboats and sailboats shimmered under the dark starlit sky. There were no cars, no crowds of people or noise. It was the most peaceful place Tammy had ever experienced.

Once they were seated at their table and the host left them to browse the menus, Tammy leaned back and took in the view. "Gosh, it's so beautiful and peaceful here. You're so lucky to wake up to this every morning. I just love coming down here."

Dwayne smiled and reached for her hand across the table. "I'm glad you like my lifestyle. I feel pretty lucky." He browsed over the menu. "Order whatever you want. It's on me. They have the best steaks here."

A few minutes later, a waiter arrived and asked them what they wanted to drink. Tammy didn't hesitate and ordered a glass of white wine. She'd gone all day without alcohol and was feeling the effects. And she convinced herself she'd need it to tell Dwayne about the accident. It seemed like a pretty good excuse.

Dwayne didn't comment on her choice of drink and she appreciated it. After Dwayne ordered himself a Pepsi, the waiter left them alone to browse the menu some more. Tammy took Dwayne's recommendation and ordered a sirloin steak, and as usual, Dwayne ordered a seafood platter.

After seeking the support of three glasses of wine and with dinner almost over, Tammy finally had the courage to tell Dwayne what had been on her mind for weeks. She took the last bite of steak and before laying down her fork, she took in a deep breath. "Dwayne, there's something I have to tell you."

For a moment, he stopped eating and looked up. "Uh-oh. This sounds serious." Unsure of what she was about to tell him, he released a nervous laugh. "Let me guess, I worked you too hard today and you saw how hard lobster fishing really is and you want nothing more to do with it. You're breaking up with me. Is that it?" he asked, his nerves hidden behind an anxious smile.

Tammy quickly shook her head. "No. No. I love everything about what you do. This is about me." She paused and looked down at the table. "There's something I've been hiding from you and I think it's time you knew."

Sensing this was hard for her, Dwayne reached over the table and took her hand in a firm hold. "You can tell me anything, Tammy. Surely it's not as bad as you are thinking."

Tammy gripped his fingers for support and began the dreaded task of telling him.

"Before I met you, I got into a car accident. My car was totaled and I woke up in the hospital. Thankfully, no one else was hurt, but it could have been a lot worse."

Dwayne looked puzzled. "Why are you afraid of telling me about a car accident? Is it because it was your fault?"

Consumed with guilt, Tammy looked away to avoid his eyes.

"Yes, it was my fault. I was drunk. It was my birthday and I had too much to drink. I know that's no excuse, but I drove while intoxicated and could have killed someone because of my stupidity. The thought haunts me every day."

"Go on," Dwayne urged, sensing there was more to the story.

Tammy took in another deep breath. "When I woke up in the hospital, there was an officer there and he gave me a DUI. I've been to court twice to try and take care of the fine, and I have to appear again in August. It's my final extension and I'm not sure what will happen. I'm not asking for your help; I just think you should know." Tammy waited nervously for Dwayne's reaction.

He didn't answer right away. Instead, he mulled over Tammy's confession. "Is there more you want to tell me?"

Tammy creased her brow. "What do you mean? No, that's it."

Dwayne chose his words carefully. He admired her honesty and wanted to keep her on track. "Okay, so is it a concern of yours that you continue to drink even after the accident, and the fact that you could have killed innocent people doesn't stop you from drinking?"

Tammy felt herself sinking into her seat. She hadn't admitted to him that part of the story but he clearly understood her. Feeling embarrassed, she answered while again avoiding eye contact. "Yes."

Dwayne tilted his head to try and catch Tammy's eye. Showing his continued support, he didn't let go of her hand. "Do you think you have a drinking problem?"

Tammy could feel the tears beginning to pool in her eyes. She felt ashamed and unworthy of him. Finally, she looked up and met his stare. "Yes, I do." She let her tears flow and wiped them away from her cheeks. "And I don't know what to do. I'm an awful person and I don't deserve you."

Dwayne spoke to her like he had spoken to many others, all of whom had come to the realization that they were alcoholics. "Tammy, you took the first step. You admitted to yourself and to me that you have a drinking problem. Do you realize how much courage that takes?" He squeezed her hand. "I'm so proud of you."

Tammy took in a deep breath and smiled through her tears. She knew she had nothing to be afraid of. Dwayne wasn't going anywhere.

"That means a lot. Thank you."

Dwayne knew exactly how she was feeling. After all, he'd been there over ten years ago when he found himself in the same predicament and had decided to quit drinking. Knowing she needed a shoulder to cry on, he left his seat and took the empty one next to her. Tammy welcomed his embrace and buried her face in his shoulder while allowing her tears to drench his shirt.

"What am I going to do?" she asked between sniffles.

"Well, I think you already know the answer to that. You tell me. It's not

up to me to tell you."

Tammy was quiet. He was right; she did know the answer. "I don't want to drink anymore. But why am I so scared? Why does the thought of not drinking petrify me? My biggest fear is that you won't like me anymore. That I may be too boring."

Dwayne laughed. "Do you hear yourself? Do you realize how

dependent you are on alcohol? Think about it. I don't drink. Am I boring?"

Tammy soon realized how pathetic she sounded and all she was

doing was trying to find excuses to drink. Dwayne was right. If anything, she'd probably be a better person if she didn't drink. The problems and insecurities she was experiencing all stemmed from her drinking habits. It was like a light bulb switched on in her head. She suddenly saw herself from another perspective and it all made bloody sense.

She raised her head in triumph and for the first time, she was excited about her future. "You're right! I don't need alcohol. I can do this. From now on, I'm not going to have another drink. I'm done." She turned to Dwayne and kissed him passionately on the lips. "Thank you."

Dwayne gave her a warm smile. "You don't have to thank me. I just

listened. You are the one making all the decisions. You've got this. I can tell you, at times, it won't be easy, but I'm here for you. Whenever you want to talk, I don't care if it's in the middle of the night, you know how to get hold of me. Talking instead of drinking is the key."

Determined to be successful and now having made the commitment not

to drink, Tammy proudly pushed away the glass of wine in front of her and smiled. "I think I'll have a cup of coffee."

Dwayne smiled back and flagged down the waiter while pushing her

glass to the edge of the table to be picked up.

Tammy managed not to drink for the rest of the weekend, but she never realized up until that point how much she craved a beer or a glass of wine throughout the day. At times, she felt herself becoming irritated and found herself snapping at Dwayne for no apparent reason. Thank god he understood it was the absence of alcohol that was causing her mood swings. Once the cravings had subsided, she made a point of apologizing, and he made the extra effort to take time out and talk to her about what she was feeling. He was giving her all the support she needed. Tammy wondered how she was going to handle the cravings once she was back home and Dwayne wasn't around.

She saw how easy he picked up smoking again when she smoked around him. A wave of guilt swept through her at the thought. She knew she would be returning home to Judy who, like herself, loved to drink. She would have to be a lot stronger and not cave in to the addiction. She couldn't let it be more powerful than her own determination.

By the end of the day, she was feeling exhausted. Not only

mentally from the head trips of no alcohol but also physically. She and Dwayne had spent all of Sunday working outside in hot temperatures on the lobster gear. Her muscles were sore, her body ached and her hands were stiff from endless hours of cutting and bending wire. She'd used muscles she never knew she had, and in an odd way it felt damn good. Never had she worked so hard and had such a feeling of accomplishment. She was proud of herself, not only for not drinking but also for doing what most would call 'a man's job.' And she had loved every minute of it and couldn't wait to return and do some more.

By the end of the day, they had fifty traps built, all the buoys painted, one hundred and fifty bait jars prepared, rope cut to the appropriate lengths and more wire cut to start on the next fifty traps.

"I want to come back next weekend," Tammy said while packing her bags on the boat.

Dwayne couldn't get over her enthusiasm. It excited him every time. "Sure! I'd love it if you would. I can't believe how much we got done this weekend. We make a great team." He walked over to her, pulled her away from her bag and took her in his arms. "You're a natural. You're good at this stuff. Damn, you might even be better at it than me some day. You're a fast learner and you never cease to amaze me."

Tammy stayed in his arms, loving the security they brought her. "Oh, I could never be better than you. But I love this stuff! I mean, my nails are a mess." She held her hand out flat. "Look, they're all broken. My hair is all matted from working in the sun and I'm sweating like a pig. My body is the sorest it has ever been but as weird as it sounds, I feel bloody fantastic. I'd take this any day over waiting on tables."

"Well, there's still plenty of work to do. I still have another hundred traps to build so I could use all the help I can get."

Tammy beamed him a smile before breaking away. "Great! I can't wait. Can I bring Matt? I promise he won't be in the way."

"Of course you can bring him." He leaned down and grabbed Tammy's bag off the bed. "Come on, I'll walk you to your car."

Always hating this part of her visit where she had to say good-bye, Tammy hesitated before putting the car in reverse. She looked up at Dwayne, who was standing by her window leaning down and looking in. "I'll miss you," she said.

"I'll miss you too. Now remember, you can call me whenever you want if you're having a hard time with the not drinking thing."

"Thanks. I will. It's going to be tough with Judy drinking, but I'll be strong. I've got this."

Dwayne squeezed her shoulder. "I know you do. You'll be fine. I'll see you next weekend."

"I can't wait," Tammy replied before reluctantly putting the car in reverse. It was time to return to the life in the city where she no longer wanted to be.

CHAPTER 16

ammy arrived home after dark, feeling exhausted and regretting she hadn't taken a shower at the boatyard. But she had already left later than she had intended to and wanted to see Matt before he went to bed.

"My god, woman, you're a mess," Judy said as soon as Tammy walked through the door. Judy was sat in her usual spot on the couch nursing a glass of wine. All three kids were sat together on the floor engrossed in a movie.

Tammy laughed while closing the door behind her. "Ha! Thanks. I love you too."

The minute he heard his mother's voice, Matt was up off the floor and ran into her arms. "Mommy!" he squealed.

Tammy gave him a huge smile as she knelt to greet him and swallowed him up in her arms. "Hey buddy. I've missed you too," she said while planting a big kiss on his cheek.

Judy rose from the couch. "You look like you need a drink."

Matt soon returned to his movie, allowing Tammy to stand. "Actually, nope. I've quit drinking."

Judy froze, her mouth agape, stunned by Tammy's announcement. "What? Why? We always have wine together. Is it because of Dwayne? Did he tell you to quit?"

Upon hearing Judy thinking Dwayne was to blame, Tammy raised her hand to cut her off before she went on a rampage. "No, it's not because of Dwayne. He has nothing to do with this. I've just been doing a lot of thinking, and I think it's stupid that I've continued to drink after I almost killed myself while driving drunk. Next time, I might not be so lucky."

Judy shook her head in disbelief. "You can't be serious? You don't even drink that much. It's not like you wake up in the morning and drink all day. Don't you think you're overreacting a little bit?"

Tammy was disappointed by Judy's reaction. Instead of being supportive like Dwayne, she was actually trying to find fault with her decision. "Judy! I almost killed myself, and if you think about it, I drink every day after work and on my days off, I drink even more. I'm a mother and I need to be more responsible. I don't want to ever risk doing that again. I drink to escape my crappy life, but I don't want it to turn into a full-blown addiction where I need alcohol every day, which is where it's heading. I'm nipping it in the bud now so it doesn't slowly begin to consume me. I've seen how addiction can destroy someone's life. So have you for that matter. The fathers of our children lost us and their kids because of their drug addiction. Alcohol can do the same thing. I'm not going to let that happen."

Judy had never seen Tammy so defiant about something. "You're serious, aren't you?"

"Yes, I am. No more alcohol. I'm done. And I know this is your home too, but I'd appreciate it if you'd not drink in front of me for a while until I can get a grip on not wanting that glass of wine that is sitting in front of you."

Judy was suddenly flooded with guilt by Tammy's words. She looked down at her glass and quickly picked it up. "Oh, sure. Not a problem." She scurried out of the room with the glass. "I'll empty it down the sink. I've had enough anyway."

"Thanks. I'm going to take a quick shower and then cozy up with my little man before he has to go to bed."

For the next week, Tammy struggled with her constant cravings for alcohol, but she was so proud of herself when she succeeded and didn't drink a drop. It was much harder than she had anticipated; she was astounded by how many times throughout the long days she thought about having a drink. After work was the most difficult, because she and Judy would normally end their day with chit-chat and a glass wine or a gathering of co-workers at their local bar. For now, she was going to stay away from bars. The temptation was just too strong. Instead, she chose to go straight home and for the first time, she was home every night to tuck Matt into bed. It was something that never occurred to her—drinking had stolen that away from not only her but also her son.

She suddenly found herself more productive. No longer did she lounge on the couch sipping wine. Instead, she had quality time with Matt, playing games, going for evening walks, cooking home-made meals, reading stories to Matt and even reading books for herself, which was something she had always loved to do. She soon realized it had been a long time since she had picked up a book.

Tammy found herself wanting to keep busy to keep her mind off drinking and in the process, she discovered how much she was missing out and how much she had been neglecting Matt.

She even made a spontaneous trip with Matt on her day off in the middle of the week to visit her sister Donna, who she hadn't seen in months. She always had lame excuses for her absence, but in reality, she was too busy sitting at the bar or hanging out at home nursing a beer or a glass of wine.

Her sister lived only an hour away so it was inexcusable that she hadn't made the effort to see her more often. Donna never learnt to drive and depended on Jason for rides, but he had recently started his own tree trimming company and was working ten to twelve hour days; it was close to impossible for Donna to get him to take her to Tammy's house. Tammy understood that and blamed only herself for not visiting more often.

Tammy had other motives for visiting Donna. Still in the back of her mind was the idea of going fishing with Dwayne to San Clemente Island. Matt was only four and wouldn't start school until next year. She would need someone to watch him full time while she was gone for at least seven days, according to Dwayne, and she thought of asking Donna. But the idea soon crumbled when Donna reminded her of the one and only time she had ever watched Matt, which turned out to be a disaster. It was the year before, close to Christmas, and Tammy was visiting her sister. She saw the opportunity to get some Christmas shopping done without Matt and decided to leave him with Donna for a few hours.

While in the care of Donna, Matt took a bad fall, which resulted in his lip getting split open. Tammy returned to find Donna, in floods of tears and clearly in a panic, sitting on the couch with Matt while holding a cold washcloth to his lip. After cleaning off the blood, which made it look worse than it was, Tammy inspected the cut and didn't feel it was necessary to take him to the hospital.

But, as a result of that event, Donna was now too afraid to watch Matt for any length of time, afraid he may get hurt again while in her care.

For the first time on this most recent visit, Tammy shared with her sister about the car accident and the shame she felt.

"Why did you wait so long to tell me, Tammy?"

"I'm sorry. I've been so embarrassed by the whole thing. I can't believe how bloody stupid I was."

Donna got up from the couch where they were sitting and grabbed her cigarettes off the kitchen counter. "Well, you're really lucky you didn't get more seriously hurt." She held out the pack of cigarettes. "Do you want one?"

"Sure, thanks," Tammy said. "Yes, I am lucky. But one good thing came out of it."

"What's that?' Donna asked between drags.

"I quit drinking."

Donna returned to the couch and gasped. "You're kidding? Wow! I was wondering why you hadn't asked for a beer yet. I was about to offer you one. Sure glad I didn't now," she said with a laugh.

Donna had been her only hope. She couldn't ask Judy because she had to work. Only then did it occur to Tammy that poor Judy would have to find someone to watch her own kids if Tammy did manage to find a way to go to the island. Although she and Dwayne had agreed Matt could go along for the weekend, there was no way she could take him with her for a full week. It would be too dangerous. Dwayne had explained to her that he would be living on the boat for the entire time because the Navy owned the island and there was no access to the public. Tammy knew there would be no way she could keep Matt confined to a boat for a week.

Tammy was determined to find a solution. But she also realized she couldn't make any concrete plans until she learnt the outcome of her court appearance, which was coming up in the next few months. She knew if she didn't pay the fine, there were no more extensions and she would probably be facing jail time. She had no idea how much time the judge would sentence her to, but there was a possibility she might be in jail when it came time for Dwayne to go fishing. The thought petrified her.

She wanted to go to San Clemente Island more than anything. She was learning everything there was to know about preparing for lobster season, listening to Dwayne's stories about his previous adventures and how much fun it was to pull up traps and find them loaded with lobsters. He said it was better than Christmas. After spending hours prepping the gear with Dwayne, Tammy wanted to experience that gratification first hand.

She called Dwayne every day during the week to give him a progress report on the no-drinking project and also for moral support. He had a way of talking to her where everything made sense. The times she had broken down on the phone and told him she couldn't do it anymore, he knew exactly what to say and put everything back in perspective.

There was one time she had called him late in the evening. It was after Matt had gone to bed and there was nothing on the TV. Judy was out with her boyfriend and their friends, and she was home alone babysitting. She had tried to focus on reading, but the cravings were super strong. And she knew Judy's beer was in the fridge. Three times she had opened the fridge and just stood there staring at the cold cans, listening intently as they screamed at her to pick them up and take them back to the couch.

Not knowing what else to do and not wanting to give in to her cravings, she lit her fourth cigarette and called Dwayne. He stayed on the phone with her for an hour, talking to her about anything. What had she done that day? How was Matt? How was work? What was she wearing? That last one got a chuckle out of Tammy.

He didn't let her hang up until he was convinced she no longer craved a beer and promised she would go straight to bed. She kept her promise and after hanging up the phone, she turned off the lights and went to sleep. Her last thought was about how lucky she was to have Dwayne in her life.

CHAPTER 17

Over the next month, Tammy switched her days with other servers so she and Matt could spend every weekend with Dwayne. Their productivity was much slower now that they had a four-year-old to keep occupied, but Dwayne wasn't concerned. He was still way ahead of where he would have been without Tammy's help.

They spent the first two weekends cutting wire, making traps, painting buoys and cutting ropes. By mid-July, Tammy felt like she belonged in the community and received a lot of admiration from the crew working in the boatyard as she worked alongside Dwayne.

Many stopped by the corner of the yard on their breaks to watch the duo in action. Some even helped by entertaining Matt. He had become the little buddy of many, and the guys seemed genuinely excited to see him when he came dashing through the yard, anxious to see Dwayne and all the boats.

Everyone in the boatyard knew Dwayne was on a tight schedule to get ready for lobster season so they all pulled together like one big family, eager to help by taking time out from their own jobs to spend some time with Matt. Some played soccer with him in the middle of the yard, some showed him the boats they were on and gave him little easy jobs. Others brought him a cheeseburger and spent their lunch hour with him. Like Tammy, Matt was beginning to enjoy being in the marina more than at home and couldn't wait until the next weekend arrived.

By the end of the second weekend, all the traps were built and stacked neatly in the corner of the yard. The piles of wire scraps had been tossed, the ropes were coiled and hung up and buoys were stacked along the side wall. Tammy stood back, leaning against the workbench to admire their work while Matt bounced a buoy around at her feet. "Look at that. It's only mid-July and you have all your traps built. What are you going to do for the next month?"

Dwayne laughed at her comment. "Sweetheart, those traps aren't even close to being finished. When you come next weekend, we're going be unstacking fifty of them, cementing them and dipping them in tar. We can only do fifty at a time because we have limited space in the yard. And, trust me, it will take all weekend to do fifty."

Tammy cocked her head in confusion. "Wait. What do you mean by cement and dip them?"

Dwayne released another laugh as he approached her and gave her a playful hug. "The traps have to be weighted so they will sink to the bottom of the ocean. That's what the cement is for. And I dip them in tar—just like what's on the roads—so they don't rust and will last longer in the ocean."

Tammy stood for a moment while she tried to work out the process. "So you mean to tell me we have to unstack all these traps again?"

"Yep. By the time you get here next week," he said, pointing to the space at the end of the work bench, "there will be a cement mixer over there and next to it will be a large dip box full of tar. The best bit? You get to play with both cement and tar. So prepare to get messy. Oh, and be sure to bring some long pants and long sleeve tops. The older the better. You can't be dipping in shorts. The tar is really tough to get off your skin."

"Oh boy, I can't wait. I'm sure Matt's going to love it too."

Thinking she had learned everything there was to know about building lobster traps, Tammy muddled the next part of the process for most of the following week. It actually sounded like fun. For weeks, it had been the same repetitive chores, so she was looking forward to doing something different. Even if it meant getting covered in cement and tar.

Yet again, she found herself anxious to be a part of the fishing industry and couldn't wait for the next weekend to come around. Matt mirrored her excitement, to the extent that her days in the city were now spent listening to Matt asking when they were going to the boat again. It seemed neither of them enjoyed the city life anymore.

Per Dwayne's request, Tammy and Matt arrived at the boatyard super early on Saturday, just in time to see the sun come up. He wanted to get the dipping part done before the day got hotter so the dip would have time to dry. Dressed in her oldest worn-out jeans and an already stained shirt, she found Dwayne at the corner of the yard amongst twenty plus bags of cement and a shiny new orange cement mixer. Tammy gasped. "God, that's a lot of cement. Are we going to use all that?"

Facing away from Tammy and Matt, Dwayne was startled by her question and was almost knocked over by Matt's enthusiastic hug when he rushed over and locked his arms around Dwayne's legs. "Yep, we certainly are," he said, bending down to give Matt a loving hug. "We might even need more."

She turned and looked at a large plywood box. It stood as tall as her waist, was at least four feet wide and wasn't there last week. "What's that?"

"That's the tar dip."

"I can't wait," Tammy said sarcastically, even though she was intrigued by the whole operation. Eager to get started and learn something new, Tammy rubbed her hands together. "Okay, tell me what to do. I'm all yours."

"All mine, eh? I like that." Dwayne laughed before getting down to business and giving Tammy the rundown on what needed to be done. He walked her over to a huge blue tarp that was lined with rows of dipped traps. "I had the afternoon off yesterday so I was able to get these dipped. They're pretty light without the cement." Dwayne touched one and rubbed his fingers to check they were still clean. "They're dry now so we can cement them."

Being early, the yard was quiet, which meant no one was around to entertain Matt, but Dwayne had a way of making it fun for him so he enjoyed being involved. At this stage of the building process, being just wire, the traps were super light to handle and Matt was made to feel important by helping Dwayne carry a trap over to the dip box.

Wanting to beat the rising temperatures, Dwayne wasted no time in turning on the cement mixer and getting Tammy to help him hoist up the first one-hundred-pound bag of cement and empty it into the mixer.

"Fuck, that's heavy," Tammy yelled over the din of the motor. Once relieved of its weight, she stood back and watched Dwayne cut the bag and pour the contents into the mixer. As soon as he did, a large cloud of dust blew out of the opening and settled all over Dwayne's face.

Dwayne quickly turned his head and shouted, "Hold your breath. Don't breathe
this stuff in."

Tammy only needed to be told once. She quickly pulled Matt away and gave him a pile of buoys to play with; they always seemed to entertain him.

They repeated the process and lifted another two bags into the mixer, and then Dwayne added water using a long hose that stretched through the yard from the nearest faucet. After a few minutes, Dwayne felt comfortable that the cement was mixed to the right consistency and turned off the mixer. Tammy's ears struggled with the sudden silence as Dwayne grabbed two five-gallon buckets. "Now the fun begins." He winked at Tammy with a playful smile. "Here, hold one of these buckets under the mixer as I pour some cement into it. I'm only going to fill it halfway, otherwise they will be too heavy."

Using both hands, Tammy held the bucket tight, but the sudden weight of the added cement being poured in caused her to almost lose her grip. "Damn it!" she yelled as she quickly adjusted her grip to compensate for the extra weight. She lowered it to the ground with a thud when Dwayne was done pouring. "Now what?" she asked.

"Grab the other bucket. We're going to fill that one too."

After the buckets were filled, they each took one over to the traps. Dwayne then showed her how to pour a little cement into each corner of the bottom of the traps until the wire on the base was covered with cement. Two buckets did three traps. Already feeling the strain in her back, Tammy stretched her muscles and scanned the rows of remaining traps. "Only forty-seven more to go."

It took most of the day to complete the task, working under the cruel heat of the sun with no shade and few breaks. Again, the community of the boatyard came together and helped by keeping Matt busy. Lifting the cement bags, carrying the weighted buckets and bending over each trap was so back-wrenching that by the time they had reached the last trap, Tammy struggled to move.

With a joyous sigh of relief, she threw down the bucket, grabbed an ice-cold water from the cooler and collapsed on the ground next to the workbench. "I can't believe we got them all done," she said as beads of sweat poured down her face and glistened in the sun. Enjoying the cool sensation of the cold water gliding down her throat, she poured some over her head to break the intensity of the heat rushing through her veins. "God, that feels good," she said while shaking her head. Matt, who was now with them, laughed at his mother drenching herself in water, her hair soaked.

Dwayne joined her on the ground, patting her wet hair as he lowered his body. "It was a team effort. There's no way I could have gotten all of them done on my own." He gave her a peck on the cheek. "Thank you."

Tammy lowered her head on his shoulder but quickly pulled it back. "Ouch! God, even my neck is sore. My entire body is one big sore." She laughed. "And you don't have to thank me. Even though my body aches, my muscles are beyond strained and I feel like I have no fingerprints left, I love doing this stuff."

"Well, I'm glad you do. I don't know too many women that would do this. You are an exception. Even the guys in the boatyard are amazed by your strength and stamina. No pun intended, but you're quite the catch."

"Awww, you are too, and I truly mean that."

Still exhausted from their day of intense labor, they decided to do absolutely nothing for the rest of the evening except take showers and hang out on the deck of the boat with Matt until, at around nine o'clock, they were too tired to stay awake.

CHAPTER 18

The next morning, Tammy could barely get out of bed. Holding her back, she pulled herself upright and released a moan of agony. "Man, I feel like I've been run over by a train."

Dwayne and Matt were nowhere to be found in the small cabin, and no clock hung on the wall so she had no idea what time it was. She struggled some more to get her wounded body out of the bed. Her joints creaked as if they needed oil, her hands were rough like sandpaper and her neck and shoulders hurt from the inside out. When she finally managed to stand, which was a long drawn-out process consisting of repetitive moans and sharp screams of pain, she made her way up on to the deck and scanned the boatyard and slips.

She heard Dwayne's voice off in the distance.

"Hey! You're awake," he yelled.

Tammy turned her head in the direction of his voice and spotted him fishing off the dock with Matt. What a way to wake up—coffee and fishing. It couldn't get any better.

An hour later, around eight, they were back at the corner of the yard. After two large cups of coffee and keeping herself moving, Tammy's body was beginning to loosen up and she was ready to face another day of intense labor. Dwayne didn't seem fazed by yesterday's strenuous tasks and was raring to go.

After taking a sip of his coffee, he led Tammy far across the yard to another stack of traps.

"These are traps from last year. We have to dip these too."

Tammy stared at the pile. "But these already have cement on them. Aren't they going to be heavy?"

Dwayne nodded and gave her a smirk. "Yep, 'fraid so. It's gonna take the two of us to dip these." He looked at the stack and folded his arms. "These are gonna take a lot of dip, so I think we should dip them before we finish the new ones."

Tammy let out a huge sigh. "Okay, let's get to it. Where are we going to put them? You're taking up half the yard already."

"That's okay. It's the weekend." He looked over at the traps they dipped yesterday. "We can lay a tarp next to those and line them up alongside."

It took them well over an hour to unstack the traps and lay them in a row on the ground, by which time, Tammy's back was already beginning to hurt again.

"God! How much do these things weigh?" she asked while rubbing her side.

"About seventy pounds. You going to be okay?"

"Yeah, I'll be fine. Let's do this."

Dwayne had Tammy help him remove the heavy plywood lid on the dip box. Tammy looked inside and scrunched her face at the black gooey liquid.

"Eww. This looks like it could be messy."

Steering an eager Matt away from the box, as he was anxious to look inside, Dwayne laughed. "Yeah, you could say that." He handed Tammy a large pair of black rubber gloves. "Here, put these on. You don't want to get any of this stuff on your hands."

With the over-sized gloves now in place, Tammy couldn't help but feel like the mad scientist. "Okay, what are we doing?"

After setting Matt up with buoys and blocks of wood to keep him occupied, she'd given him strict instructions to keep away from the wet traps. Dwayne handed Tammy a rod of rebar. "We first need to stir the tar up really well, and then we're going to dip each trap into the tank and put them back on the tarp to dry overnight."

"Wow! This will take a while; it's so much work. I sure hope you catch some lobsters after all this."

"Fishing is the easy part. Getting ready to fish is the hard bit."

"No kidding. I had no idea there was so much involved," Tammy said as she began to stir the thick black liquid, being careful not to splash any on her clothes.

After a good thirty minutes of stirring, they were finally ready to dip the first trap. Anxious to get the first one in the box, Tammy attempted to lift a trap on her own but quickly changed her mind. "Damn! These are heavy."

"Yep. The cement just added another thirty pounds of weight to them. Each trap now weighs about sixty. Come on, we'll both take an end and lift them together."

Tammy couldn't imagine how she was going to feel by the end of the day after lifting all these traps, and she decided it was best she didn't think about it. After setting the first trap on the edge of the box, they slowly lowered it into the dip box until it was completely covered. Tammy watched as the liquid gurgled and the trap sunk beneath the surface. It reminded her of quick sand. "That's pretty cool. Now, how do we get it out?"

Dwayne raised his gloved hands. "With these."

"Seriously? And I thought the cement part was messy."

Dwayne looked at Tammy as he took his place at one side of the box. "Ready?"

"Let's do this," she replied as she positioned herself on the other side. Next, she reached inside the box and slid her gloved hand into the tar in search of the top of the trap. "God, it's so thick."

"It has to be so it will stick to the wire."

Suddenly, she felt the trap and quickly wrapped her hand over the wire, making sure she had a good grip and hoping her glove wouldn't slip off. "Ah-ha! Found it," she yelled in triumph.

"Good. Now, hold on tight. We're going to pull it up together and rest it on the side of the box to let all the excess tar run off."

"Okay. I'm ready."

"One, two, three…and lift."

Using all her strength, Tammy lifted at the same time as Dwayne and was amazed at the effort it took to get the trap up onto to the edge. As they pulled, the liquid tried to suck the trap back down; she thought it would be easier if they were pulling it out of quick sand. By the time it was out of the tar and dripping, Tammy was leaning over trying to catch her breath.

"Man, that was heavy." She glanced at the rows of un-dipped traps. "And we have to do all these?"

Dwayne threw her a cocky smile. "Yep. Come on, let's walk this one over to the tarp and grab another one."

Because it was Sunday and most of the workers took the day off, the yard was empty besides them. Thankfully, though, Matt was doing a really good job of entertaining himself while they dipped the traps. Sometimes riding his bike that Tammy had brought down, or playing with his ball or the buoys or eating snacks. The boatyard was like a huge playground he had all to himself, and he never once seemed bored. More importantly, he stayed where they could keep an eye on him at all times.

By noon, they had managed to get thirty-five of the traps done and Tammy's body was feeling it immensely. Not only did every part of her body ache to the core, but her clothes from the waist down were caked with dry tar along with smears of it on her face where she had unknowingly wiped it with the glove. Parts of her hair were even glued with tar. "God, I'm a mess," she proclaimed. "I need to take a break."

"I think you look cute. But sure, I need a break too. I'm having a hard time keeping up with you. I thought you'd never ask."

Tammy groaned as she removed her gloves and walked her aching body over to a lounge chair, where she called Matt over for a snack and some juice. A few minutes later, Dwayne's pager went off with a high-pitched beep. He pulled it out of his front jean pocket and looked at the display. "I gotta make a phone call. It's one of my clients. I'll be right back."

"Okay, I'll be right here. I'm not moving." Tammy took a sip of cool water and lit a cigarette.

Dwayne returned ten minutes later with a distraught look on his face.

"Everything okay?" Tammy asked.

"No. Not really. I gotta go. A client of mine is in a sailboat race tomorrow and his bilge pump isn't working." His face flushed with anger. "Damn it! I really wanted to get these traps done before the yard fills up with workers tomorrow. I was hoping to get them all stacked in the morning after they've had a chance to dry and before the boatyard opens." He looked over at Tammy, who appeared stunned from his sudden outburst. Clearing his throat, he continued in a calmer voice. "Maybe it won't take that long and we'll have time to finish up when I get back. I need to get out of these dirty clothes and change. Will you guys be okay until I get back?"

"Of course. Do what you have to do. We'll be fine."

Tammy understood his annoyance and disappointment; after all, she was feeling it too. They were on a roll and could have probably knocked out the last batch of traps in an hour and been done for the day.

After Dwayne left, a feeling of defiance crept over her. She refused to be defeated by the fact that Dwayne had to leave. Plus, it would be fun to surprise Dwayne if she could dip the traps by herself. She began to toil with the idea in her head. The main obstacle would be lifting them out of the box. She'd have to use her upper body strength for leverage and brace the trap against her stomach to move them on to the ground to dry, which meant she really would be covered in tar. Then she had an idea.

Determined to complete the task singlehandedly, she pulled out a roll of over-sized, extra strong black trash bags and tore one off the roll before holding it lengthwise in front of her body. It reached below her knees. "Perfect! This will work." She then proceeded to make a hole, just big enough for her head in the sealed bottom, and two on the sides for her arms. Once she was satisfied with her creation, she pulled it over her head and slid her two arms in like a smock. Her entire body was now protected. Matt laughed at her new idea of fashion.

"You look funny, Mommy." He chuckled as Tammy made her way over to the traps. Using both hands and all her strength, she heaved one of the traps over to the dip box and up on to the edge. Out of breath already, she had to pause before lowering it into the box. "I can do this," she proclaimed between gasps for oxygen. After catching her breath, she lowered it into the tar and watched it sink beneath the surface. "Okay, now how the hell am I going to get this thing out and over to the other traps to dry?"

On her first attempt, she failed miserably. It was just too heavy and she soon found herself exhausted. A couple of minutes later, she had an idea. She tried picking the trap up by its short end and standing it on its side while still in the dip. From that angle, she had more leverage and could pivot the trap out of the dip and onto the top corner edge. Once there, she could let it sit and drip while she caught her breath again.

Pleased with her progress so far, she now how to figure out how to carry the trap over to the drying area without wiping most of the tar off. She couldn't hold it against her body because the side touching her would be wiped clean of tar, and again she thought about using the short side, just like she did when it was in the dip box.

Using the wonders of gravity, she inched the trap to the edge of the box and grabbed the two short sides. While holding it, she pulled it way from the box and allowed gravity to take over until the trap was just inches from the ground. From this position, even though it was a struggle, she was able to walk the trap over to the others and slowly lower it onto the ground to dry.

Matt cheered at her success. "Do another one, Mommy," he hollered from his spot in the deck chair, amused by his one-man-team mother and her terrible attire.

Now that she had the system down, Tammy knew she could get the rest of the traps done on her own. She knew she'd probably regret it afterwards and would be hurting for days to come, but she was driven by wanting to see the look on Dwayne's face when he returned and saw all the traps were dipped and laid out to dry. It would be well worth it.

He returned a few hours later, just when Tammy was dipping the last trap. Matt rushed across the yard on his tricycle to greet him. The shock on Dwayne's face was priceless as he scanned over at all the dipped traps.

"You've got to be fucking kidding me! How the hell did you manage to do all those? And what are you wearing?" He looked up and down at the trash bag now soaked with tar covering her body.

Tammy beamed him a smile. "It's a trash bag, and it worked great to protect me from the tar. Now watch," she said, excited to show him her method as she began pulling out the last trap from the box.

Fascinated and amazed, Dwayne watched as she completed dipping the last trap and set it down to dry. "Wow! You're amazing! I can't believe you did all those by yourself. Come here and give me a kiss."

"You're welcome. I knew I could do it. And now you don't have to worry about getting the rest dipped before tomorrow. They'll

all be dry by the morning. I'm just sorry I won't be here to help
you stack them," she said as she slowly tore the sticky bag away
from her body and tossed it into the trash can.

"Oh, don't worry about that. I'll manage. You've done enough,"
he said, still in shock over what she had done. "Now, where's that
kiss?" he asked while taking her into his arms.

"Ooh...ouch!" Tammy screeched as Dwayne squeezed her tight.
"Not so hard. My shoulders are killing me."

"Oh god, you're going to be hurting later. I wish I could be
home with you to give you a full body massage later. You're going
to need it."

"I know. I'm going to soak my body in the tub as soon as I get
home. I'm beginning to feel the pains of my labor already.
Speaking of which, and I hate to say it because of how much I
want to stay here and help you, I must return to my boring life in
the city. I have to go to work tomorrow. But I'll be back next
weekend."

"Great! Because it's gonna be just like this weekend. We're
going to dip fifty more traps."

A genuine smile blanketed Tammy's face. "I'm actually looking
forward to it. Call me crazy, but this beats waiting tables any day."
She rubbed her back. "By then, my body should be healed and
ready for the next round."

It was becoming harder to leave the marina when it was time
for her to go home. She was returning to a life where she felt she
no longer belonged and had absolutely nothing to look forward to.

As usual, she found Judy on the couch, and Tammy immediately zoned in on the glass of wine on the coffee table and a
sudden craving for alcohol began to poke at her mind. For the
entire weekend, she had been too busy to think about drinking,
but as soon as she walked through her front door, the temptations
were all around her. Judy followed Tammy's eyes and instantly felt
the tension between them as Tammy quickly looked away from
her glass.

"Sorry, I'll get rid of it," Judy said as she scurried away to the kitchen.

Exhausted from the weekend, Tammy simply nodded. "Thanks."

But she was starting to realize that she and Judy were beginning to take different paths in life. It was a realization that she didn't want to confront so instead, she headed to the bathroom for a soak.

CHAPTER 19

ammy and Matt returned to the marina the following weekend and just as Dwayne had warned her, it was exactly like the previous one where they spent both days cementing and dipping another fifty traps. And, just like before, her body was screaming with pain by the time they were finished.

Judy wasn't home when she returned. She and her kids were spending the weekend at her boyfriend's house. But she promised she'd be home later that night to watch Matt the following day while Tammy worked. Tammy was expecting Judy to announce any day now that she was moving in with Joel—that's how much they'd grown apart. They only saw each other to drop off their kids when one of them needed to work.

Tammy had no idea how she would manage on her own if Judy moved out. She depended on her for a lot of things, from child care to splitting the bills, and with her upcoming court date that had been constantly occupying her mind, she was relying on Judy to take care of Matt if needed.

That date was coming up fast. She only thought about it when she was home, just like all the other worries that consumed her.

But she still hadn't managed to save any money for the fine. How could she? She was barely making enough to make ends meet as it was. During her recent visits with Dwayne, she never mentioned it to him because she always tried to leave her problems behind. Otherwise, her weekends would be ruined.

When the eve of her court date was upon her, Tammy still didn't know what to tell the judge. She knew she was out of extensions and would be facing either jail time or community service.

Feeling the urge to have a drink to calm her nerves, Tammy decided to call Dwayne, who always seemed to make her feel better during testing times. She paged him and waited for him to call her back, which he did within ten minutes.

"Hey, you okay?" he asked with concern.

"Yeah. I just wanted to hear your voice. It's a rough night. I've got court tomorrow and I'm a nervous wreck, so of course I want a drink. Because, as we both know, alcohol fixes everything." She laughed.

Dwayne sounded shocked. "It's tomorrow? Why didn't you tell me?"

"Yes, it's tomorrow, and I'm telling you now," Tammy said with a hint of sarcasm.

"But I want to be there. What time is your hearing? And which courthouse is—"

"Now wait just a minute, Dwayne. What do you mean you want to be there? What if I don't want you there? I'm kind of embarrassed by the whole thing as it is, and I'm not sure if I want you seeing me standing in front of a judge."

"Oh come on, Tammy. You're being silly. I want to give you some moral support. Can you at least allow me to do that?"

Feeling guilty for her stupidity and realizing he was willing to take time out of his busy schedule to be with her, she immediately softened her tone.

"I'm sorry. You just took me by surprise. I had no idea you

wanted to be there. Thank you. That's really sweet of you. Have you got a pen? I'll give you the details."

After giving him the address of the court, they remained on the line for a while longer until Tammy's cravings for alcohol subsided. Once she'd hung up the phone, she decided to watch the news before turning into bed. It was then that she came to a decision on what she would tell the judge tomorrow.

One of the headline stories was about Civil Brand, the women's jail in downtown Los Angeles. Apparently, they were releasing many inmates early due to an excessive problem of over-crowding. Some were only doing ten percent of their time. Tammy was glued to the set, a seed of an idea growing as she told herself what she was going to do. She just needed Judy to get home so she could talk to her. After all, she was part of the plan.

Struggling to stay awake, Judy finally arrived home sometime after eleven. Before she even had a chance to take off her coat or peek in on her sleeping kids, Tammy stopped her in her stride. "Sit down. I need to talk to you."

"Can't it wait? I just got home," Judy stated in an irate voice. The odor of alcohol resting on her breath didn't go unnoticed either.

Tammy ignored her request and motioned her to sit down on the couch. "The kids are fine. They are all sleeping. This is really important."

Judy rolled her eyes. "Fine. What's up?"

"I'm going to jail and I want to make sure you'll be able to take care of Matt."

Judy's jaw dropped. "What? Are you crazy? What do you mean you're going to jail?"

"I know it sounds crazy but I've been watching the news. They're releasing people early because of overcrowding. If I turn myself in tomorrow, I bet I'll only do a few days."

"And if you don't? What if they keep you in for most of your sentence? Which, by the way, might be weeks or even months for all you know. I'm sorry, but your idea sucks." Judy had heard enough. She shook her head in protest before attempting to leave the couch, but Tammy grabbed her arm and pulled her back down.

"Hold on a second, Judy. I have no other choice. I can't do community service. That would take up endless hours of time and I can't afford to take so much time off from work. If this goes to plan, I'll only miss a couple of days. Tell me you can watch Matt?" Tammy pleaded.

"Matt will be fine. I'll work it out with Joel. Between us, we'll be able to take care of the kids. If worst comes to worst, I can always ask my mother. But I can't believe you are seriously considering this. What does Dwayne think?"

Tammy lowered her head. "I've not told him." Then she raised her voice a notch. She was not going to argue about this. "And I'm not going to tell him. He will only try and talk me out of it like you're doing. My mind is made up."

Judy raised her hands in defeat. "Okay. It's your life. I just hope your plan works. They might keep you in for weeks. You know that, right?"

"There's a slim chance that might happen, yes. But as long as I know Matt will be okay, I'll get through it."

"Tammy, you've never been to jail. You have no idea what you're in for. I hope for your sake you're not there too long." Realizing Tammy had made up her mind and there was no more to be said, she again attempted to stand. This time, Tammy didn't stop her. "Okay then, I guess I will see you when I see you. Call me from the inside when you can, and good luck. I'm off to bed."

"I will, and thanks," Tammy said as she took Judy's hand. "You're a good friend."

Judy scuffed the top of Tammy's hair. "And don't you ever forget that." She laughed before leaving the room.

Tammy pondered her decision for a few moments and told herself she was okay with it. She was tired of the fine hanging over her head. It had been dragging on for almost eight months. She wanted to be done with it so she could move on. This was the only way.

Other than going to jail, her only other anxiety was how was Dwayne going to react. He'd only find out Tammy's plan when she told the judge.

CHAPTER 20

$\mathcal{T}$ammy had to be in court by 9:00 a.m. She gave herself plenty of time in the morning, to shower and get ready. She wore her best jeans that were not faded and free from any holes. Knowing she was going to jail she wanted to be comfortable. She chose not to wear any jewelry, considering the fact that she was turning herself in, and she told Matt a little white lie, that she was going to be gone a few days with Dwayne. At first, he was upset but only because, of course, he wanted to go too, but Tammy bribed him with a movie date when she returned.

She arrived at the court building a half-hour early and after parking her car, she began scanning the parking lot for Dwayne's truck. But it was a huge lot with tons of white trucks just like Dwayne's so she soon gave up. After entering the court building, she glanced down the corridors at the crowds of people sitting on wooden benches along the walls. Some were reading official documents, others were talking to well-dressed men and women—who Tammy assumed were their attorneys—and many were pacing up and down the corridors with excessive nervous energy.

Tammy was disappointed to see there was no sign of Dwayne.

She thought maybe he got an emergency call from a client. And then it suddenly occurred to her that there was no way to call him from jail. He only had a beeper. She hoped he would call the house and Judy could fill him in.

While waiting for the courts to open and with no empty seats, Tammy stood against a wall and kept to herself. At the end of the hallway, a woman was crying as she clung to who Tammy believed was her husband. The man tried to console her but failed miserably, and more people began to stare in her direction as her cries became louder and more frantic. Tammy wondered if he was going to jail today also.

Distracted by the woman's cries, Tammy hadn't noticed Dwayne walk in, and she jumped when he squeezed her shoulder. "Fuck! You scared me," she roared while holding her chest.

Dwayne chuckled. "I'm sorry. I thought you saw me."

"That's okay." Tammy leaned in and gave him a peck on the cheek. "Thanks for coming. But you didn't have to, you know?"

He wrapped an arm around her shoulders and pulled her in close. "But I wanted to be here. You don't have to thank me." He glanced down at his watch. "It's almost nine. You should be going in soon. Are you nervous?"

"Yes, I'm nervous. I just want this to be over."

"And it will be," Dwayne reassured her.

Tammy considered telling him her plan, but after no more than a few seconds, she decided against it. She knew he'd only protest and would try every possible way to talk her out of it. Once in the courtroom before the judge, she knew he couldn't say anything.

A few minutes later, the doors of the courtrooms were opened and people began to shuffle in. Tammy swallowed the lump in her throat and tried to calm her accelerated nerves. "Ready?" she asked Dwayne while taking his hand.

He squeezed her hand tight. "You'll be fine. I'll take you out for a fancy lunch afterwards."

Tammy knew he wouldn't be able to, but she simply nodded as

they walked hand in hand into the courtroom and took a seat near the back next to a much younger man and an older couple, who Tammy assumed were his parents. For the next five minutes, Tammy watched as people of all races and ages continued to file in and claim their seats, all waiting to hear their fate from the judge.

The noise level steadily increased as people took their seats and talked with each other and their attorneys. Tammy and Dwayne remained quiet. Occasionally, Dwayne gave Tammy a comforting rub on the shoulders and asked if she was okay, and Tammy gave him a simple nod.

A few minutes later, everyone stood and the room fell into complete silence as the judge entered and took his seat of authority. Tammy swallowed another lump in her throat before sitting again. Her nerves were now at their peak, but she managed to hide them successfully from Dwayne.

For the next hour, they listened to cases mostly about traffic violations—speeding, parking violations, and DUI's like Tammy's case. One girl cried before the judge as she stood next to her attorney—something Tammy couldn't afford—and listened as the judge gave her a final extension. Tammy wondered if she too would be turning herself in to jail in three months.

Another guy said he could pay the fine, sending vibes of jealously through Tammy, and the last guy chose community service and was required to do five hundred hours. Tammy gasped and calculated the amount of days that would be. She whispered in Dwayne's ear, "Wow! That's over twelve weeks."

"Maybe he had priors?" Dwayne whispered back.

"I don't think so. Not with a DUI."

Suddenly, Tammy heard her name echo through the courtroom. "Shit, I'm up," she said under her breath into Dwayne's ear while handing him her purse.

Dwayne gave her arm a gentle rub as she squeezed past him and made her way to the front of the courtroom, feeling all eyes upon her. She stood in silence before the judge as he peered over his glasses and read her case. She could do nothing but wait for him to speak.

As she waited, a thousand questions raced through her mind, none of which she had no answers to. *How will Dwayne react? Will Matt be okay? Will I still have a job?* She hadn't told her boss because he had the next two days off and was hoping she'd be out of jail by the time she had to go back.

The judge interrupted her thoughts and gave her a stern look as he read the DUI charge to her. Then, with a cold, harsh stare, he asked, "What is it going to be, Miss Mellows? Today, you must either pay the fine, do community service, or do jail time."

Tammy hesitated before answering. Was she doing the right thing? She had no other choice.

"Miss Mellows?" the judge asked again.

Tammy looked straight ahead, not taking her eyes off the judge. "I'll...um...I'll do jail time, Your Honor."

Suddenly, Tammy heard an outburst from the spot behind her where she knew Dwayne was sitting. "What!" he screeched, along with gasps from many others.

Tammy didn't look at Dwayne. She couldn't. She would only weaken, and she couldn't allow that to happen.

The judge ordered silence and stated, "So be it, Miss Mellows. I sentence you to twenty-one days in the county jail."

Tammy was shocked by the amount of time the judge had ordered her to serve. It was much more than she had anticipated. What had she done? She would never be out in a few days with that much time to start with.

There was another outburst from Dwayne. "Wait. I can pay the fine!" he yelled. Tammy turned and saw him pulling out a wad of bills from his front pocket and holding it up to show the judge.

The judge gave Dwayne an angry stare. "One more outburst from you and I'll hold you in contempt of court."

"But..." Dwayne said in a softer tone as he returned to his seat, realizing the judge was not going to listen to him.

Tammy felt her eyes beginning to mist. Struggling to hold it together, she quickly turned back towards the judge. If she looked at Dwayne again, her knees would just buckle beneath her and she refused to let him see her that way. She committed the crime, and there was no way she was going to allow Dwayne to bail her out. She had to take responsibility for her own actions.

Once the court was back in order after Dwayne's outburst, the judge focused on Tammy again. "Miss Mellows, did you want to begin serving your sentence immediately or do you need some time to arrange things at home and turn yourself in at a later date, which I would set today?"

Again, while rubbing her sweaty palms across her stomach, Tammy hesitated and swallowed hard before answering. "I would like to begin my time immediately, Your Honor."

Again, Dwayne couldn't refrain himself. "What! Tammy, you—"

"Silence!" the judge ordered before turning to the bailiff and instructing him to take Tammy into custody.

Tammy couldn't hold back her tears any longer and allowed them to fall as the bailiff approached her. Showing no sympathy, he ordered her to put her hands behind her back. Waves of whispers rolled through the courtroom as Tammy felt the cold metal of the handcuffs grasp her skin. She shuddered when she heard them snap closed.

Without looking back, her heart tore at what she was putting Dwayne through, leaving him to witness her being led out of the courtroom in handcuffs. She wished now she had insisted he hadn't come. What thoughts would be going through his head as he drove home alone with only her purse sitting next to him? Tammy wouldn't blame him at all if he didn't want to see her ever again.

CHAPTER 21

*D*wayne was numb from what he just witnessed, and for the next hour he sat lifeless in the courtroom with images of Tammy in handcuffs haunting his mind.

She knew all along she was going to turn herself in. Why didn't she tell me? Why didn't she let me pay the fine?

He looked over at her purse, alone on the chair next to him where Tammy had been sitting just a short while ago. He pictured her sitting in a cell, crying and scared. He wasn't angry with her. He was disappointed that she hadn't confided in him or asked for his help. He knew she was independent and hard-headed, but yet again her pride got in her way. She didn't have to go to jail. They could have worked this out.

Oh, Tammy, what have you done? How am I supposed to go back to my life knowing you are locked up for the next twenty-one days?

Lost in his thoughts, the distant voice of the judge calling, "Court is dismissed," followed by the loud knocking of the gavel on his wooden desk brought Dwayne back to reality. He hadn't been expecting to leave the court alone. He wasn't prepared for this. He didn't want to abandon Tammy knowing she was probably still somewhere in the courthouse. But she had left him no other choice.

Before standing, he took one last look at the door where she had been led away and with a heavy heart, he picked up her purse and forced himself to leave for the lonely drive home.

~

Once Tammy had been escorted out of the courtroom, she let her tears fall. The tears weren't from fear of what lay ahead for her. They were for Dwayne. The thought of him sitting alone, oblivious to her plan and watching as she was taken into custody, unable to do anything about it. It pulled at her heart strings. She knew she had hurt him and regretted now not telling him. It was selfish of her for putting him through that and she wondered if he would ever forgive her. Did she just destroy the best thing that had ever happened to her? Sadly, she wouldn't know until she was free again. The not knowing was going to be harder than being locked up in jail.

She was led to a room where some other female inmates of various nationalities sat waiting. Some were Hispanic, two were of color, and the remaining four were white. Tammy was relieved the guard had removed the handcuffs before locking the door behind him.

She was greeted by silent nods and screening stares from the other females. She nodded back and made her way to a desolate corner and quietly took a seat, keeping to herself.

She remained in the room for the next four hours. Two other women were brought in during that time. One was Hispanic and crying, and the other was a petite blond who Tammy knew was high just by looking at her dilated eyes. Past experiences had taught her that was a dead giveaway. She had seen the look too many times with Steven.

Not knowing what to expect, Tammy remained tense for the

entire time she was in the room. The constant sound of her heart hammering against her chest prevented her from talking. A couple of the women nodded in her direction, usually followed by the words, "Hey, what are you in for?" After she had told them a DUI, they again nodded and left her alone while they chatted with other women. Tammy got the impression it wasn't their first time in jail.

The room where they were being kept was small, and the lack of air quickly became apparent. Many of the women, Tammy included, began wiping their sweaty brows with their sleeves. Others walked back and forth, complaining of the heat while fanning their faces with their hands. Outer layers of garments were removed and tossed in corners, and everyone expressed a need for water to quench their elevated thirst. As the hours dragged on, some of the women became irritated and began yelling.

"Hey, we need some water here!" one shouted from the other side of the tiny room.

"This is fucking bullshit. I wouldn't keep my dog in these conditions," another shouted with her face pressed against the door.

But nobody came.

Tammy cowered in the corner as their ranting continued. A young Hispanic girl sat next to her and they both muttered a few words, each sensing they were not a threat to one another. They remained seated next to each other for the rest of their time in the room.

When the sound of footsteps could be heard approaching the door, silence swept over the room and smiles of relief replaced the frowns on most faces. With anticipation, all eyes focused on the door, waiting for it to open. Two sheriffs entered the room, both with their hands cupped over guns hanging from their hips, ready to grab them if necessary. "Okay, everybody form a single line."

Immediately, all the women stood to attention and faced the officers. Tammy was at the back of the line and watched as each girl was handcuffed with their hands in front of them before being led out in single file. Tammy cringed when she felt the familiar sensation of the cold metal touching her skin and the snap of the cuffs binding her wrists.

They were led out into a narrow corridor, with one of the sheriffs in front and the other at the end of the line behind Tammy. After a maze of corridors and locked double doors, they ended up outside at the back of the courthouse. Tammy breathed in heavily, filling her lungs with the welcoming fresh air that greeted them. Parked at the curb was a black and white jail bus with all the widows barred. One by one, the women were instructed to board the bus in single file. Just like the room, the bus was hot and stuffy. Tammy took an extra moment to breathe in and fill her lungs one more time with the fresh air before being told to "move it" by the sheriff standing behind her.

The noise level on the bus was deafening. All the women seemed happy to finally be out of the hot room, and the small amount of fresh air they'd managed to grasp in transit seemed to have perked them up and put them in better spirits. Tammy quickly scanned the bus for the girl she sat next to in the holding tank and spotted her in the middle on the right. She was relieved to see the seat next to her had not been taken and quickly scurried over to her. The woman smiled when she recognized Tammy and patted the seat next to her with cuffed hands.

Within two minutes, the engine of the bus began to roar and the doors slid closed. The two sheriffs at the front exchanged a few words before the driver put the bus in gear and drove out of the covered parking lot, onto the main street and into congested traffic.

While sitting idle at the traffic lights, Tammy looked out of the window over her new friend's shoulder and noticed all the people in the cars surrounding them. She found herself envious of their freedom. They were going about their daily lives, traveling wherever they pleased and whenever they wanted with no restrictions.

Some were with friends or loved ones. Others had their children in the back seat.

Tammy thought of her son. Was he missing his mom as much as she was missing him? What was he doing right now? She choked back her tears at the thought of not being there at night to tuck him into bed. *I'm sorry, Matt. Mommy will be home soon.* Tammy remained silent with her thoughts as the bus meandered through the traffic on its way to Civil Brand, the women's county jail.

Tammy guessed it took about an hour to arrive at the back entrance of the jail. Once the bus had come to a complete stop, the doors were opened and the women were ordered to exit. They were led by the two same officers, again one at the front and one at the back, through a large metal gate and then through several sets of double doors, all of which had to be buzzed opened. Standing on the other side were two hefty female guards dressed in brown uniforms. They stood straight, with their feet apart and their fingers curled around the leather of their belts. Their stares were cold and their bodies were stiff. Immediately, one of them took authority and yelled at the women.

"Okay, ladies! Follow me in single file and there will be no talking."

Obeying her orders, the women fell silent and followed her down the cold lime-green hallway. They had to go through three more locked metal gates before they reached the holding tank where they would wait until booked. A guard stood at the doorway of the holding tank and removed the handcuffs from each woman before she shuffled away.

When it came to Tammy's turn and her wrists were free, she began rubbing them vigorously to relieve the constant urge to itch that she had been experiencing for the past hour. The room was about the same size as the one at the courthouse but painted the same ugly lime-green like the hallways, and like the other holding tank, it had no windows. Concrete benches hugged the walls, and there were just enough seating spaces for the dozen or so women, although a few chose to stand in the middle of the room.

Tammy sat across from the same woman as before and nodded when she saw her. The woman nodded back and then folded her arms and closed her eyes. Tammy tried again to keep to herself, but a colored woman sitting next to her, dressed in a skimpy black dress, black stiletto heels and wearing heavy make-up, nudged her arm. "Whatcha in for, girl?"

Tammy felt the lump rise in her throat but swallowed it before answering. Unable to hide the nervousness in her voice, she softly answered, "DUI."

"Your first one?"

"Yes."

The woman nudged her arm again. "They got me for prostitution. Third time I've been 'ere in a month." Again, she nudged Tammy's arm. "A woman's gotta make a living, right?"

"Right," Tammy quickly agreed, wishing the woman would leave her alone.

"So what's your name, girl?"

"Tammy."

"You're a shy one, ain't you?"

Tammy didn't reply. Instead, she looked down at her feet and rubbed her arm, which was now sore from the constant nudges she had been receiving.

"Everyone calls me Raven," the woman said before letting out a loud laugh and putting her face close to Tammy's. "That's because I'm dark and mysterious." To block the stench of alcohol coming from the woman's mouth, Tammy quickly turned her head and held her breath. She rolled her eyes as Raven continued to talk. "You'll be fine, girl. Just keep to yourself and don't piss anybody off. They ain't gonna keep you here long. Before you know it, you'll be out."

"Thanks. I hope so," Tammy replied before folding her arms

against her chest and closing her eyes, hoping the woman would sense she wanted to be left alone.

To her relief, she did, and she began talking to the woman on her other side.

Finally left to her thoughts, Tammy sat quietly, her eyes still closed and her mind filled with thought of all the things she took for granted: her son, her home, Dwayne, and most of all, her freedom. She wondered how long it would be before she would be able to experience any of that again.

She was overcome with shame when thoughts of family entered her head. Her father, Joanne, her mother, and her two older sisters. What would they think of her if they could see her now? She didn't want to know the answer to that. She had let everyone down, including herself. Once she got out of this wretched place, she was going to make sure she'd never be back. Even though she had managed not to drink alcohol for almost two months, she now knew for certain she would never touch the stuff ever again.

She didn't know how long they were kept in the holding tank, but it felt like hours. She had lost all track of time. She had no idea if it was still daylight outside or night time. She was hungry, her mouth was dry from her long-suffering thirst and her body was stiff from sitting on the hard, cold benches. When a few of the women were called and escorted out of the room, Tammy wondered where they were being taken. Were they released or being moved to another part of the jail? Every time a guard entered the room, the chatter of the women ceased in the hopes they would hear their name called. Tammy held her breath, wondering if she'd be call next. Utters of disappointment and a few cuss words were exchanged amongst the women when they were left behind. Tammy's heart sank at the notion that she was to remain in the same room for much longer. Being idle for so long was killing her. She wasn't use to wasting her days away by just sitting in one spot for hours on end.

Tammy wasn't sure how much time went by until a guard entered the room again. "Tammy Mellows," she heard through the fog in her mind. All heads scanned the room, looking to see who the name belonged to.

"Here," Tammy said nervously while rising to her feet.

"Come with me," was all the guard said.

As Tammy made her way to the front of the room, some on the women patted her on her shoulder as she walked by.

"Bye, girl," she heard from Raven.

She was led down a maze of corridors and through more metal gates until they reached a counter with a small window at head height. The guard instructed her to stand by the window. Tammy did as she was told and remained motionless, afraid to make any sudden moves that might startle the guard. A middle-aged woman, heavyset with dark brown hair and dressed in the same uniform as the others, appeared at the window and handed Tammy a plastic bag.

"Place all your valuables in the bag. Jewelry, cash, wallet, purse."

"I have none," Tammy quietly said.

The woman retrieved the bag. "Okay then." She looked Tammy over. "What size are you? About a medium?"

"Yes, I think so," Tammy replied.

The woman disappeared and returned a few minutes later with an orange jumpsuit and handed it to Tammy. "Here you go. This should fit. Follow the guard down the hall."

Tammy picked up the jumpsuit and proceeded down the hallway behind the guard. Her stomach rumbled as she walked. She wondered when they were going to feed her. She hadn't eaten or drank anything in hours. What she wouldn't give for a glass of water right now.

The guard led her in to a room on the left, where another guard with glasses and blond hair pulled up into a bun was waiting. The room was painted in the same lime-green, and a wooden desk sat in the center, piled high with papers. The box of rubber gloves sitting on the edge didn't go unnoticed. A pile of large plastic bags sat on the floor next to the desk, and a black and white chart showing measurements in feet hung on the back wall.

The guard that had brought Tammy in nodded to her co-worker.

"I'll take it from here," the co-worker said while looking at a file. She paid no attention to Tammy.

After the other guard left, Tammy stood in the middle of the room, her heart pounding beneath her skin, her bones rattling from the cold, desolate room. The guard still hadn't looked at her. She might as well have been a crumb on the floor.

"Are you Tammy Mellows?" the guard finally asked while continuing to look at the papers in her hand.

"Yes."

"Okay then. Approach the desk."

Tammy did as she was told and waited for the next order.

The guard opened one of the desk drawers, pulled out a fingerprint kit and a book and laid them on the surface of the desk. "I need your right hand," the guard said in a flat tone.

Tammy lifted her hand and allowed the guard to maneuver it across the ink. But the guard struggled to get it in the exact position she wanted. "Relax your hand," she commanded.

Tammy tried her best, but she could still feel the tension in her muscles as she watched the guard first roll her index across the ink and then her thumb.

"That's good enough. Now go stand against the wall in front of the chart and face me."

With nothing to wipe her inked fingers on, Tammy rubbed them across her jeans as she walked over to the wall. She blinked as the flash of a camera took her by surprise. She didn't need to ask what she looked like in the picture, but she didn't dare ask for a re-take.

"Okay, I need you to strip down and put your clothes in here." The guard handed Tammy one of the plastic bags.

"You want me to take *all* my clothes off?"

"That's what I said, isn't it? Now come on. I've not got all day."

Tammy was horrified that she had to remove all her clothing and stand naked before this woman. How humiliating. Up until now, she had managed to hold it together, but this was the worst feeling in the world. She had never felt so degraded and unimportant. This was just wrong. She felt the tears welling up in her eyes as she slowly began to undress, first her shirt, and then her jeans. She folded them carefully and placed them in the bag along with her tennis shoes and socks. She felt a sudden chill, as her skin was now exposed to the cold, damp air of the room. Hesitating, she remained standing in only her bra and panties, and she slowly lifted her arms to cover her chest.

"Come on. I need the underwear too." The guard seemed agitated.

Tammy looked away and closed her eyes, trying to stop the tears from falling. Taking a deep breath, she removed first her bra and then her panties. She dropped them in the bag, her hands now shivering from the cold.

The guard set down the papers and pulled a flashlight out of her back pocket. "Open your mouth," she instructed as she strode across the room, flashlight in hand.

Tammy obeyed and looked up while the guard shone the bright light into her mouth and then into her eyes. Next, with a puzzled expression, Tammy watched as the guard put on a pair of rubber gloves. "Now face the wall and spread your legs apart," she said as if it were a perfectly normal request.

"What?" Tammy squealed in disbelief.

"Just do it."

Tammy wanted to do nothing but run into a corner and hide. Never had she felt so humiliated and violated by another human being. She realized now they were searching her for drugs. Wanting to get this over with as quickly as possible, she walked over to the wall with her arms covering her breasts and did what the guard instructed. Once the intrusion was over, she heard the words she'd be longing to hear. "Okay, you can get dressed now."

Tammy couldn't pull the white cotton underwear and orange jumpsuit on fast enough. She wrapped her arms around the ugly suit, enjoying the protection from nakedness it gave her.

Once dressed, the guard led Tammy out of the room, where another guard was waiting beside the door. She was once again led through a maze of corridors and brought to a huge hall full of cots. There must have been at least fifty of them. Each had one flat pillow and a brown blanket. At the entrance of the hall was a booth surrounded by glass and a small hole to speak into. Inside the booth, Tammy saw four female guards.

"This is where you'll be spending your time. You're assigned to bed twenty-eight." The guard pointed to the middle of the room. "Over there."

Tammy scanned the room. There were only three other inmates inside, and all were looking her way.

"But where's everyone else? This place is empty," Tammy said with uncertainty.

"Yep. We did a bunch of early releases this week. Now, go claim your bed. They'll be calling you for dinner pretty soon."

Tammy's heart sank and tears gushed down her cheeks.

What have I done? They've already done all the early releases. I may be in here for weeks, Oh god...Matt, Dwayne, I'm so, so sorry.

CHAPTER 22

*D*wayne didn't know how long he sat in his truck in the parking lot of the court. In fact, he didn't even remember walking to his truck. When he'd left the courtroom, he was feeling so numb that he was oblivious to everything around him. He remembered staring out of the window of his truck and just looking over at the court house, knowing Tammy was still in there somewhere.

He believed she wasn't aware how much she had hurt him. She had obviously put some thought into turning herself in today, because he knew she would've had to arrange for someone to watch Matt while she was locked up. Dwayne assumed it was Judy. So, if Judy knew what she was going to do, who else knew? "Why didn't you talk to me, Tammy?" He crashed his fist down on the dash and looked over at her purse before yelling some more. "You should be sitting here next to me. We were supposed to go have lunch!" He couldn't help but feel disappointment toward her. He thought their relationship had reached a level where she could trust and confide in him. Obviously, he had been wrong.

He was steered away from his thoughts by a screaming mother, who was chasing a young child through the parking lot while yelling at him to stop running and wait for her. Dwayne watched as the child turned and looked at his mother, laughed, and then began running again. He waited until they were far enough away from his truck and fired it up. He turned and looked at Tammy's purse one more time, shook his head, put the truck in gear, and pulled out of the parking to head back to the marina. Alone.

~

Tammy was lying on her assigned bed with her stomach in knots from hunger and her mouth so dry that she was finding it hard to swallow. A loud female voice suddenly came over an intercom.

"Stand up next to your beds. Dinner is in fifteen minutes."

The thought of food and liquid gave Tammy an instant boost. She jumped to her feet and realized she must have dozed off when she saw there were now at least a dozen other women in the hall, some she recognized from the holding tank.

The guards followed the same procedure as before and led the women in single file, one in front and another in the back, to a massive food hall two hallways down. The fowl stench of the food hit Tammy's nostrils as soon as she entered the room. It reminded her of the smell of school dinners, something she always used to hate. She gasped at the number of inmates crowded in the hall. There must have been hundreds of them, all wearing orange jumpsuits, sitting twenty to a table, ten on each side. Tammy tried not to make eye contact with anyone as her group was led to the front and made to stand in line with a plastic plate. But she could feel the daunting stares as she nervously walked by, keeping her eyes fixed to the ground.

Tammy watched with disgust, curling her lip, as dollops of

mashed potatoes, creamed corn, and what she thought was some sort of meat dish in a disgusting tanned color sauce was plopped on her plate. Not to mention the three cooks drenched in sweat that were responsible for serving it. The last cook handed her a carton of milk and a bottle of water. With her food in hand, her group was led to a table near the back of the room and ordered to sit.

Tammy sat next to an Asian girl who seemed harmless enough and nodded in her direction as she took a seat. The Asian girl rolled her eyes, muttered something under her breath and then turned the other way.

Tammy felt hurt by being shunned; she was just trying to get along with whoever crossed her path while locked up in this hell-hole. Tammy decided to give her the same treatment and ignored her for the rest of mealtime.

The girl across from her, who she found out was called Charley, seemed okay. She smiled at Tammy when she sat down, said hello and immediately asked her name. She was about Tammy's age and was in for shoplifting. Apparently, it was her fourth time committing the same crime.

Consumed with hunger, Tammy cleaned her plate of the vile looking food within minutes. She would have eaten a frog if it was put in front of her. She gradually felt the stomach pains begin to subside and after drinking the bottle of water in one continuous gulp, she was beginning to feel like herself again.

After her meal, she chatted some more with Charley before being interrupted by the same guard that had brought her and the group to the hall. She stood at the end of the table and instructed them to pick up their plates and stand. Tammy said a quick goodbye to her new friend and followed the guard and the others to the trash bins to throw away their plates before being led back to their beds.

When they returned to the hall of beds, Tammy thought she

was in a different place. The room was now over half full with inmates. Some were curled up sleeping, others were grouped on beds laughing and singing, and a few sat on their own sobbing. Tammy couldn't believe how quickly the room had filled up in just a few hours. Her spirits were suddenly lifted with hope. *Maybe there is a chance of getting an early release after all.*

She spotted her friend from earlier sitting on the edge of a bed, talking to another girl. She saw Tammy walk in and waved her over. Relieved to have someone to talk to, Tammy immediately took her up on the invite and scurried over to join them. Conversations between them were light and friendly. She found out the other girl's name was Amelia. Oddly enough, it was the first time in jail for all of them. Six unpaid parking tickets for Amelia, and a DUI for the other new girl called Sandra—who, ironically, also swore she would never drink again.

Suddenly, an outburst from the back of the hall startled Tammy and the rest of the women

"You, fuckin' bitch! I'm gonna kick your ass!" a rough-looking fair skinned woman yelled at the top of her voice to a petite young colored woman.

Everyone else froze and turned to watch the commotion in silence. Only the two women could be heard. Tammy watched in horror as the heavyset woman grabbed the other woman by her hair and threw her to the ground.

Others close by began to chant, "Fight! Fight!"

"Isn't anyone going to stop them? They'll kill each other," Tammy shrieked to Amelia and Sandra.

Within a few seconds, a loud horn went off and an angry voice came over the intercom as five guards hurried out of the booth.

"Back to your beds. Now!" the voice yelled.

Tammy leapt to her feet and dashed over to her bed and sat on the edge. She watched as the guards raced over to the two women, who were still in a raging fight on the ground, and yanked them apart.

"Okay! Break it up!" one of the guards yelled.

Tammy was astonished it took all five guards to break up the fight and drag the two women out of the hall.

With the commotion over, the room soon began to return to normal and sounds of chatter and laughter filtered around the remaining women. But a few minutes later, the angry voice came over the intercom again.

"Okay. You ladies don't know how to behave. Lights out in five minutes."

Tammy heard the protest from many of the women around the hall, yelling cuss words and using finger gestures to express their disapproval. But they were ignored and in five minutes, as promised, all the main lights went out, leaving just a few dim ones to illuminate the room. Tammy curled up in her bed and fell asleep listening to the whispers and subtle giggling of the few that refused to go to sleep.

~

She wasn't sure how long she had been sleeping and thought she was dreaming when she heard loud voice calling her name.

"Tammy Mellows! Wake up!"

Tammy stirred in her sleep but still hadn't opened her eyes.

"Tammy Mellows!" the voice shouted again.

She realized she wasn't dreaming and remembered where she was. Groans and complaints came from the other women, as they too were now awake from the yelling of the guard. Tammy sat up and rubbed her eyes, and then she spotted the guard standing two beds away.

"Get up, Mellows. You're going home."

"What?" she asked. But she didn't need to be told twice and jumped out of bed as fast as a bolt of lightning. "Are you serious?"

"As serious as I am standing here. Get up and follow me."

With her eyes now focused and adapted to the dim lights, Tammy scanned the beds and saw every single one was occupied. *My god! This place filled up in a matter of hours.*

"Come on! Move it!" the guard yelled.

"Coming. Coming," Tammy quickly replied, her heart racing with excitement.

As the guard marched toward the door, Tammy hurried to catch up with her. Once in hearing range, she found the courage to ask, "What time is it?"

Without looking back, the guard replied, "A little after midnight."

Tammy calculated in her head that she'd only served under twelve hours from the time she was first handcuffed in the court-house until now. She chuckled to herself. That worked out to be over a hundred dollars an hour of her fifteen hundred dollar fine. Unlike before, she was now chuffed to bits about her decision to turn herself in. No one could argue with the outcome. Finally, the DUI that had been hanging over her head for months was now finally behind her. She had done everything the courts had requested her do and now she could move forward with her life.

Lobster fishing was the first thing that came to mind. She was now free to figure out a way to go fishing with Dwayne. That is if he still wanted to be with her after the stunt she pulled in the courtroom.

The release process took a few hours, but by 2:00 a.m., Tammy found herself standing on the streets of Los Angeles at the back of the jail. She was happy to see it was a full moon, the night air was warm and the street was well illuminated with lights.

To her right, she saw a row of phone booths, conveniently placed for the newly released inmates like herself. But panic consumed her at the sight of the phones. She hadn't thought this far ahead in her plan. She had no money! She couldn't call Dwayne, as he only had a pager and couldn't call collect on it. The only option she had was to call her house and wake up Judy, but she couldn't expect her to pack all the sleeping kids into the car and come to pick her up. She didn't want to put Judy or the kids through that. Tammy thought long and hard.

She had an idea and walked over to one of the phone booths and reluctantly dialed zero to call the operator. After two rings, a woman's voice came on the line.

"This is the operator; how may I help you?"

"Yes, I'd like to make a collect call," Tammy quickly replied.

After giving the woman the number to her house, Judy answered the phone after a few rings in a sleepy voice and had apparently accepted the charges.

"You're now connected," the operator confirmed before leaving the line.

"Judy! Judy, it's me. I'm so sorry to wake you, but there was no one else I could call. I'm out! Can you believe it?"

Judy snapped out of her drowsy state. "What? You're kidding me?"

"Yes! My plan worked. How is my baby boy? I can't wait to hold him. Listen, I want you page Dwayne and punch in this phone number when it alerts you for a call back number. I don't want you to wake the kids to come get me."

"Sure, not a problem."

"Thanks. It's late, so I'm not sure if he will return the page tonight. He may think it's a job and wait till morning. I'll give him twenty minutes. If he doesn't call me by then, I'm going to have to call you back and I'm afraid you'll have to come pick me up."

"That's fine. I'm just glad you're out. Will you be coming back here?"

"Yes! I want to see Matt in the morning." Tammy then proceeded to give Judy Dwayne's pager number and the number to the phone booth.

"Okay, I'll make the call and then I'm going back to bed. Call me if you need me."

"Will do, and thank you."

After hanging up the phone, Tammy looked at her empty wrist and realized she wasn't wearing her watch. "Damn it!" she whispered under her breath and began pacing the sidewalk, desperately hoping the phone in the booth would ring soon. Knowing Dwayne would have to get dressed and walk across the boat yard to return the call, Tammy gave him some time.

After what seemed like hours, although it was probably only ten minutes, the phone still hadn't rung. "Come on, Dwayne. Call me back," Tammy pleaded out loud as she huddled her body in her arms and continued to pace back and forth to keep warm.

Suddenly, a car pulled alongside the curb and a window wound down.

"Hey! You need a ride?" yelled a male voice from inside the car.

Tammy froze. "No, I'm good. Thank you."

"It's awfully cold out here. I can take you any place you wanna go," said a

young colored man, who Tammy guessed was probably in his late twenties.

"I have a ride. Thanks again."

The man leaned out of the car window. "I don't see no car here."

Suddenly, a loud ring came from one of the phone booths. "That's him. I gotta go." Tammy rejoiced before dashing over to the phone. In the distance, she heard the car speed off and released a huge sigh of relief.

She swiped the receiver off the hook so fast she almost dropped it. "Dwayne! Dwayne! Are you there?"

"Tammy! Yes, I'm here. How are you able to call me?"

"I'm out! I'm standing outside the jail and I need a ride. Can you come get me? I'm all alone and it's pretty creepy out here."

"You're out? Oh my god! Yes! Yes! Of course I can come get you. It's going to take me a while to get there. Hang tight, okay?"

"Okay…and, Dwayne?"

"Yes?"

"I'm so sorry for not telling you I was going to turn myself in."

"It's okay. You can explain later. Let me get on the road. I'll see you soon."

"Okay, and thank you," Tammy replied in a soft voice before hanging up.

CHAPTER 23

*T*ammy knew it would take Dwayne at least an hour to get to the jail from the marina and spent her time pacing the sidewalk to stay warm, hoping no more strangers would stop to offer her a ride. She kept herself occupied by trying to think of ways to go fishing with Dwayne in September—if he allowed her to, that was. Tammy racked her brains, trying to come up with a solution on who could watch Matt. *There has to be a way!*

Suddenly, after what seemed like an eternity, she saw bright headlights coming down the road. Unable to see the vehicle, Tammy shielded her eyes from the glare and backed away from the curb with uncertainty, not knowing if it was another stranger.

As it approached the curb, Tammy clearly recognized it as Dwayne's truck and raced over to meet him. Once it was in park, she saw Dwayne lean over and unlock the passenger side. Tammy yanked open the door and immediately saw her purse sitting on the seat. She picked it up and hugged it. "My purse! Thank you for taking it," she said while hopping into the truck.

"Well, you left me no choice." Tammy sensed his sarcasm and knew he deserved an explanation. He leaned over and gave her a hug. "Welcome home," he said with what Tammy felt was a forced smile. It wasn't the welcome she had hoped for and felt she needed to smooth things out before they could move forward in their relationship.

Dwayne put the truck in drive and casually said, "I'll take you home."

With no mention of him spending the night, Tammy felt the tension between them. She reached over and placed her hand on his thigh. He didn't reciprocate, which had Tammy worried.

"Dwayne, I'm sorry I didn't tell you I was going to jail. I knew if I did, you'd talk me out of it somehow and I couldn't let that happen."

He turned and gave her a stern look. "Why would that have been so bad, Tammy? You didn't even give me the chance to help you. I had the money. This could have been prevented. You didn't have to go to jail. And yeah, my feelings were hurt. I thought you could talk to me."

"I know that now. You know the crap I went through with Steven. I've always had to figure out stuff for myself, and I guess I've become hard-headed because of it. I'm so used to my one-man army that I don't know how to ask for help. And besides, why should you pay for a crime I committed? That's not right."

Dwayne released a slight chuckle, which lifted Tammy's spirits a little. "First of all, I'm not Steven, and second, I would have made sure you paid me back. I wasn't going to make it that easy." He reached over and took her hand. "From now on, if something's bothering you, know that you can talk to me about it. Okay?"

Tammy finally relaxed in her seat. He was right. She should be able to trust him and reach out to him. "I'm sorry. I'll try and change my stubborn ways."

Dwayne laughed. "That's better. Now come over here and give me a kiss. I've missed you, woman. Don't ever pull something like that again."

"I won't. I promise." With a huge grin, she hastily scooted over to his side, snuggled into the embrace of his arms and gave him a hard kiss on the cheek. It felt good to be close to him again. She breathed in his scent and knew this is where she belonged. She thought for a moment and with hesitation decided she was going to share what was troubling her. "You know, there is something that is bothering me. It has for a while and I don't know what to do about it."

"Really?" Dwayne sounded pleased she was about to confide in him. "Well, go on, tell me. Maybe I can help. It begins by sharing. See?"

The butterflies she was feeling were somewhat calmed by his humor. "I don't think you can help, but maybe you have some ideas that will help me." Tammy took a deep breath. "You know, for the past month or two, I've been working really hard with helping you get ready to go fishing and I've loved every minute of it." She stalled for a moment.

"Go on," Dwayne urged her.

"Well, I'd like to be there when you start reaping the rewards."

Dwayne took his eyes off the road for a second and looked at her. "You mean you want to go fishing with me?"

"Yes, if you'd let me."

"I would love it! Why should that bother you? Do you think I wouldn't want you to come with me? I was actually going to ask you this week. But apparently, you had other plans of going to jail." He laughed, but Tammy could hear the excitement in his voice.

"Really? I would love to go!"

"Tammy, I love the idea of you being out there with me. It gets so friggin' lonely. So what's the problem? Why does it bother you? Do you think I was going to say no after you've been right there next to me, working just as hard as me? I wouldn't do that."

"No, that's not it. I can't just take off for a week. Who's going to watch Matt, and what about my job? That's what's been bothering me. I have no one to watch him and my job isn't going to allow me to take a week off. Not only that, I can't afford to lose a week's pay."

Dwayne's tone suddenly became flat. "Oh, I see what you mean. That is a problem. Hmm, we're going to have to think about this one."

"I've been thinking for weeks now and can't come up with a solution. Judy can't watch him; not only will she have to work, she will have figure out who will watch her kids if I do go. I thought about asking my sister, but she's afraid of watching him ever since he fell at her house one time and split his lip. There is no one else. And I can't take him with us. It's too dangerous."

Dwayne suddenly mentioned an idea that hadn't occurred to Tammy. "What about your parents?"

"My parents? You mean my dad and Joanne?" Tammy creased her brow. "You do know they live in Florida, right?"

"I know. Maybe they would like to spend some time with their grandson. When was the last time they saw him?"

"Oh, I don't know, Dwayne. That's an awfully long way to go, and I'd have to put him on a plane. I don't think I can do that. And besides, there's still the issue with my job."

"Well, that's easy. Just quit. You'll get a cut of the money we make fishing, so you'll still be getting a paycheck."

"Quit?" Tammy was horrified by his suggestion. "I can't quit! What will I do when I get back?"

Tammy suddenly realized they were pulling into her driveway. She had been so busy talking about her hopes of going fishing that she hadn't been paying attention to their drive. Once the truck was in park, Dwayne turned to her and gave her a passionate kiss on the lips. "You know there really is a simple solution to this."

"There is?" Tammy replied with her eyes narrowed.

"Sure. Quit your job, you and Matt come live with me on the boat, and you can become a commercial fisherwoman. There are only a handful in California, you know?"

"Is that a word? Fisherwoman?"

"It is now!" Dwayne laughed.

Tammy was stunned by his idea. Quit her job? Leave Judy and move in with Dwayne on a boat? She had to think about this. "Oh, Dwayne, I don't know. It all seems so sudden. I've been known in the past to make hasty decisions. And it still won't solve the problem with Matt for the fishing trip. And do you think there's enough room on the boat for all three of us?"

"Sure there's enough room. The dinette table folds down into a bed. Matt could sleep there. I'll admit, it will be a little cramped, but hey! It will be an adventure." He laughed and gave her a cheeky wink. "Call your parents. I'm sure they'd love to have him over for a visit."

Tammy shook her head in despair. "Can we go inside and talk about this? I'm freezing sitting out here. You're spending the night, right?"

"You bet I am." He laughed. "I need to talk some sense into you."

CHAPTER 24

*I*f felt good to be home. Dwayne and Tammy tip-toed through the house so as not to wake anyone, and before running a much-needed bath, Tammy quietly stood over her son as he slept and gushed at the sight of him. Overjoyed to see his innocent face, she carefully leaned over and gave him a gentle kiss on his forehead. "Mommy's home. I've missed you, buddy," she whispered softly.

Dwayne joined Tammy in the bath, where together they erased all lingering scents of the jail from Tammy's body and quietly made love. Afterwards, they huddled on the couch until 5:00 a.m., where they finally fell asleep in each other's arms, discussing Dwayne's idea in whispered voices.

Tammy still couldn't wrap her head around upending her life so drastically and suddenly. She needed time to think about it. But time was running out. Dwayne would be leaving to set the first round of traps in a month.

Even though he was exhausted from little sleep, Dwayne had to leave the next morning for work. He left Tammy with her thoughts and in the company of her son, who screamed with joy when he saw his mommy sleeping on the couch.

Over the next few days, Tammy's life began to fall back into its normal routine of waiting on irate customers, babysitting kids and picking up toys. She needed more out of life than this and made the decision to at least mention Dwayne's idea to her dad. She convinced herself it couldn't do any harm. *Dad will probably be too busy with his writing anyway.* But she finally picked up the phone.

After three rings, he answered. "Hello, John speaking."

"Dad, it's Tammy."

"Tammy! How have you been?"

"Good. Hey, listen, I have this crazy idea and thought I'd run it by you."

John's tone suddenly changed from joyful to serious. He'd heard too many crazy ideas from Tammy in the past. "Go on."

Noticing the sudden change in his voice, Tammy stalled, wondering if this was a bad move. "Well, you see, I've met this guy and I want to go fishing with him." After blurting out the first thing that popped into her head, Tammy realized how stupid she sounded.

"Fishing? Since when have you liked fishing?" her dad asked in a questionable tone.

Tammy couldn't hide her enthusiasm when he asked and began to ramble on excitedly. "Oh, Dad, I love it! It's amazing! I'm not talking about regular fishing with a rod. This is commercial lobster fishing. That's what Dwayne does, the guy I've been seeing, and for months now I've been helping him get ready for the season and I absolutely love it. He's taught me so much and well, you see, I want to go pull the lobster traps with him. But the thing is, he fishes off an island sixty miles out at sea and stays there for a week. I can't go unless I have someone to take care of Matt."

"My daughter wants to go fishing sixty miles out at sea." John laughed. "Well, Tammy, you never cease to surprise me. Have you thought this through? What about your job? Have you talked to them? And where do I come in?" John asked, assuming she might be asking for a loan so she could take time off from work.

Tammy didn't want to mention the rest of the idea or that she might be quitting her job so she ignored that question. "Dad, I wanted to ask if you and Joanne might want a visit from Matt?" There was silence. "Dad?" Tammy asked nervously. "Dad, are you there?"

"Yeah. Yeah, Tammy, I'm here. Well, I can tell you genuinely like this fishing thing. How long are we talking about?"

Tammy was surprised that he was even considering it. "I think a week. I'd have to check with Dwayne."

"Hold on a second. I'm going to put Joanne on the phone. She's the one you'll have to ask. After all, she'll be the one that would have to watch him, and Andrew already keeps her busy enough as it is."

Tammy waited with her heart pounding in her chest, wondering if this was a bad idea. A few moments later, Joanne came on the line and again Tammy recited what she had just told her father. Joanne was just as amused as her father when she mentioned her quest to go fishing, and she showed her motherly concerns regarding Tammy's typically hasty decision.

"What if you don't like it, Tammy? You said you've only helped him get the traps ready but you've not actually gone fishing. You'll be stuck out at sea with no way to get home. You can't ask your boyfriend to stop what he's doing to bring you back, you know, especially when you're that far out."

Tammy understood Joanne's concerns, but her recent shark fishing trip came to mind. "If it's any consolation, I went shark fishing with Dwayne not so long ago and absolutely loved it."

Joanne gasped. "Did you say shark fishing?"

Tammy giggled at her reaction. "Yep, I sure did, and it was an amazing experience."

"Well, I wasn't expecting to hear that." She laughed. "Oh, Tammy you are full of surprises. Maybe you have found your calling."

"I know I'll love it, Joanne. I can feel it."

"Tammy, I do know one thing. When you've made up your mind about something, it's impossible for anyone to change it." She paused for a moment. "Sure, we'll watch Matt."

Tammy sensed the smile in Joanne's voice. "Really?"

"Yes. Besides, it's about time Matt met his uncle." Joanne laughed. "Doesn't that sound odd? But Andrew is Matt's half-uncle, even though he's only two years older."

Tammy chuckled at the thought. "It does seem kind of weird."

Tammy spent the next few minutes thanking Joanne many times for agreeing to watch Matt if she decided to go with Dwayne. She explained that there were other issues to iron out before committing herself completely but she would keep her posted.

After hanging up the phone, Tammy remained stunned on the couch for a few minutes. She hadn't expected her parents to say yes. The only thing holding her back now was her job. She asked herself how much she actually enjoyed her job. And if she quit her job, would that mean she'd have to move onto the boat with Dwayne? Was she ready for that? Could she really live on a boat? She had so many unanswered questions.

She had a few more days to think things through properly, which was something new for her. She wasn't going to make any drastic decisions this time. She had to be sure this was something she and Dwayne both wanted and that their relationship was going places. Without a doubt, she knew she loved him, but she had never confessed her true feelings to him. Not yet. Was it because she didn't know how he felt about her?

It also occurred to Tammy that if she did this, she'd be giving up everything. Her and Matt's home, her job, and most of all her independence—all things she had worked really hard for. If it didn't work out between her and Dwayne, his life would just go on like it did before they'd met. He'd still have his boat, his home and his jobs, whereas Tammy would have to start over yet again. She'd lost count of how many times that had occurred in her life because of stupid decisions. She didn't want this to be another one.

CHAPTER 25

By the time Friday rolled around, Tammy still hadn't decided what to do. She had too many 'what ifs' tormenting her head. She needed some reassurance from Dwayne that he was in their relationship for the long-term. This weekend, she intended to find out. Dwayne had warned her that it was going to be another intense weekend of getting the last of the gear built and dipped. He only had three weeks left before he headed out to the island to drop off the first round of traps, and he still had a ton of work to do on the boat.

Tammy was anxious to get back to the familiar surroundings of the boatyard and the friendly people, so as soon her shift was over at three, she hurried home to change and pick up Matt. In no time at all, she was back on the road and heading for the marina.

She found Dwayne shirtless, looking as sexy as ever at the corner of the yard, and wasted no time diving into the work that needed to be done. Matt knew the drill and busied himself with riding his bike around the yard.

They worked hard into the night, allowing Matt to stay up late and gaze at the stars he never got to see in the city.

Tammy hadn't mentioned anything about talking to her dad. She'd wanted to wait until she had Dwayne's full attention. Once their work was done for the night and Matt was finally asleep on the boat, she felt it was time to talk. She grabbed a blanket from the bottom of the bed and laid it out on the deck before Dwayne returned from his shower.

When he came back, wrapped in his bathrobe, he found Tammy stretched out on the blanket, staring up at the sky with its stars like jewels. He immediately joined her and snuggled his body next to hers. Breathing in the fresh scent from her recent shower, he embraced her and looked up. "Beautiful, isn't it?"

Tammy laid her head on his chest and embraced him. "It's absolutely stunning and so peaceful. I love how the water glistens from the moon and the sounds the ripples of the water makes. I hate leaving this place."

Dwayne rubbed her shoulder and kissed the top of her head. "Well, you don't have to, you know."

Tammy sat up and placed her hands on his chest. "I talked to my dad about watching Matt."

Dwayne's eyes shot wide open. "You did? And?"

Tammy beamed him a smile. "They said they would love to watch Matt. I couldn't believe it. You know what this means, don't you?" she said excitedly without waiting for a reply. "I can go fishing with you."

"So what's stopping you? I know you'll love it, and you're so good at building traps. We'll have a blast out there. Pulling the traps is the easy part."

"Oh, Dwayne, I really want to go but I need to know that this is not just a fling we are having. I'd be giving up everything to do this."

Dwayne sat up and took Tammy's hand. "Tammy, I don't ask every woman I've dated to move in with me. She has to be pretty special." He laughed. "And you are. I've never told you until now, but I love you and would love nothing more than to share my life with you."

Tammy heard what she needed to hear. "I love you too," she replied before closing her lips on his and folded her arms around him. There was no going back. This was the life she wanted and it was where she felt at home. She was going to take the plunge and move in with Dwayne. She broke away from their now passionate kiss and sat up. "I'm going to do it!" she said excitedly. "I'm going fishing with you! But not just that. If the invitation is still on the table, I want to move in with you and live my life with you."

Dwayne's eyes beamed with happiness. "Really?"

"Yes! I belong here, and so does Matt."

Dwayne pulled her in close and kissed her hard on the lips. "You won't regret it. I promise."

"I know. This feels right. I've never been so sure about anything in my life. The hardest part will be sending Matt off to Florida. Joanne suggested having him stay there until Thanksgiving. She wants me to make sure I really want to commercial fish for a living."

Dwayne nodded. "I think she's right. A week isn't enough."

"But Thanksgiving's over two months away. I'm not sure if I can do that."

Dwayne felt the uneasiness in her voice. "Tammy, he'll be with family, and he will probably love spending time with his grandpa. It's likely you will have more of a hard time than him. Kids adjust real easily."

She knew she was doing this for their future, but she had to be sure this was what she wanted to do for a living and Joanne was right, a week wasn't enough. "Okay! I can do this! I'm calling my parents tomorrow," she exclaimed excitedly while throwing herself into Dwayne's arms.

"Oh, Tammy, I love you so much. Go grab another blanket so we can get hide beneath it and get frisky under the stars." His devious smile had returned.

"Okay!" Tammy said cheerfully as she hurried down into the cabin in search of a blanket.

~

With her mind made up and feeling excited about the future, Tammy left the marina with a spring in her step. She had three weeks to get everything in place before heading out to the island with Dwayne. Her first concern was telling Judy. They'd been through a lot with each other, and she couldn't deny the sadness and the sense of guilt she was feeling, knowing she was abandoning her.

Since Tammy quit drinking, they no longer had their midnight chit-chats over a glass of wine. In fact, Tammy couldn't remember the last time she had an in-depth conversation or just joked around with Judy. With all the sudden realizations while driving home, Tammy knew it was time to move on.

When she arrived at her house, Judy was still up in her usual spot with a glass of wine and immediately rose from the couch to go pour it down the sink. Tammy hated that she made her feel that way.

"It's okay. You don't need to do that. I'm fine," Tammy told her. "Sit down. We need to talk. I'll just go and put Matt down."

"Okay," Judy said, looking worried as she returned to her seat.

A few minutes later, Tammy entered the room with a chilled Pepsi and sat on the couch next to Judy. With her curiosity piqued, Judy spoke first.

"So, what's up?"

Tammy stalled with her reply by circling the rim of her can with her fingertips. "Dwayne has asked me to move in with him." She took Judy's hand. "And I really want to, but I hate the idea of messing things up for you. You are my best friend, and we've always had each other's backs. I feel like I'm abandoning you. But I also think we're beginning to go our separate ways. Am I right when I say that? You've been seeing a lot of more of Joel, and I've been spending more time with Dwayne..."

To Tammy's surprise, Judy started laughing.

"What's so funny?" Tammy asked.

It took a moment for Judy to calm herself and wipe the tears from her cheeks. "I'm sorry. It's just that Joel and I have been talking about moving in together too, but I just didn't know how to tell you. Well, you just saved me the trouble." She laughed again.

Tammy eyes became wide. "You're kidding me!" she yelled before joining Judy in her laughter. "Oh, so I have nothing to be worried about? Have you guys found a place yet?"

"No. We were planning on starting after I had found the courage to tell you. So I guess we can start right away. His place is too small; it's only a one-bedroom so we can't live there."

Tammy thought for a moment. "Well, wait a minute. Why doesn't Joel just move in here after I've moved out? There's no reason for you to move, Judy. This is your home."

Judy suddenly realized how everything was falling into place. Releasing a satisfactory smile, she eased back into the couch. "You're right! It will work out perfect for everyone. There's just one downside to all of this."

Tammy looked worried. Had she overlooked something? "What's that?"

"I'm going to miss the hell out of you. Come here and give me a hug."

"Aww, we'll still see each other. I promise. After lobster season, I'll see if Dwayne will take us all out on the boat."

"Really?" Judy squealed. "The kids have never been on a boat. They would love it."

Tammy went on to tell Judy all about her plans for the big move, which included quitting the restaurant and becoming a full-time commercial fisherwoman.

"You and Matt are going to live on the boat?" Judy asked,

sounding skeptical. "Is there enough room for all of you? And what about all your stuff?"

"It will be cramped, but we'll make it work. I've lived in worst places, as you well know. It's beautiful in the marina, and it'll be worth sacrificing the house just to be able to wake up in the middle of such a magnificent environment. Matt will love it. I know he will. He's adapted so well to the boat life and has learnt so much. It will be tough having my parents watch him for a few months, but it's something I need to do if I'm serious about giving this lobster fishing a try."

Judy shook her head. "Damn, girl! I can't believe you're gonna be a frigging fisherwoman. Who'd have thought? I'm really happy for you and if anyone deserves to be happy, you do." She held out her arms. "I need another hug."

"We both deserve these changes in our lives. I'm excited for you and Joel as well. You are about to start a new life together too."

Both girls felt the tinge of sadness lingering in the air. It was an emotional and scary time for them. The Tammy-and-Judy era was slowly but surely coming to end. Neither knew what the future held, but they were anxious to find out.

CHAPTER 26

*O*ver the next week, Tammy knuckled down with organizing everything so she would have her life and her belongings in place by the time Dwayne left for his first trip to the island. It wasn't the first time she had made a quick decision to move; in fact, she was somewhat concerned that this seemed to be a common occurrence in her life. First, there was her rushed move to the States from England, and then the expedited decision to be with Raymond when she discovered she was having his child. When her thoughts switched to Steven, Tammy shook her head in disgust. She'd lost count of how many times she'd had to move with him.

Her last shift at work was done and the day she officially moved out of the house had finally arrived. She'd already put most of her belongings in storage, leaving all the furniture for Judy—much to Judy's protest. But Tammy got her way and after one last family meal with the kids and a tearful farewell, Tammy and Judy's path together had finally come to an end.

She spent what she thought was going to be an emotional night with Matt on Dwayne's boat before taking him to the airport the following morning, but he was so excited about flying on an airplane for the first time that the only person having anxieties was Tammy. All three of them stayed up late telling stories to Matt under the bedcovers via flashlight until Matt finally fell asleep in their arms, which is where they huddled together until sunrise.

It was just a short ten-minute ride to LAX airport from the marina, and Tammy had a hard time containing Matt's excitement over his upcoming plane ride and the only tears that were shed, were Tammy's. Once they were checked in, they were greeted by a flight attendant who assured Tammy that she would be sitting next to Matt for the entire trip and would be personally handing Matt over to Joanne at the other end.

Tammy watched through her tears as her son disappeared through the crowd. Once he was out of sight, she let the tears fall uncontrollably while burying her face in Dwayne's chest. "Oh, Dwayne! Am I a terrible mother for doing this?"

Surprised by her outburst, Dwayne held her tight. "No, you're not. Now don't be saying that about yourself. He's going to be fine. He's visiting family so Mom can learn a new career. You're doing this for him."

As always, he had a way of making her feel better and helping her take note of the brighter side of situations. "Thank you," she whispered while wiping her now swollen eyes.

"Let me take you out for breakfast. Tonight, we can call your family and you can talk to Matt. Okay?"

The thought brought a smile to her face. "I'd like that. Come on, let's go. I'm hungry."

For Tammy, living on the boat was like an endless camping trip, except they were on water. Tammy didn't deny that their living quarters were cramped, but she really didn't feel the effects because they spent all their days outside, evenings were spent relaxing on the deck with other fellow boaters and meals were cooked on the barbeque. It was a lifestyle she knew she would never get tired of.

Sending Matt to Florida for the next few months was going to be difficult, but she couldn't deny that she was enjoying her temporary freedom from motherhood. For the first time in four years, she could do as she pleased without worrying about Matt. But her biggest relief was her money anxieties. Once she moved out of the house, they had all disappeared. She suddenly found herself free of rent and all the other overwhelming obligations that came with living in a house. Tammy embraced it and gave one hundred percent of herself to Dwayne and helping him get ready for the season.

With only two weeks left until they were due to head out with the first load of traps, they worked around the clock finishing up the gear and stacking it so it was ready to be loaded onto the boat when the time came. Dwayne spent hours going through both boats thoroughly, making sure everything was running smoothly and that he had extra supplies and tools to fix anything that may go wrong while out at sea.

It was too late to get Tammy a commercial lobster permit for the current year so instead, Dwayne got her a deck-hand permit, which allowed her to be on the boat and participate in the actual pulling of the traps. Having not considered it before, Dwayne thought it was probably a better idea for her first year. The deck-hand permit was much cheaper and it gave Tammy a chance to see if she liked it before committing to the expense of a commercial license.

Everything was going to plan and they were right on schedule. The last two days before their departure, Dwayne took Tammy on an amusing shopping excursion for her official bright orange slickers, rubber boots and matching rubber gloves. They also shopped for groceries and filled the boats up with fuel. The only thing left to do was to load the traps onto the boats, which ended up taking most of the last day.

Each trap weighed close to sixty-five pounds, but between them, they loaded fifty traps on to the *Baywitch* and ten traps onto the *Little Boat*. Once all the traps were tied down and secured, leaving them with no deck space whatsoever, Tammy dropped her exhausted aching body onto the dock next to the boats to admire their work while Dwayne returned the handcart to the corner of the yard.

When he returned, she had a question for him. "So how are we going to take out both boats? Are you going to be towing the little boat?"

Dwayne chuckled because he knew she'd be asking this question. He just thought she would have asked it much sooner. "Nope. I can't tow a boat with a load of traps. That's too dangerous."

Tammy thought for a moment. "So who's going to drive the *Little Boat*?"

A devious smile appeared across Dwayne's face. "You are."

ammy never rose to her feet so fast. Even with her sore body, she had to talk some sense into Dwayne immediately. "Are you insane? I can't drive that boat to the island. It's over sixty miles!" she protested in a panicked state.

"Yes, you can, and you will." He held a slight firmness to his tone. "On the next trip, we will just take the *Baywitch*, but this is my first time to the island and I want to use the *Little Boat* to explore. I can't do that with the *Baywitch* because it doesn't go in shallow waters, which is why I need you to drive the *Little Boat*."

As much as Tammy appreciated his confidence, she wasn't feeling it. "No, I can't! I've never driven a boat that far. That's a long way." She began pacing the deck as her nerves started to take over. "I've only driven the *Baywitch* a few times outside the harbor, and that's been with you on board. I've never even driven *Little Boat* before. And you expect me to drive it by myself, sixty miles across the goddamn ocean? I can't do it, Dwayne!"

Dwayne approached her as she continued to pace the dock and stopped her in her tracks by placing a firm grip on her shoulders.

"If you want to commercial fish, you're going to have to learn how to drive a boat. It's part of the trade. You can't fish by car."

Tammy slapped his arm and shoved him away. "This isn't funny. It's sixty bloody miles. That's a long way. I have no idea what to do and not only that, I'll be by myself. What if something goes wrong?" She didn't wait for an answer and continued to express her anger. "You're telling me this now. Why didn't you tell me sooner so I could have at least prepared myself?"

"This is exactly why I didn't tell you until now. If I had, you'd have been stressing over it the whole time and working yourself up into a frenzy, just like you are doing now. Yes, sixty miles is a lot of ocean, but it's also a great opportunity to learn how to drive a boat. By the time we get to the island, you'll be a pro." He approached her and grabbed her hand, speaking in a softer tone. "And as far you being alone goes; you will be following me, and I won't let you out of my sight. If it makes you feel any better, we will be in radio contact, and we can talk on the radio the whole time if you want." He shook her hand vigorously. "You can do this. I know you can."

"Oh god, I don't know, Dwayne. I'm scared. I'll be driving the boat for nine hours. That's a long time."

"That's nine hours of practice time. Like I said, you'll be a pro by the time we reach the island. There's nothing but open ocean. You can make all the mistakes you want. You're not going to hit anything. Look at it like a big adventure. Come on, what do you say? You'll be fine."

Tammy folded her arms across her chest. "Well, it looks like I don't have a choice. But I'm still not happy about it."

Dwayne pulled her in and gave her a hard kiss on the lips. "That's my girl. Now come on, let's get some sleep; we have a long day head of us tomorrow."

"Okay…I guess we will see how I do tomorrow." Still feeling concerned, she followed Dwayne into the cabin of *Baywitch*.

Tammy understood why he hadn't told her sooner about

driving *Little Boat*. He was right. She'd spent a sleepless night worrying about it and was now afraid she wouldn't be able to stay awake for the entire crossing. After four cups of coffee and an obscene number of cigarettes, her nerves were still getting the better of her. Feeling the chill of the morning air, she left to use the bathroom for the last time, knowing a bucket would be her only source of relief for the next few days. Dwayne fired up both boats while she was gone.

When she returned, Dwayne met her at the bottom of the ramp and led her over to the *Little Boat* and took her to the helm. "The only thing you need to know about is the throttle. It works just like the *Baywitch*. Forward, neutral and reverse. You'll be following me so you won't need to read the compass, but pay attention to it and take note of the direction of where we're heading for practice." He lifted the mic from the VHF radio. "This is the radio. You can call me anytime by pushing this button and talking into the mic. Release the button to hear me talk and press to talk again when you're ready. Got it?"

Tammy nodded. "Got it."

I'm going to pull the *Little Boat* out of the slip and put it on the end tie so you don't have to deal with steering it out of the slip. Once I've passed you on the *Baywitch*, you simply untie the boat from the cleats, push yourself off away from the dock and follow me slowly out of the harbor." Dwayne saw the worried look on her face. "You'll be fine. Give me a kiss and go wait for me at the end of the dock."

Tammy leaned in and welcomed his affection before heading over to the end of the dock to wait for him. Left in her own thoughts for a few moments, she tried desperately to calm her escalating nerves. *You can do this, Tammy.*

She glanced at her watch. It was almost ten. She knew they were leaving later than intended, but last-minute details had set them back. Tammy calculated the time of the crossing and knew they wouldn't arrive until after dark. The thought of driving the boat into the night didn't help matters.

The sight of seeing Dwayne turn out of their basin and head toward her snapped her out of her daydream. With ease, he pulled alongside the dock where she stood and threw her a line. Despite her shaking hands, Tammy caught it and tied off the *Little Boat* onto the cleat. The outboard motor rumbled as Dwayne stepped on to the dock and gave Tammy's shoulders a firm squeeze. "Are you ready?"

"As ready as I'll ever be."

"You'll be fine. I know you will. Give me a few minutes to get the *Baywitch*. As soon as I pass you, simply untie the boat and follow me slowly out of the harbor." Dwayne gave her a lingering kiss on the lips. "I'll see you at the island." And before she could summon any further protests, Tammy suddenly found herself alone on the dock.

She stepped on to the boat—her boat—and stood motionless for a few seconds to steady herself as the boat rocked from her presence. Her body trembled viciously, and it wasn't from the cold. *Come on, Tammy, pull yourself together. You've got this.*

But as hard as she tried, she couldn't control her fear or the high levels of anxiety she experienced while waiting for Dwayne.

About ten minutes later, she heard Dwayne's voice over the radio. "You should see me coming out of the basin in about a minute."

"Okay," Tammy hollered, but then she remembered Dwayne's instructions about pushing the button to speak. She shook her head at her stupidity and lifted the microphone out of the cradle before pushing the black button on the side. "Okay," she hollered again, remembering a few moments later to release the button. "This is going to take some getting used to," she said to no one in particular.

Dwayne's voice crackled over the radio again. "You got me, Tammy?"

"Yes."

"There you are. You've got to remember, it's not like a regular phone. To hear me, you have to release the black button."

The sound of his voice brought a smile to her face. "Yeah, I know. I'll get used to it. Where are you at?"

"You should be seeing me in just a few seconds. As soon as I've passed you, untie the boat and ease away from the dock. The *Baywitch* has a heavy load so we will be going slow the whole way. It will give you plenty of practice time."

Tammy chuckled at his comment. She needed all the practice she could get. Standing at the helm, she fixed her stare at the basin where he said he would be coming and sure enough, she spotted him almost immediately as he turned into the main channel. The *Baywitch* was a much larger boat than the one she was driving and looked even greater with traps stacked five high on the deck. The *Little Boat*, on the other hand, sat low in the water. In fact, Tammy could reach over and put her hand in the chilled water if she wanted to. She patiently waited for Dwayne to pass her, and he waved and gave her a huge smile as he slowly eased by. Tammy waved back, took a deep breath and proceeded to untie the boat. Once free, she gently pushed away from the dock with her hand. "Here we go!" she whispered nervously before scurrying over to the helm and gently easing the throttle into gear. "Fuck! I can't believe I'm doing this."

The zigzags started as soon as she began inching forward to follow Dwayne.

"You're over-steering," she heard Dwayne say. "Don't try and compensate by steering the other way. That's why you're zigzagging. Give the boat a minute to respond."

With both white-knuckled hands clenched on the steering wheel, Tammy didn't want to let go to pick up the mic of the radio. "Yeah, yeah, I know. Give me a minute," she hollered into the air, not that there was a chance of Dwayne hearing her over the roar of both motors. Feeling thankful no wake was allowed inside the harbor, Tammy continued to follow Dwayne at the slow pace of about four knots, zigzagging the whole time.

Along both sides of the channel was a bike path, where joggers, dog walkers and bicyclists roamed. Many stopped to look at the boats leaving or entering the harbor. Some waved at Tammy as she passed but, not wanting to let go of the wheel, Tammy simply nodded and threw them a nervous smile. But she couldn't help feeling a sense of pride as these people watched her driving a boat.

"How are doing back there?"

Realizing she had no other option, she let go of the wheel with one hand and picked up the mic. "Fine. Trying to get use to this steering. I'm still zigzagging."

"You're doing great. You've got sixty miles of open ocean to practice. By the time we get to San Clemente, you'll be driving as straight as an arrow."

Tammy laughed. "I'm not too sure about that. This is really hard. My hands are already tired and we've not even left the harbor yet."

"It will get easier. It's only because you are over-steering right now. Hang in there. I'm going to let you go so you can concentrate."

"Okay," Tammy replied before hanging up the mic.

It took about fifteen minutes to exit the harbor but even then, Tammy wasn't feeling any more relaxed. Still clinging onto the wheel, she gave the boat a little more speed as they came around the break wall and into open waters. She instantly felt the choppiness of the waves beneath her, which intensified the rocking motion of the boat. "God damn it!" she yelled, trying to steer the boat in anything that might resemble a straight line. But she was losing her battle fast. The wind was much stronger and cut through her hair with force, blowing it back away from her face. Sitting closer to the water than the *Baywitch*, she actually felt the spray of water against her face and arms. On the brink of tears, she kept trying to compensate her steering as if she was driving a car, which only resulted in more zigzagging. "I can't do this!" she cried in desperation. Looking at the compass on the dash, she assumed it was obviously just as confused as she was on the course she was trying to keep.

Frustrated with her attempts so far, Tammy took a deep breath and stopped steering, allowing the boat to straighten itself out. Dwayne was probably about five hundred feet in front of her. She envied how he handled the *Baywitch*. She wanted to be just as good as him but also realized he'd spent his entire life around boats.

Once the boat seemed to be going in something like a straight line, Tammy took the wheel again and paid close attention to her steering. She looked at the compass and saw they were on a course of one hundred eighty degrees and used that as her guidance. Concentrating and watching the compass seemed to help, and she soon noticed she was keeping on course and doing less of the zigzagging. "I'm getting this!" she squealed triumphantly. But as soon as she became more relaxed, she found herself going off course again. "Fuck!" she yelled before correcting her steering for what seemed like the hundredth time.

Tammy had been so engrossed in her steering and the wheel that she hadn't paid much attention to her surroundings. Feeling a little more comfortable, she scanned the ocean. There were a few sailboats in the distance off to her port and starboard side, and numerous fishing boats anchored off shore. She looked behind her and saw the coastline of Santa Monica and Venice in the distance. She could make out the Ferris wheel on the Santa Monica pier and people lazing around on the beach. She wondered when she would be walking on land again.

About an hour into the trip, Tammy was feeling a little more confident and extremely proud of herself. She was driving a boat all by herself across the Pacific Ocean. "Fuck, this feels great!" she yelled at the top of her voice. The sense of freedom she was feeling was exuberating and she wanted to share her joyous mood with Dwayne. After picking up the mic, she held down the button and hollered over the sound of the motor, "Dwayne! You got me?"

A few seconds later, he replied, "I got you! How's it going back there? I've been watching you. You're doing much better. Looks like you're getting the hang of it."

"I am! This is fucking awesome! How far have we gone?"

"Oh, I'd say about eight miles. And, Tammy, watch your language. This is an open channel. Every boater on this channel can hear you out there."

"Oops...sorry. Hang on, only eight miles? It feels like we've gone a lot farther."

"It always does on a boat. We're only going about eight knots. We won't get there till after dark."

"Yeah, I know. Not sure how I'm going to like driving at night."

"Don't think about it right now. That's hours away. Just enjoy the ride and keep up the good job."

Over the next few hours, they conversed over the radio periodically. Hearing Dwayne's voice comforted Tammy and instantly put her at ease. She was no longer zigzagging and was able to keep on course pretty easily without even thinking about it. It was beginning to come naturally for her. Dwayne was right. This was the perfect opportunity to learn how to drive a boat.

By the third hour, she had the radio turned up full blast and found herself screaming out the song "I am sailing" by Rod Stewart when it played over the speakers. While enjoying the feeling of confidence and complete freedom, she noticed something splashing in the distance on the starboard side of her boat. It wasn't just one splash; it was hundreds of them, and they were moving closer to the boat. "What the hell is that?" she asked herself. When the splashes came close enough, she suddenly realized they were dolphins and squealed with delight before calling Dwayne on the radio. "Dolphins! On my right. I'm going to go check them out," she hollered over the radio.

Being a smaller boat, it was easier to steer, so Tammy took a detour and headed over to the school of dolphins while Dwayne slowed down the *Baywitch* and waited for her. In one swift movement, Tammy gave the wheel a sharp turn and headed off to the right where she had seen the splashes. Within minutes, she found herself surrounded by a school of dolphins racing through the water and jumping two to five feet out of the water. There must have been at least a hundred of them. Many came up alongside the boat, where Tammy could actually reach into the water and touch them as they swam by playing and following the wake. "This is amazing!" she cried out loud as she watched in awe the beauty before her. *This is what it's all about!* As she lost herself in the world of dolphins, she became a part of their world for just a moment.

After they had blessed her with their presence and moved on, Tammy called Dwayne on the radio. "Did you see that? That was amazing. I've never seen anything like it."

"I saw with my binoculars. That was pretty cool. You'll be seeing a lot of that in the future. Ready to keep going?"

"Yeah. I'm back behind you," Tammy confirmed.

She had taken Dwayne's advice and kept her jacket and snacks handy on the dash to grab and eat while she drove, but her arms and hands were beginning to tire from steering for so many hours and she was in desperate need of a bathroom break. She looked behind her at the mainland and saw it was now only a speck on the horizon. There were no longer any boats close by; it was just her and Dwayne. The vast size of the ocean suddenly hit home and she wondered how anyone could possibly find them if something happened out here; how would they ever survive? The ocean would just swallow them up in a matter of minutes. Tammy shuddered at the thought and while doing so, suddenly spotted land up ahead in the distance. *Surely we can't almost be there already?*

Tammy picked up the mic. "Dwayne, you got me?"

"Yeah, I got you. Everything okay?"

"I see land up ahead. That's not San Clemente, is it?"

"No, that's Catalina Island. I'll take you there sometime. There are all kinds of fun things to do like snorkeling, scuba diving and beach combing. You'll love it. We'll be passing the west side in about an hour."

"That would be great. We could bring Matt too. Listen, I really need to take a break and give my arms a rest. Is that possible?"

"Sure! Catch up to me and put your motor in neutral. Then you can shut off the boat and we'll bob around for a little while."

Tammy followed his instructions and beamed a huge smile when she could see Dwayne waving at her from the helm of the *Baywitch*. She waved back and shut off the motor. The sudden silence brought her peace. After hearing the constant roaring of the outboard motor for several hours, a welcome calmness embraced her. She stood for a moment and listened to the sound of the ocean crashing against the hull of the little boat. She would never get tired of the vast sense of freedom the ocean always brought. She loved the way it smelt, the constant breeze in her hair and most of all she loved being away from the pressures of the city.

After being confined to one spot on the boat for hours, Tammy took the liberty to stretch her legs and paced back and forth around the helm and either side of the boat. Even though there wasn't a lot of room, it made a huge difference to be able to walk a few steps up and down.

She was close enough to the *Baywitch* to holler and be heard without using the radio. "I'm gonna use the bucket," she shouted while laughing.

Dwayne gave her thumbs up. "Okay!"

They conversed while eating tuna fish out of a can, along with some crackers and fruit before firing up the boats twenty minutes later to continue with the crossing. Dwayne told Tammy they had another five hours to go before they reached the island. He reminded her to let him know if she needed another break. She agreed and put on her jacket before putting the boat in gear.

The small break made a huge difference and totally rejuvenated her. She now felt she had enough energy to complete the trip, but a few hours later when the sun began to go down and the sky began to darken, an eeriness crept over her. She suddenly felt so small and vulnerable amongst the ink-black sea, which was now only lit by the glow of the moon and the twinkles of the stars. She could no longer see any land, and the only part of the *Baywitch* that she could see was the small white light above the helm and two white lights on the stern.

Bracing both hands on the wheel, she held tight as the little boat cut through the waves. Afraid to take her eyes off the lights of the *Baywitch*, Tammy strained to stay focused, fearing if she turned her head for a moment she'd lose him. The ocean no longer felt like a friendly place. Images of sea monsters and what lay beneath haunted her mind. It was a different experience than driving during the day. A frightening one and a reminder just how deadly the ocean could be. If she went overboard, she would be lost for good. Dwayne would have no idea unless he tried to call her on the radio to check in, and by then, there could be miles of ocean between them. The thought petrified her, so she called Dwayne on the radio to seek some comfort and reassure herself that he was still on the *Baywitch*. "Dwayne, you got me?"

"Yep, I got you. How you holding up? You doing okay?"

"Yeah. Just a little spooked since it got dark. How much farther do we have to go?"

"We should be approaching Northwest Harbor at the island in about forty-five minutes."

Tammy released a joyous cheer. "Hallelujah!"

"You've done great, Tammy. I'm really proud of you. I knew you could do it!"

Feeling proud of herself, Tammy did a little jig while she talked to Dwayne for a few more minutes. It was the longest, most nerve-wrecking ten hours she had ever experienced. But she did it. She'd driven a boat solo, sixty miles across the Pacific Ocean, and she was feeling pretty damn good about it. Despite the darkness surrounding her, she sang her heart out to the tunes on the radio for the remainder of the journey.

Thirty minutes later, Dwayne came back on the radio. "Hey, Tammy?"

"Hey," Tammy replied after picking up the mic.

"Once we get into the harbor, I'm going to need to set the anchor. It will take me about fifteen minutes. Just put the *Little Boat* in neutral until I'm ready. When I'm done, I'm going to have you come alongside the *Baywitch* and I'll tie the *Little Boat* up against it."

A sudden gush of panic swept through Tammy. "I don't know how to pull up alongside the *Baywitch*. What if I hit it?" she asked, raising her voice.

"You'll do fine. I'll walk you through it over the radio. Hold tight. I'll come back on in a bit."

With a fresh wave of elevated nerves, Tammy hung up the mic and tried to envisage in her mind how she was going to approach the *Baywitch*—in the dark—but she had no clue and knew she could only wait for Dwayne's instructions. Once inside the harbor, she slowed the boat and then put it in neutral. She could make out the silhouette of the island ahead of her and wondered what it would look like in the day time. With no other boats in the harbor, she could hear the waves crashing against the shore.

Tammy wasn't sure how long she'd been bobbing around but was relieved when

Dwayne came back on the radio. "Okay, Tammy, I'm ready for you."

"Okay," Tammy replied, unable to hide the nervousness in her voice.

"Put the boat in gear and slowly make your way toward the port side of the *Baywitch*. When you are close to the stern, put the boat in neutral and let the current of the water drift you toward me. Make sure you have a rope tied to the cleat on the stern. You're going to throw that to me so I can tie you off."

Tammy listened carefully to everything he had said and followed his instructions precisely. Inch by inch, she headed toward the *Baywitch*, which was much easier to see since Dwayne had put the flood lights on the deck. With her heart racing and her palms sweating, Tammy put the boat in gear and slowly nosed her way toward the *Baywitch*. Feeling thankful that the water was calmer inside the harbor, Tammy was able to steer the boat with ease and when she was within ten feet of the stern of the *Baywitch*, she put it in neutral. Just like Dwayne had said, the current drifted her alongside his boat.

Dwayne had already gotten two rubber fenders in place along the side and instructed Tammy to throw him the rope, which she did right on cue. It landed in Dwayne's hands, and he rushed to tie it off before racing to the front of the boat where he and Tammy repeated the process with a second rope. "You made it!" he hollered. "Go ahead and shut off the boat and come over here and give me a big hug."

Beaming like a Cheshire cat, Tammy gladly turned off the boat, stepped up onto the *Baywitch* and almost fell into Dwayne's arms.

"Oh my god! That was nerve-wrecking and exhilarating all at the same time. I can't believe I did it."

"You were great. I knew you would be," he cheered before giving her a much-needed celebratory kiss on the lips.

Tammy remained in his arms. "I'm so tired. My arms and legs are killing me.

Please tell me we get to lie down soon."

"We sure do. We need plenty of rest before we dump this gear off tomorrow. Everything is secure. Let's go down below and make ourselves a cup of hot chocolate and call it a night."

"Sounds good to me," Tammy said with an exhausted smile.

CHAPTER 28

*T*ammy soon discovered that sleeping on a boat in the middle of the ocean was not an easy task. Between the constant rocking and rolling of the boat and the sounds of the water slapping against the hull, she got very little sleep and was envious of Dwayne, who didn't stir the entire night.

When she finally did drift off to sleep, seemingly hours after Dwayne, she was rudely awakened by the roaring of male voices somewhere off in the distance. Forgetting she was on a boat, she jumped up, startled by the noise, only to bang her head on the low ceiling of the V-berth where they slept. "Ouch! God damn it!" she seethed while rubbing her head to sooth the throbbing pain.

Dwayne stirred in his sleep, "Are you okay?"

"No, I'm not okay. I've hardly slept, I just banged my head, and there's a bunch of noise outside."

Dwayne sat up and pinned his ears. He too heard the yelling of male voices from outside. "What the hell is that? We're anchored at a desolate island!"

Being on the inside of the bed against the wall, Tammy began to climb over Dwayne, keeping her head low so as not to bang it again. "I don't know, but I'm going to go check it out."

With her feet finally on the floor, she steadied herself from the continuous rocking of the boat by grabbing a hold of the edges of the table. She glanced at the watch on her wrist. "It's only four in the morning," she grumbled while making her way to the cabin door. Once there, she inched it open and peeked through the gap, only to be startled by the sound of an airplane flying above them. "What the hell? Where the hell are we?"

Being his first time on the island too, Dwayne was also confused by all the noise and climbed out of bed to follow Tammy onto the deck. He waited patiently while Tammy precariously climbed the steps, holding onto the sides as she pushed through the cabin door. She stepped out onto the deck, leaving Dwayne down below, and started looking around for something else to hold on to. After a moment of fumbling around in the dark, she curled her fingers around the wire of one of the traps and finally found her balance.

The chill of the air made Tammy wish she was wearing more than just a t-shirt. She crossed her arms and rubbed them with her hands to try and block the cool air from hitting her skin. Suddenly, she heard the roar of an airplane again and strained her eyes toward the black silhouette of the island. That's when she saw the flashing lights of a jet as it took off from the island and disappeared into the sky. The sound was deafening, causing Tammy to cover her ears. "Wow!" she hollered once the plane had passed over them. "Dwayne, you've got to come see this."

"I'm coming," she heard him holler, and soon he appeared carrying a blanket. "Here, wrap this around you. You've got to be freezing."

Shivering, Tammy beamed at his thoughtfulness and turned her body so he could wrap the blanket around her.

"Thanks," she said, embracing the instant warmth. "Sssh. Do you hear that?"

Dwayne listened closely and could hear the sound of men hollering in the distance, from the direction of the island. He nodded, not taking his eyes off the coastline where the sounds were coming from. He pointed with his finger. "Look over there. It's a bunch of navy seals in the water."

Tammy followed his hand and immediately made out several dark shapes scurrying along the coast. Screaming and shouting, the figures ran down the beach and into the cold waters before swimming out to rubber dinghies waiting just off the shore. Tammy watched in both amazement and confusion as they then climbed in and began rowing like their lives depended on it.

"Good god! Are they nuts? That water has to be freezing. What are they doing?"

"Looks like they are training. After all, the island is owned by the government. I guess this is where the navy seals train and practice their take-offs and landings, which explains the planes. We can fish off the island but we're not allowed to go on it."

Tammy continued to watch the seals for a few minutes, impressed by their agility and strength. "Damn! Pretty impressive. That would toughen up any guy." She cocked her head back in awe as another plane flew above them.

With the rude awaking of the noise explained and now wide awake, they decided to start their day. The sun was beginning to rise and for the first time, Tammy got a glimpse of the island. It looked almost deserted with only a few buildings and trees dotted around its otherwise barren landscape. Behind her, she saw nothing but open ocean and way off in the distance, she could make out Catalina Island. But there was no mainland in sight and no other boats in the harbor. They were completely isolated from the rest of the world, other than the navy seals on San Clemente Island. It was an eerie realization for Tammy. A small sandy beach, the one where they'd seen the navy seals, sat at the far end of the harbor, and a vista of rocky cliffs spanned much of the visible coastline. Tammy was looking forward to seeing more of the island when they dropped their gear.

Once they were dressed in jeans, sweatshirts and rubber boots, Tammy managed to boil some water—holding the handle of the pan on the cooker the whole time so it wouldn't slide off from the constant rocking of the boat. While trying to keep her balance, she made two cups of coffee and poured two bowls of cereal.

Before heading out to drop the traps, Dwayne spent an hour setting a mooring so he wouldn't have to drop an anchor every time they returned to the harbor. Tammy helped with the task and because the *Little Boat* went faster and Dwayne wanted to explore, he intended to use that boat to unload the traps.

Before loading more traps onto the *Little Boat*, Tammy put on her rubber slickers for the first time. She immediately felt like an official commercial fisherwoman and giggled at her attire.

By 6:00 a.m., they had a full load of fifteen traps on the *Little Boat* and Tammy was already feeling fatigued from all the lifting. But she fought through it, and with snacks stored in an ice chest, they were ready to take off with the first load.

Dwayne explained that he would be driving the boat so it would be up to Tammy to bring a trap over to the trap table. She was then to take out the rope and buoy and clip the door open so any sea life that entered would be able to escape. On his command, she would drop the trap in the water and toss the rope in behind it. Then she'd do it all over again when he drove to the next spot. Tammy understood and gave him a nod above the noise of the motor roaring behind them.

"Go ahead and untie us from the *Baywitch*," Dwayne hollered while warming up the engine.

Having untied boats so many times now, it came naturally to her, and she did as Dwayne asked without even having to think about the task at hand. Once they were free of the *Baywitch*, Dwayne sped out of the harbor to explore his options on where to drop the gear.

The island was fifty-three square miles and twenty-one miles long. They were only allowed to fish the back-side of it and noticed buoys were already in the water from other fishermen. Dwayne had to make sure he didn't drop his gear too close to the others, so he spent some time scanning the coastline before carefully choosing his spots.

Once he'd figured out the area, it didn't take long to drop the gear and return to the harbor for a second load. It took three trips to dump all sixty traps, and they were done by noon. The warm weather had worked in their favor, with a clear blue sky and a calm, flat ocean. They were perfect conditions for making the task easier, but it wasn't going to remain that way. Dwayne pointed to a gathering of darker clouds looming on the horizon. With a storm brewing, Dwayne wanted to leave and get back to the mainland to beat the weather.

"I have to drive the *Little Boat* in a storm?" Tammy said, feeling horrified.

"No, I want you on the *Baywitch* with me," he replied. "I don't know how big this storm is going to be. The *Little boat* is empty now so we can tow it." Seeing he'd just eased Tammy's mind, he beamed her a loving smile.

"Phew! Thank god for that."

But, as Dwayne pulled alongside the *Baywitch*, he noticed a large orange flag up on the hillside of the harbor.

"Do you see that?" he asked Tammy while pointing in the direction of the flag.

"I do. What's that for?"

"I have no idea. Want to go check it out real quick? The *Little Boat* can get close to shore in the shallow waters."

Always eager to explore new things, Tammy answered with enthusiasm. "Sure. Let's go."

Curious about the orange flag and never having seen one in a harbor before in all his years on boats, Dwayne sped toward it. Within a few minutes, they were hugging the coastline in shallow waters beneath the flag. It was at least three feet across and stood midway up the cliff. Dwayne strained his eyes to see if he could make out any writing on it but saw nothing. He turned to reach for his binoculars while Tammy leaned out from the helm to see if she could make anything out.

"I don't see any kind of markings on it," she hollered. "I wonder what it's for."

As Dwayne lifted the binoculars to his eyes, an almighty boom erupted from the hillside where the flag stood, showering dirt and rocks into the waters below and barely missing the *Little Boat*.

"Holy shit! What the hell!" Tammy screamed.

"Jesus Christ!"

As Dwayne slammed the boat in reverse and revved the engine to its full capacity, Tammy ducked her head behind the windshield to take cover. They continued to watch in horror as the hillside collapsed before their eyes. Rocks and boulders, followed by mounds of dirt and rubble tumbled into the water like the aftermath of an avalanche.

Once they were a safe distance away, Dwayne put the boat in neutral and released the lungful of air he'd been holding. Tammy laughed nervously. "Damn, that scared the shit out of me!"

"Well, now we know what an orange flag means. I think it means stay clear because an explosion is about to happen." They both burst out laughing. "What else do the Navy Seals practice here?" he added sarcastically. "Come on, let's go pack up the boats and get out of here. I'm not looking forward to making the crossing in a storm."

CHAPTER 29

*I*t took them about an hour to secure everything on the *Baywitch* and rig up the *Little Boat* to be towed. It was two o'clock by the time they headed out of Northwest Harbor, and they passed another fishing boat heading in, loaded with lobster traps. Dwayne grabbed his binoculars and peered at the boat. "I know that boat. They fished Malibu last year. The captain's name is Mitch."

Tammy looked over and saw the name of the Boat was *Sea Life*. "Cute name for a boat. Nice boat too."

"Yeah, he's been fishing for decades. I had no idea he was fishing out here this year. He's a really nice guy. If we had time, I'd buzz over and say a howdy and introduce you, but we have to get out of here. Maybe we'll see him on the next trip. In the meantime, I'll give him a shout on the radio."

Dwayne continued to steer the boat with one hand while reaching for the mic of the radio. "Sea Life. Sea Life. You got me? *Baywitch* here. Over."

A few seconds later, Mitch came over the radio. "Hey, Dwayne. How's it going? You fishing out here this year? Over."

"Yeah, I am. Thought I'd give it a shot. We just dropped sixty traps. Now heading back. We're trying to beat the storm. Is this your first time fishing out here? Over."

"Yep. I hear it's supposed to be pretty good. We're gonna drop our first load in the morning. You be careful heading back. You might get caught in the storm. It's moving faster than they predicted. Over."

"Thanks, man, we will. Oh, and hey, stay away from orange flags on the hillsides. We almost got blown up." Dwayne laughed. "There's all kinds of crazy Navy Seal drills going on over here. Over."

"Someone else told me about that shit. Said a rock hit their boat. They also said that the navy do underwater explosions inside the harbor. Over."

"Really? I hope they give the boats some kind of warning. Over."

"Let's hope so, man. Thanks for the heads up. I'll catch you on your next trip. Have a safe crossing. Over."

"We will. Thanks. Over and out."

Once the exchange ended, Dwayne hung up the mic and pulled Tammy into his arms. "How are you doing, sweet stuff?" he asked before planting a kiss on her lips. "You did really good out here. I'm proud of you." He flashed her that smile that always melted her heart.

Tammy leaned into his embrace. "I'm doing good. I'm having a really good time. I love it out here. Hey, I have a question."

"Sure, what's that?" Dwayne asked, keeping his eyes focused ahead.

"When you were talking to Mitch on the radio, you both kept saying 'over.' What does that mean?"

"You don't miss anything, do you?" Dwayne chuckled and yet, at the same time, he was impressed by how much attention she paid to the details. "Well, you see, radios aren't like regular phones. Remember you have to push the black button on the side to speak and release to hear the other person talk. Well, saying 'over' let's the other person know you have finished talking. And when we say 'over and out,' that lets the other person know you are ending the call."

"Aaah, okay. That makes sense. You never told me that when we were talking."

"You're right, I didn't." He smiled. "Well, now you know."

Having left the harbor and with the weather still looking to be on their side, Dwayne let Tammy drive the boat so she could have more practice staying on course by reading the compass. He used the time to go around and made sure everything was tied down securely.

The labor intense day was beginning to catch up with Tammy. Her arms ached from lifting the sixty traps around the boats and throwing them overboard. Her feet and calf muscles were sore from a combination of standing all day and fighting to keep her balance on the rocky boat. She was super hungry from only eating snacks throughout the day, her skin was dry, and her hands were chapped and sore from the salt water. And now she had to endure a ten-hour boat ride, possibly through a storm, but her spirits were still high. She had been working alongside Dwayne for over three months now, learning everything she could about the trade, and she was loving every minute of it.

They would soon be setting the traps and reaping the rewards of their labor. The anticipation pushed Tammy to work harder in the hopes they would be successful. But she couldn't help feeling that fishing was a gamble. They had put in so much time and effort, and she knew Dwayne had spent quite a bit of money on the gear in preparation for the season. And all of it was in the hopes they would catch a good haul of lobsters at an island Dwayne had never fished before.

What would they do if their catch was poor? Dwayne told her

that he had to have a successful trip in order to catch up on the bills, which he had let slide so he could buy the gear. He was two months behind on the boat slip fee, a month behind on his truck payment, and other bills were beginning to pile up too. He also had to buy supplies for the first trip, plus bait and fuel that ran at least another fifteen hundred dollars. Everything depended on their first trip; they needed to make enough money to buy more supplies for the second trip. To say the least, Tammy was somewhat concerned about their finances. She didn't realize until now the risks that were involved.

Knowing she'd be able to call Matt as soon as they docked at the mainland made her feel much better. By the time they reached the marina, it would have been three days since she last spoke to him. She had never gone that long before and it was beginning to take its toll. She couldn't wait to hear his little voice and hear what he had been up to. Occasionally, since she said goodbye to him at the airport, rushes of guilt had consumed her. But, now she had learned the industry, she was looking forward to introducing Matt to it and hopefully having him on the boat with them.

Two hours into the crossing, the sea began to take a turn and Dwayne took the wheel. The sky had become darker and white caps were now beginning to crest on the ocean. Tammy could no longer walk across the deck without constantly holding on to something.

"Damn! It's getting rough out here," Tammy hollered as she fought with the ice chest lid, which kept slamming shut as she tried to grab two Pepsis from inside.

Dwayne turned his head to make sure she was okay. "It's just starting. It's going to get a lot worse than this. The swells are only about four feet right now, but when the boat is down in the trough of the wave, it's double, which makes it eight feet." He put one of his hands out, palm-up, around the outside of the helm. "Now it's beginning to rain. Come stand next to me after you've gotten the sodas and stay dry."

"Okay," Tammy hollered, but she was concentrating on balancing the drinks in the crook of her arm so she had a free hand to hold on to the rail while making her way back to the helm. Suddenly, the boat became airborne as the bow of the boat rose high and crested over a wave, and then it slammed back down and smacked the surface of the water. On impact, waves crashed over the side of the boat, knocking Tammy off her feet. "Damn it!" she yelled. Grabbing the leg of the trap table, she watched in despair as one of the soda cans fell from her grasp and rolled away from her before coming to a stop against the side of the boat and exploding.

Dwayne turned his head in horror. "Are you okay?" he hollered, rushing over to help Tammy to her feet.

Using all her strength to stand up, she had no choice but to let the other soda go, and that too exploded like the first. She grabbed his aiding hand to pull herself up as gushes of water continued to pool around her. "It's a good job I still have my slickers on," she yelled above the roar of the ocean. "I'd be drenched if I didn't. So much for some refreshments."

Dwayne held onto her hand tight. "Never mind the drinks. Let's get you over to the helm where it's dry and safe. I need to get back to the wheel," he shouted while ducking his head away from the now pouring rain.

By the time Tammy reached the helm, her hair was drenched and beads of water dripped down her face. While holding onto the rail of the dash, she licked the excess water running over her lips and wiped the drops of water falling over her eyes from her bangs. She looked behind her at the downpour of rain and could barely make out the *Little Boat* being towed behind them. It rocked violently from side to side, taking on water from each crashing wave.

"Is the Little Boat going to be okay? It's taking on a lot of water," Tammy yelled.

Dwayne looked back over his shoulder. "So far, it's doing okay. The scuppers that allow excess water to run out of the boat seem to be working fine, but the waves are getting bigger by the minute. I'm guessing they are at about six to seven feet right now. When we are in the trough, that's twelve to fourteen feet of water above us. Hold on, okay? I don't want anything to happen to you."

Tammy gripped the rail until her knuckles turned white. She looked out through the windshield of the helm and saw nothing but an angry ocean, with waves constantly crashing over the bow of the boat. At each breaking wave, they became airborne and Tammy had to brace for impact when the hull slammed back into the ocean. It took all her strength and every muscle in her legs to remain standing.

By nightfall and still with six hours left of their journey, the storm became ruthless and showed no mercy. The jet-black skies shielded the stars from view, and the winds howled at fifty miles an hour, throwing the downpour of rain at high speed against the windshield of the helm. The wipers couldn't keep up with the floods of water pouring down the glass. The seas had increased another foot. Each time they dipped down in the trough, Tammy cringed as the wall of water on either side of the boat crashed down over the deck. Anything that had been loose on the deck was now washed away.

Tammy looked over at Dwayne, who was at the wheel about two feet away. She was scared and wanted to be held by him, but that wasn't an option. It was impossible to move even an inch on the boat without losing her balance. Dwayne had braced himself against the side wall of the helm and was using both hands to steer the boat as best he could through the terrifying storm.

"How do you even steer in this weather?" Tammy hollered.

While turning the wheel back and forth, Dwayne yelled back, "It's not that easy, but I've spent most of my life on boats and have had plenty of practice." Suddenly, he grabbed the wheel hard with both hands and held it tight. "Shit, here comes a big wave. Hold on tight and bend your knees on impact."

Tammy looked ahead and screamed. She saw nothing but a fast approaching, solid body of water about to crash over the boat. "Oh my god! I don't want to die out here."

"Hold on!" Dwayne yelled.

Within seconds, the wave crashed into the boat and completely consumed the bow and the windshield. Sprays of water came around the sides and into where they stood, and Tammy ducked her head from the sting of the rain pelting her skin. She wanted to shield her ears from the angry roar of the ocean but was unable to let go of the rail. She turned her head just in time to see another deluge of water washing over the deck. "Oh my god!" she screamed. "There's the *Little Boat*. It's alongside of us. It's supposed to be behind us!"

Dwayne quickly turned his head and yelled, "Fuck! It's racing down the wave, causing a slack in the line."

"Is it going to be okay?" Tammy shouted back.

"As long as it doesn't hit us, it should be okay. When it's ridden the wave, the line should get tight again and pull it back behind us. Keep an eye on it."

"Okay."

Fearing the worst—that the *Little Boat* may crash into them—Tammy remained focused on it, waiting for the line to tighten like Dwayne said it would. But for the next few minutes, it remained alongside them as if in competition to beat the storm. "It's not going back!" she screamed.

"Give it a minute," Dwayne hollered while fighting with the wheel.

A few seconds later, Tammy saw the boat beginning to fall behind and released a huge sigh of relief. "There it goes."

Dwayne glanced over his shoulder. "Keep checking on it. If we get another big wave like that, it could happen again." No sooner had he said that, he yelled, "Hold on!"

Tammy looked ahead and saw yet again another huge wave

about to hit them. "Fuck!" she screamed, scrunching her eyes closed. Both she and the boat got another drenching as they rocked violently back and forth. While still trying to recover from the impact, Tammy strained to check on the *Little Boat*. "It's alongside us again, but this time it's leaning right over."

Dwayne looked over and saw the side of the boat almost submerged. "Oh shit! It may roll." Panic blanketed his face as he continued to watch the *Little Boat*. "Come on. Get back up," he shouted at the *Little Boat* with urgency in his voice.

Both he and Tammy continued to watch the *Little Boat*, which was now almost on its side as the waves continued to crash over it.

"Come on!" Dwayne yelled again.

Tammy held her breath. There was nothing either one of them could do but hope the *Little Boat* would straighten itself out once the wave had passed. If it didn't, it would be a huge disaster and both boats could go down.

Dwayne yelled again, "Come on! God damn it!"

Tammy's eyes were now clouded by a mixture of seawater and tears. For the first time, she was afraid for their lives. She didn't know how to react or what to do. She was scared. She didn't want to die, especially not out here. The thought of drowning and falling to the bottom of the ocean never to be found again, absolutely terrified her. They were sitting ducks, helpless against the force of nature and what it may throw at them.

Images of Matt haunted her mind. She wanted to be with him and hold him. For the first time, she questioned herself and her recent decisions. What was she doing out here? In a panic, she yelled to Dwayne, "Isn't there anything we can do?"

"No!" He hollered back. "Just pray it gets back up."

They continued to watch for what seemed like an endless amount of time. Eventually, they both cheered and yelled, "There she goes!"

Tammy squealed "Yes!" as she saw the side of the boat lift away from the water. A few minutes later, the line slowly tightened and the *Little Boat* began to fall back behind the *Baywitch*. "Oh my god. I thought we were goners," she said while catching her breath. But in a matter of seconds, the *Baywitch* was back in the air and Tammy lost her balance again. Taken by surprise and with nothing to hold onto, she was thrown backwards onto the deck like a discarded ragdoll and swept to the back of the boat. She came to a stop when her spine slammed into the stern.

"Arghh!" she hollered, wincing as pain shot up and down the length of her back.

Because they had been so preoccupied with the status of the *Little Boat*, they hadn't seen the next humongous wave about to slam into the boat and Tammy had failed to brace for it. Luckily, Dwayne was still wedged against the wall of the helm and managed to avoid the brunt of it. He looked in horror at Tammy, who was scrunched against the back of the boat surrounded by pools of water. He watched helplessly as she ducked her head out of the howling wind and the fierce downpour of rain beating upon her.

With one hand, she held on to the back of the boat while trying to use the other hand for balance as she pulled herself to her feet, but the force of the boat surging back and forth made it impossible.

"Tammy, are you able to get up?" Dwayne yelled over the roar of the wind.

Unable to look up, she hollered back, "No, the wind is too strong and the boat is rocking too much."

"Hold on!" Dwayne yelled back.

While still keeping one hand on the wheel, Dwayne reached over to where he had some line on a hook and pulled it loose. Despite needing to keep the boat under control at the same time, he skillfully tied a loop knot and threw the end to Tammy. "Here, grab the rope."

Straining to see the rope through the pouring rain, she missed on the first attempt. "Fuck!"

Dwayne quickly pulled it back in and threw again.

"Got it!" she yelled.

"Okay. Hold on tight to the rope. I'm going to pull you in."

"Okay!" Tammy yelled, grasping the rope tight with both hands and wrapping it around her fists. Using the rope for leverage, Tammy was finally able to pull herself to her feet and using all his strength, Dwayne began pulling her in. As she inched her way back to the helm, she could feel the rope cutting into her flesh. As soon as she was within reach, Dwayne grabbed her and pulled her into his arms and held her tight. She was a mess. Her hair was soaking wet and matted, streams of water were running off her slickers and her cheeks were ice cold.

Dwayne took a hold of the wheel with one hand while still holding onto Tammy with the other. "My god, are you okay?"

Tammy fought to loosen the rope from around her fist. "No, I'm not okay," she cried, letting the tears stream down her face. With one last tug, she finally broke free of the rope. In a rush of fear and frustration, she bundled it up in a ball and threw it on the dash before fixing her cold, numb fingers back on the rail again.

She leaned in to Dwayne, who squeezed her tight and said, "You're okay now."

Tammy buried her face in his chest, trying to seek warmth from the frigid cold of the stormy night. "I was so scared and I'm freezing. I can't even feel my hands."

Dwayne rubbed her shoulders and pulled her in even closer, not wanting to let her go. "I'm so sorry that happened to you. You're safe now, I promise."

Still holding the wheel, he strained his eyes to see out through the windshield. Even though gushed of water still pounding against it, he couldn't miss what was coming. Releasing his hold from Tammy, he held on tight to the wheel and yelled, "Hold on with both hands and don't forget to bend your knees on impact. A big one is coming."

"God! I'm sick of this! When is it going to end?" she screamed while gripping her hands around the wooden rail of the dash. "I'm exhausted."

Within seconds, they became airborne as the *Baywitch* rode over the wave. Tammy braced herself for the impact; she didn't know how much more her body could take. She wouldn't be surprised if she had bruises the following day from the beating the ocean was giving her. As the *Baywitch* plunged into the water, Tammy let out a loud, painful grunt to ease the force of the impact. She turned her head to check on the *Little Boat* and saw it had snuck up closer but wasn't alongside them this time.

"You okay?" Dwayne shouted once the wave had passed.

Too tired to speak, Tammy gave him a nod and continued to look straight ahead.

For the next ten minutes, the boat continued to rock viciously and sprays of water continued to flood the deck, but the waves seemed to be decreasing in size.

"I think we're through the worst of it," Dwayne shouted from the wheel.

For the first time in a while, a slight smile breached Tammy's face. "God, I hope so. I was seriously scared for my life back there."

Dwayne could tell she was still concerned about their safety and left the wheel for a moment to embrace her. "I'm so sorry that your first experience out here was a life-threatening event. Trust me, I would never let anything happen to you. I knew we had a storm coming, but it traveled a lot faster than I anticipated and it was much stronger too. But, Tammy, you've been a trooper and handled it better than most people I know."

Tammy hugged him back, enjoying the security of his masculine arms around her. "It's okay. You can't control nature. I feel safe with you. I know how experienced you are, and I wouldn't be out here with anyone else but you." She chuckled.

Dwayne leaned in and gave her a wet, salty kiss on the lips. "I love you. You're the best."

"I love you too."

Feeling better and with the seas beginning to die down, Dwayne took the helm again, and Tammy returned to holding the rail and looking straight ahead.

By the time they were about an hour out of the harbor, the storm was behind them. It was around ten o'clock in the evening. Clouds still lingered in the sky, allowing a few stars to appear, but the rain had stopped and the wind was only a slight breeze. The waves were now a comfortable three-foot swell, and the *Little Boat* was where it was supposed to be, in tow behind them.

Tammy's body ached from head to toe. She couldn't wait until the boats were tied up to the dock so she could do a complete body check and look for bruises. She had a feeling she would find a few. Her hands were sore from clenching onto the rail for hours, to the point that it was too painful to move or bend her fingers, and every muscle in her legs ached and her feet were numb from standing for the entire trip.

Looking for any kind of relief and wanting to be close to Dwayne, she snuggled close to him for the last hour at the wheel. He held her close and rubbed her tired body with his free hand while she tucked her head onto his shoulder.

"I'm so tired. I can't remember ever feeling this exhausted," Tammy said in a sleepy voice.

Dwayne kissed the top of the head. "We're almost there, sweetheart. As soon as we're tied up, you go crawl into bed, okay? I'll take care of the *Little Boat*."

"No argument from me." But then a thought occurred to her and she raised her head. "You know, it just dawned on me that we're already home. We live and work on this boat. When we tie up, we don't have a home to go to. It's here. That's a strange feeling."

Dwayne nodded. "Yep, you're right. It kind of takes the stigma away of actually going home."

"It does. It feels kind of weird. Depressing in a way. No big bed to go home to or the space that a house offers. Something else I'll have to get use to I guess. It just never occurred to me until now."

She confessed to herself that the idea wasn't so appealing.

CHAPTER 30

They finally pulled into the dock around eleven o'clock, where the waters were calm and the winds were non-existent. Tammy dragged her feet and struggled to step onto the dock to help tie off the boats. She giggled when her feet came into contact with the hard surface of the dock. Even though they swayed a little bit, it was nothing like being on a boat for the past two days. She had to stand for a moment to become reacquainted with dry land. Her legs felt like jelly and she had to think before putting one foot in front of the other.

"This feels weird." She laughed while cleating off the *Baywitch*.

"You'll get used to it. Wait until we come back after being out for seven days." Dwayne laughed while shutting off the engines of the *Baywitch* and jumping off to deal with the *Little Boat*.

Once both boats were secured, Dwayne joined Tammy in the cabin. Having wasted no time, she was already undressed, wearing only her bra and panties and was busy inspecting her body on the edge of the bed.

"God, no wonder my body hurts. Look at me. I'm a mess!" she said while twisting her leg at obscure angles to see her thigh.

"Here, let me take a look." Dwayne leaned in to help. "Damn, girl! You're not kidding."

After a closer look, they found a total of eight bruises on Tammy's body. The worst being on her back and upper thighs, which probably happened when she fell and slid across the deck. Her back was scraped up from the rough finish of the non-skid on the deck, and the thigh that had slammed onto the surface was bruised a deep purple. She had more bruises on her hips where she banged into the dash of the helm a few times, and a couple more on her arms.

"God, Tammy, I didn't realize you got so banged up," Dwayne said while rubbing the back her thigh softly. "Are you going to be able to go back out?"

Adamant about not being a quitter, Tammy became defensive. "Of course I'll be able to go back out. Nothing a good night's sleep can't take care of." She softened her tone and kissed Dwayne on the lips. "They're just bruises. I'll be fine."

"Okay. I just worry about you. Come on, let's get you into bed and I'll massage you until you fall asleep."

CHAPTER 31

The next morning, Tammy could barely move. She turned her head on the pillow and saw Dwayne was already up and busy making coffee. It was the sweet aroma that had woken her. Rolling to the edge of the bed, she winced in pain every time she had to move a muscle. "God, doesn't your body ache? I feel like I've been run over by a steam roller." She reached round to rub the small of her back, but she pulled away again when her arm flinched in pain.

"I'm a little sore, but I didn't get thrown across the boat like you." He turned and took Tammy's hands. "Here, let me help you."

Slowly, Tammy raised herself to her feet. "Ouch!" she screamed, followed by grunts of pains. "Oh man, I wish you had a bath tub. You have no idea what I would do to be able soak in a tub right now."

Dwayne helped her up on to the deck and into a chair before bringing her a cup of coffee. "Are you sure you'll be able to go back out? I don't want you to overdo it. I care about you." He seemed genuinely concerned about the agony she was going through.

"I'll be fine. I just need to loosen up a bit. After my coffee, I'll get dressed and walk a few laps around the yard."

Dwayne leaned in and gave her a gentle kiss. "Okay. If you're sure. I know how stubborn you can be." He chuckled.

After a few sips of her coffee, Tammy was already feeling the magical effects of caffeine and feeling more alert. "When do we leave again?" she asked.

"Tonight."

A look of shock blanketed her face. Tonight!"

"I'm afraid so. We only have a week to get all these traps out. We need to do two more trips. But we're only taking the *Baywitch* this time. I wanted to take the *Little Boat* on the first trip so we could explore the island. I figured we'd go get fuel and groceries today and when we get back, we can load traps on to the boat and do a night crossing. We'd leave here about six and get to San Clemente around three in the morning. There are no storms in the forecast, so it should be a nice crossing," Dwayne added, knowing how anxious Tammy must be about going back out there again. "We can rest up for a bit before the sun comes up and then go dump the traps." A devious smile appeared on Dwayne's face as he knelt in front of Tammy and began rubbing her thighs. "Tell you what. Why don't I take you up to the showers and caress those bruises of yours? I can gently wash every inch of your body. How does that sound?"

Tammy beamed a radiant smile. "Hmm, that sounds wonderful. But after the amazing shower that you are promising me, I want to call Matt. I can't wait to hear his voice. That will make me feel better."

"Good idea! I want to say hi to the little guy too, and I'll give Justin a call while we're there." Dwayne took her hand. "Are you ready?"

"I am. Let's go."

∾

Over the next week, Tammy and Dwayne made two more trips to the island. Both were much easier than the first. A friendlier ocean and taking only one boat allowed them to trade off driving and take breaks so they could actually sit down for a while. But each trip was made back to back, and the work was intense from the minute they tied up at the dock to the time they left again. There was so much to do when they returned that there was little time left for sleep.

On one of the trips, Tammy finally got to meet the captain of *Sea-Life*. He was about the same age as Dwayne but heavier set and wore a red baseball hat with the name of his boat on it. His arms and face were tanned from spending endless days on the ocean. He was friendly toward Tammy and welcomed her to the fishery. He wished her luck and offered his help to them both if they ever needed it.

After making the last trip and returning in the early hours of the morning, they managed to get a good night's sleep of at least seven hours. It was the most they'd had in over a week. But then they had to gear up for the actual fishing trip, which was scheduled for the first Wednesday in October. They had only five days to get ready. This is what Tammy had been waiting for and just the thought was enough to energize her. She couldn't wait to get started.

As always, her priority at the beginning of each day when they were on land was to call Matt, which always put her in a better place. He had adjusted quickly and well and was enjoying his new playmate Andrew. Tales of him doing new things that Tammy hadn't yet seen tore at her heart. She laughed with tears while Joanne told her about the day he got stuck up in a tree. It was his first time climbing a tree. Another time, her father said Matt had been helping him to plant some bulbs. Tammy had never done any gardening with Matt, but it brought back forgotten memories of gardening days with her dad.

That morning, Tammy and Dwayne moved with great difficulty. The grueling week had finally caught up with them, and they tried to capture as much rest as possible before going at it again. After Tammy's phone call to Matt, they spent a few quality hours together on the deck of the *Baywitch*, enjoying the morning rays of sun with an overdose of caffeine.

Even though the time spent together was short, it was something they both needed and had missed. While working on the boat, it had been nothing but intense labor from sun up to sun down and a few hours in between to catch some sleep. Tammy savored every minute of Dwayne's affection and cuddles, knowing as soon as they got up, they wouldn't stop again until the traps were baited and set at the island.

Dwayne had explained what needed to be done before they headed out, and the list was long. They had just enough money to make it back out, but after buying all the supplies, he told her they would be broke. Everything relied on a successful catch.

The first task was to fuel up both boats, and they would also need extra barrels of fuel on the boat to fill up the *Little Boat* while they were out at the island. Next would be a trip to downtown LA to pick up five hundred pounds of frozen bait and load it on to the boats. A week's worth of groceries needed to be bought, and twenty-five lobster receivers needed to be stacked onto the boat.

"What are those?" Tammy asked.

"They are plastic crates that float in the water and are tied up to the *Baywitch* in the harbor. We use them put the lobsters in and keep them alive until we return. We only get paid for live lobsters, so keeping them healthy is critical. After a few days, I'm hoping a few of the crates in the water will be full of lobsters."

It took two days to get all the tasks completed, but now that the last knot was tied and everything was secured on the boat, they had just enough money left over to treat themselves to a nice dinner at the nearby steak house. It would be their last big cooked meal for seven days, Dwayne reminded Tammy.

At the restaurant, they sat side by side. Tammy cuddled in Dwayne's arms as she devoured every last morsel on her plate, enjoying the simple pleasures of a hearty meal.

"That was delicious. I'm stuffed," she said as she pushed her plate away. "And I'm so tired."

Dwayne pulled her in closer and gently pulled her hair back away from her face before kissing her softly on the cheek. "How are you holding up? Are you sorry you decided to go fishing with me?" He added a nervous chuckle, not sure of her reply.

Tammy pulled herself up away from his chest and turned to face him. "Oh gosh, no. Never! I'm loving every bit of it. Even our victory at sea." She laughed. "I love spending our entire days and nights together, working with you and learning all these new things. I just hope we catch some bloody lobsters after all this hard work."

"Hearing you say that makes me happy. You're a trooper, Tammy. I've never met anyone like you. I was afraid I'd worked you too hard and probably scared you off. I thought you'd never want to fish again. Having you around makes fishing enjoyable. I love you."

Tammy leaned in and met his kiss. His lips felt rough from being on the ocean but she didn't care; she loved everything about him. "I love you too."

Their kiss lingered for a few minutes and grew passionately with their tongues exploring each other's mouths. Holding her tight in his arms, Dwayne broke away in a panted breath. "Come on, let's go back to the boat. I want to make love to you. It might be the last time for a whole week."

"Sounds like a beautiful way to end the day," Tammy replied in a soft voice.

CHAPTER 32

The next morning, they left before the sun was up, feeling refreshed and fully rested. They rode together on the *Baywitch* with the *Little Boat* in tow. The ocean remained their friend and granted them a glorious crossing with calm waters, blue skies and plenty of sunshine. They made good time and reached the island by three o'clock, and they found they were no longer alone in the harbor. There were six other boats already anchored.

Tammy recognized the *Sea-Life* and Dwayne pointed out three others that he knew: *Patience, Lobster Fest* and *Out to Sea.* He had gotten to know them when he had fished Malibu but hadn't seen any of the captains since last season. "We'll have to go for a cruise around the harbor so I can introduce you after we've cut up all the bait and gotten organized."

Remembering how friendly Mitch was at their introduction, Tammy liked the idea of meeting the other captains. She agreed with great enthusiasm.

By five o'clock, Dwayne and Tammy had all the bait cut, the bait jars filled and everything ready to start baiting and setting the traps tomorrow. They had just enough daylight to go and say hi to the captains Dwayne already knew, and to introduce themselves to the others. They jumped on the *Little Boat*, which was easier to maneuver, and drove off.

They stopped first at the *Patience,* a boat about the same size as the *Baywitch* but with a bright red hull. Patrick, the captain, walked to the stern of the boat as Dwayne pulled up. Tammy saw he had one other crew member who was busy coiling up line and gave Dwayne a nod before returning to his task. Patrick was also about the same age as Dwayne, in his thirties, and he gave them both a friendly smile. Much to Tammy's surprise, he made her feel welcome.

"It's nice to finally see a woman out here. I'm sure you'll show us how it's done and put us in our places," he hollered across the water with a hearty laugh.

Tammy couldn't help but laugh back. "I'll do my best!"

To Tammy's disappointment, the captains on the other two boats, Tom on the *Lobster Fest* and Lester on the *Out to Sea*, weren't so friendly. She sensed their doubts regarding her ability, and she felt a little hurt when they both told her they'd be surprised if she lasted the season.

"I've never seen a woman fish out here in all my forty years. There's a reason for that you know," Lester said.

"Well, she's not like other women," Dwayne corrected. "She's going to be just fine out here. You watch. She surprised the hell out of me and she will do the same to you." He threw Tammy a smile as he bragged about her.

"I'm curious to see how long she'll last. Well, good luck to you both," he said before they took off.

With the sun setting fast, they made it to one other boat to say hi to the eldest of the captains called Dale. His boat was named *Dreaming*, a boat Dwayne didn't know. He didn't seem too happy to see them and was also surprised to see a woman out at the island. Tammy could tell he doubted her abilities to fish and live on a boat for five days straight, which is what they would be doing once the traps were baited and set. He asked her the typical questions. Had she ever fished before? Does she know what she's in for? All his questions were followed by a sarcastic laugh.

She could tell he had spent his entire life on the ocean fishing. He was probably in his sixties, with a crew of three deck hands handling the traps stacked on the boat. His skin had clearly been exposed to years of sunlight, having a look of tanned leather. Deep wrinkles and crow's feet surrounded his eyes, his nose was peeling and his lips were dry and chapped. As he spoke from his boat, his shoulder-length, mangled gray hair blew in the wind. He also stroked his gray beard the entire time, which Tammy thought was a little creepy. But she wasn't going to allow herself to be intimidated by anyone. She knew she was capable of handling anything that was thrown at her, and she would prove herself to the rest of the fleet fishing the island.

During the interrogation, Tammy was grateful Dwayne had her back and beamed him a smile when he began bragging about her to Dale while holding her tightly around the waist. Dale seemed surprise by Dwayne's praises and had backed off a little by mumbling, "Well, all's I can say is good luck."

Dale went on to tell them he'd been fishing San Clemente for over ten years, and more boats showed up every year. He complained that pretty soon the island would be fished out. "There's not enough lobsters for all these damn boats."

Dwayne took it all in his stride. Being one of the new boats Dale had complained about, he didn't want to be on the old timer's shit list. He'd heard many stories of angry fisherman who had been known to cut off your traps if you fished too close to his, or if he was envious of your catch, he would steal them for himself, or even worse, pull your line and open all the doors to your traps.

Life as a commercial fisherman was competitive and at times ruthless. Dwayne wanted no trouble; he just wanted to fish, and even though the guy came across as an asshole, Dwayne bit his tongue. "Sorry you feel that way. We just stopped by to introduce ourselves." Dale had already turned his back on them and proceeded to move gear around on the deck of his boat. "We'll let you get back to work," Dwayne hollered before steering the *Little Boat* away. "What a jerk," he whispered in Tammy's ear.

By the time they got back to the *Baywitch*, the sun had already set and the night sky was dominated by a full moon, which Dwayne liked because, according to legend, it made the lobster crawl.

Bright deck lights from all the other boats illuminated the harbor while Tammy sat on the deck, surrounded by boxes of fresh-cut bait and frozen mackerel.

"God, this bait stinks," she said to Dwayne.

"That is the smell of money," he said, inhaling a lungful of the stench through his nose. "I love that smell. Wait till the end of the week when most of this lot has defrosted."

"Speak for yourself," Tammy tried to say while holding the end of her nose closed.

Dwayne took her hand and rubbed it softly. "I'm so happy you're out here with me. I'd be so lonely if you weren't. Thank you for coming."

"You don't have to thank me. I want to be here. I'm loving every minute of this new adventure you brought me on. And you are a great coach by the way."

"You have gone far beyond my expectations and you never cease to amaze me. As for the guys on the other boats, don't let them get to you. They can be real assholes at times."

Tammy shook her hair and held her head up high in defiance. "Oh, I won't. I'll show them."

While enjoying the little time they had to relax, they spent the rest of the evening watching the crews on the other boats doing their last-minute chores before the big day of baiting and setting traps. Like Dwayne, some were finished and could be seen hanging out on their decks, the sound of their laughter carrying across the water.

Dwayne went over their plan for the next day. They would be using the *Little Boat* every day. He would be driving the boat and Tammy had the job of deck hand. As Dwayne pulled up to each buoy, her job, he explained, was to hook the line using a long-handled gaff and wrap the line around the pulley. Dwayne would then work the pulley wheel and pull the trap up. Once it was on the table, Tammy would bait it and close the door while Dwayne drove the boat to the desired fishing location. Once at the spot, it was up to Tammy to push the trap overboard and throw out the line and buoy. They had a hundred fifty traps to do. They worked well together and both were confident they could get them all done by the end of the day.

The next morning, before sunrise at four thirty, Dwayne and Tammy were the first to leave the harbor. Dressed in their slickers, rubber boots, gloves and a layer of t-shirts with a sweater beneath, they took off in the chilled darkened morning for the first trap. It was only five minutes away on the east side of the island, where it was always calm for the first half of the day.

With her gaff in hand, Tammy stood alert behind Dwayne, looking out for the first buoy floating on the water. A few minutes later, she spotted their red and black colors and squealed while pointing with her finger. "There it is at two o'clock!"

Dwayne followed her finger and as they approached it, he slowed down the boat to allow Tammy to gaff it, but she missed and yelled, "Damn it!"

"That okay. You'll get the hang of it after doing this all day," Dwayne said as he began turning around and coming back up on the buoy. "Okay, try again," he hollered while trying to keep the boat steady.

With one swing of the gaff, she nailed it. "Got it!" she yelled in triumph.

"Great! Now grab the rope, wrap it around the pulley and throw the buoy on the deck."

It didn't take Tammy long to bait up the trap and seal the door closed. By the time Dwayne was at the fishing spot, she was ready to drop it back in the ocean and on command, she pushed it overboard and tossed out the line and buoy.

Dwayne gave her a high-five. "Good job!" he shouted over the noise of the outboard. "Hold on, we're gonna speed up to the next one. A hundred forty-nine more and we'll be done."

As they headed toward the next trap, Tammy hollered to Dwayne, "Look over there! It's a sea lion. He's following us," she squealed with excitement.

"Yeah, he's after the bait. Whatever you do, don't feed him, otherwise we'll never get rid of him."

They hustled all day, and with no time to rest in between each set of traps, they snacked on whatever they could grab and ate quickly before they reached the next trap. Tammy missed with the gaff a few more times, but like Dwayne had said, she soon got the hang of it. Periodically, she noticed the seal was still following them and when Dwayne wasn't looking, she tossed him a mackerel. *What harm can it do? The poor guy is hungry.*

By mid-afternoon, they had succeeded in baiting and moving one hundred twenty traps, but the last thirty were becoming a challenge. The wind had picked up and the swells had increased. Keeping the boat steady to allow Tammy to gaff the rope wasn't easy, and the time spent at each one was becoming longer. They were beginning to tire; their bodies were sore and their feet ached from standing all day. Tammy found she had to brace her knees hard against the hull of the boat to steady herself from the increased rocking of the boat as she leaned over to hook the line.

The *Little Boat* had low sides that only came up above their knees and, afraid she might fall overboard, Dwayne held onto the back of her sweater as she leaned over. "I gotcha!" he hollered each time she swung out the gaff.

By the time the sun was setting over the horizon, they were pulling up to the last trap. Feeling rejuvenated that their quest was finally coming to an end, and that they had accomplished what they had set out to do over fourteen hours ago, they pulled up on the final buoy cheering at the top of their lungs. "Don't miss!" Dwayne laughed. "I don't want to prolong this anymore."

"Got it!" Tammy cheered.

"That's my girl!"

Once the last trap was back in the water, Dwayne turned off the boat and made his way over to Tammy. "Give me a kiss, partner. You were fantastic today."

Tammy held up her hands. "Don't get too close. I'm a slimy mess." She looked down at her slickers, now coated in blood and what she could only describe as gunk. "Look at me. I'm covered in fish guts."

Dwayne ignored her warning and took her in his arms. "You smell like money." He laughed before giving her a hard kiss on the lips.

Tammy welcomed his affection and smothered him in wet, salty kisses. "Thanks. You weren't too bad yourself. I can't wait to see what we have tomorrow. You're right, this is just like bloody Christmas Eve."

CHAPTER 33

 hen they returned to the harbor, it was nightfall and the moon was just as bright as it had been the night before. The sky was clear and hundreds of stars glistened above them. "Man, what a beautiful night," Tammy said, admiring the illuminated skies above her from the deck.

Most of the boats were already back in and anchored down for the night. Dwayne and Tammy waved as they cruised by toward their mooring.

"I gotta find a way to clean up. I stink," Tammy proclaimed while tying up to the cleat of the *Baywitch*.

"I wouldn't bother until we've scrubbed down the little boat and cut up enough bait for tomorrow's pull. That's gonna take a few hours."

"Damn...does it ever end? Tell you what, I'll chop bait while you take care of the *Little Boat*. I'm already stinky." She laughed.

Dwayne was right. It took them another two hours to do the last remaining chores of their long day, by which time, Tammy was beyond desperate to find a way to clean herself up. There was no shower on the boat, or any hot water for that matter.

"I'm going to go say a howdy to Mitch on the radio before it gets too late and see how his day went. You can always dip a towel in the ocean and use that to wash yourself off with."

"I'll think of something. Say hi to Mitch for me."

Ten minutes later, while Dwayne was involved in a conversation with Mitch on the radio, he heard a loud splash from the back of the boat and quickly turned his head, just in time to see a spray of water hit the boat. "What the hell?"

Mitch came over the radio. "Was that your girl I just saw jump into the water naked?"

Hearing cheers and whistles from the other fisherman echoing from the surrounding boats, Dwayne dropped the mic and left it dangling by its cord while he rushed to the stern to see what all the commotion was about. With a confused look, he peered over the side and saw Tammy raise her head out of the water.

"God, this feels bloody fantastic!" she yelled with a huge grin painted across her face.

Dwayne was stunned. "Are you crazy? What the hell are you doing?"

"I'm taking a bath. It feels wonderful. Want to join me?"

"No!" Dwayne said defiantly. "Great whites swim in that water. Come on, get out."

Behind them, the other fisherman continued to cheer and raise whatever drink they had in their hand. Dwayne looked up and laughed at the excitement from the growing audience of guys, who were probably enjoying a memorable moment of seeing a naked woman swimming in Northwest harbor for the first time in their lives. "Well, that's one way to get the guys to like you." He chuckled. "They're never going to forget this. You're crazy, girl!"

"Ha!" Tammy squealed while floating on her back with her breasts protruding toward the stars. "I feel liberated. You gotta try it!"

"No thanks. I'm good. Besides, I'm enjoying the view like

everyone else," he said with a mischievous wink. "Isn't the water cold?"

"Nah. It's feels great. Sure you don't wanna come in?"

Dwayne shook his head again. "Thanks. I'm sure."

Tammy rolled off her back and continued to tread water as she spoke. "Okay, but you're missing out. I'm going to go for a swim. I'll be back in a bit."

"Stay close to the boat where I can see you. I'm going to stay right here and watch you. I'm sure everyone else will too," he added.

Tammy granted Dwayne's wishes and didn't swim too far away. Periodically, she waved to the loud fishermen, some of whom were now viewing the spectacle through binoculars. She liked the attention, and it seemed Dwayne was getting a kick out of it too. She swam around for a good ten minutes before the chill started to set in, so she made her way back to the swim step where Dwayne stood anxiously with a towel in hand. As she pulled herself out of the water, her naked body on full display, the whistles and cheers grew louder.

"Well, you've certainly made their night," he said with a grin. He handed her the towel over the side of the boat and she quickly wrapped herself in it. "Come on, take my hand, I'll help you up," Dwayne told her.

Once she was on the boat, Tammy started to shiver, so Dwayne took her in his arms and began rubbing her shoulders vigorously.

"That felt good. But damn, I'm freezing now. I'm going into the cabin to warm up." She looked up at Dwayne while still in his arms and gave him a smooch. "I love you."

"I love you too, you crazy woman you." He slapped her behind as she broke away from his hold. "Now go on. Go get warm while I put some soup on for dinner."

Soup was the quickest and easiest meal to heat and eat on a boat, especially when they were too tired to do anything else. Dwayne knew this from experience and within ten minutes, he had two servings of clam chowder in metal cups ready along with a couple of rolls.

"Soup's ready," he hollered from the deck.

"Coming," she replied from the cabin while pulling a comb through her wet, mangled hair.

A few minutes later, she joined Dwayne on the deck dressed in clean sweats. "I'm bloody famished. The soup smells good," she said, taking the empty seat next to him. She scooped a cup out of his hands and a roll from his lap. "Thank you."

"Let's eat this and call it an early night. What do you say? Tomorrow's the big day. I want to take off around five in the morning."

"Sounds good to me. I'm bloody knackered," Tammy said in between spoonfuls of soup, each one instantly warming her to the core. Other than her quick dip in the ocean, this was the first time she had been still all day, and she cherished the short moment of quiet while savoring every delicious taste of her hot soup. The winds were absent and the boat rocked gently, making it easier to eat. She glanced out at the other boats and noticed a few already had their lights turned off, telling her they also were planning for an early start.

Dwayne had told her that the opening day of lobster season is usually the best. The lobsters hadn't been fished in six months and the crawl should be heavy. It's the day that they should make the most money. After that, it would start to drop off. Every boat was counting on a good catch on that first day, because most were probably in debt, just like they were.

The anticipation of pulling the traps tomorrow was not only exciting but also nerve-wracking. What if they didn't catch enough lobsters to cover their expenses and get caught up with the bills? What were they going to do? She never realized how much they were depending on this first catch until Dwayne had explained their finances.

"I hope there's a bunch of lobsters crawling in our traps right now," she said while taking her last spoonful of soup.

"Me too. Come on, let's go to bed. We will find out tomorrow."

Fifteen minutes later, they were curled up in each other's arms beneath the covers, both trying desperately to fall asleep. But the anticipation of tomorrow's pull prevented them. Lying restless in Dwayne's arms, Tammy thought she heard a loud thud out on the deck of the boat. "Did you hear that?" she whispered to Dwayne.

"Hear what?" Dwayne asked in near sleepy state.

"I think there's someone out there."

After almost being asleep, Dwayne was now wide awake again and feeling somewhat irritated because he knew it would be a challenge to go back to sleep again. He answered with an edge to his voice. "Tammy, we're in the middle of nowhere on a boat. There's no one out there. Now go to sleep."

Suddenly, they were alerted by another loud thud on the deck. They both sat bolt upright, straining their ears for any more strange noises.

"See, I told you there's someone out there!" Tammy whispered.

"What the fuck?" Dwayne whispered back. "Wait here."

Tammy remained in the bed while Dwayne reluctantly ducked his head and crawled out of their tiny sleeping quarters. Flashlight in hand, he cautiously eased his way to the cabin door and again heard another thud. Looking over his shoulder at Tammy, he whispered, "There's definitely something out there."

Unsure of what Dwayne was about to face, Tammy swung her legs out of the bed and sat nervously on the edge, her legs dangling in the cold night air. Dwayne turned on the floodlights of the deck before swinging the cabin door open. Shocked by what he saw, he had only two words. "Holy fuck!" he shouted and quickly closed the door again

Now on her feet, Tammy asked, "What is it?" A loud grunting noise came from the deck. "What the fuck is that?"

"There' a fucking five-hundred-pound seal on the deck of our boat," Dwayne hollered back while searching frantically for some sort of weapon to shoo the beast off the boat.

"What? You're kidding?"

Dwayne froze mid search and turned to Tammy with an inquisitive stare. "Wait. Did you feed the seal today while we were baiting the traps?"

Tammy shied away from his stare and chewed on her lip for a moment, contemplating her answer. "Well...maybe a couple of times. There was a seal following us and he looked hungry, so I tossed him a couple of fish."

Dwayne knew he should be angry with her for not following his rules when it came to feeding the sea lions, but he just couldn't. Maybe now she'd understand why. Instead, he simply shook his head and laughed. "Well, your buddy is wanting more fish. Now do you see why I told you not to feed them?"

Showing his impatience, the sea lion bellowed in the direction of the cabin door. Tammy jumped back from the beastly sound while hanging her head in shame. "I'm sorry. I had no idea. I promise I won't feed them again." She looked up toward the cabin door and then at Dwayne. "What are we going to do?"

"We've got to figure out a way to get him off the boat."

"Can we throw a mackerel in the water? Maybe he will jump off to get it," Tammy suggested.

Dwayne chuckled. "No, because he will just come back for another one tomorrow." He began searching the boat again, but he soon realized all his long poles were on the deck.

"What about saucepans? You can bang them together."

Dwayne smiled with an agreeable nod. "Good idea! Hand me a couple."Tammy quickly retrieved two metal saucepans from a drawer and gave them to Dwayne, who inched his way back toward the door. Standing closer behind him, with one hand on his shoulder, she held her breath as Dwayne slowly pushed open the door. Shocked by what stood before them, Tammy almost fell backwards and clung onto Dwayne's shoulder to keep her balance.

"Fuck! He's huge!" she screamed, finding herself face to face with the biggest creature she had ever seen.

The stench that came from his breath as he let out another fierce roar caused Tammy to quickly turn her head and hold her nose. "God, he stinks," Tammy yelled in disgust.

Not wanting to give the beast a chance to enter the cabin, Dwayne wasted no time in furiously banging the pans together while yelling at the top of his voice, "Get out of here! Go on. Go!"

For a few seconds, the seal stayed put in his puddle of water on the deck and simply stared at Dwayne. Seeing Dwayne as the only thing standing in his way of the mackerel, the seal argued his case with another deafening roar. But Dwayne stood his ground. Hitting the pans together harder, he continued to shout and step slowly up to the deck.

Tammy followed close behind, joining Dwayne in his yelling. "Go on! Go!" she growled in a vicious tone.

The seal began to retreat and inch by inch, he slid his body toward the stern of the boat. Dwayne and Tammy continued with their yelling and screaming, backing the seal away. They herded him backwards until he had nowhere to go but over the back of the boat. With one last clash of the pans, the seal roared again before sliding his body around and leaping onto the ledge of the stern. By this time, flashlights from other boats were aimed in their direction, all wondering what the commotion was about.

"Go on! Shoo!" Dwayne yelled, now within a foot of the intruder. Defeated and clearly upset, the seal pushed himself off the ledge and landed in the ocean with an almighty splash. He instantly disappeared beneath the surface.

With a heaving chest and an adrenaline rush still raging through his body, Dwayne bent over and locked his hands on his knees to try and catch his breath. "Damn, that was close."

Tammy flopped into the deck chair close by, her legs limp like a jelly fish, her breathing heavy like Dwayne's. "Man, I've never seen a seal up close like that before. I can't get over how big he was. He was bloody massive."

Dwayne's panting began to subside and his demeanor began to soften. Raising his back, he released a cocky laugh. "Now do you see why I said not to feed the seals?"

"Yes. I'm sorry." Tammy gave him a flirtatious smile to strengthen her apology.

Feeling relieved from the departure of the seal, they headed back toward the cabin to attempt to go back to sleep, but they stalled when they heard Mitch's voice over the radio.

"Dwayne, everything okay over there? Do you copy?"

Dwayne said to Tammy, "Mitch probably heard everything. Sound carries over water. Let me talk to him real quick. He's probably wondering what all the commotion was about. I'll be right there."

Tammy nodded. "Okay," she replied as she headed down into the cabin.

"Hey, Mitch, I gottcha. Over."

"Hey, Dwayne, everything okay? I heard you guys hollering and making all kinds of noise. Are you guys having a domestic?" He laughed. "Over."

"No. A giant seal decided to pay us a visit on the boat. He's gone now. Tammy learnt the hard way about why we don't feed the seals. Over."

"Oh, man. Yeah, they're aggressive buggers. Glad everything's okay. Tell Tammy hi. I'm out."

"Sure will. Thanks for checking in. Over and out."

"Well, that was embarrassing," Tammy said from under the covers as Dwayne entered the cabin. "Now I'm gonna be the laughing stock of the fleet."

Dwayne joined her in the bed and gave her a comforting hug. "No you're not, silly. You're not the first one to feed the seals. Out here, everything is a learning curve. Through trial and error, we learn what to do and what not to do. And you've just had your first lesson on what not to do." He pulled her in closer. "Come over here and give me a kiss. We've got a big day tomorrow, so try and get some sleep and dream of thousands of lobsters crawling into our traps."

CHAPTER 34

*A*fter months of preparation and hauling gear across the ocean, Tammy was too excited to sleep. She knew she'd regret it tomorrow, but everything they had worked so hard for led up to the opening day. This is what it was all about, and the anticipation kept her awake most of the night. Afraid of waking Dwayne, who slept peacefully next to her, she lay motionless, staring at the berth's ceiling for most of the night and feeling anxious for the alarm to go off. When it finally did, she shook Dwayne's arm vigorously.

"Dwayne! It's time to get up. We get to go fishing today!"

Startled by her force, Dwayne was awake in seconds. "You're not excited, are you?" he said while rubbing his eyes and pulling himself to an upright position.

Tammy was wedged between the wall and Dwayne. The only way to get out of the bed was to either climb over Dwayne or wait for him to get up and move out of the way. "Come on, get up. I want to get dressed and get our snacks together."

Dwayne laughed at her enthusiasm. "Hold on a sec. Can I open my eyes first?" He chuckled while slowly pulling himself out of the bed.

In a dash, Tammy rolled out and squeezed past Dwayne while grabbing her clothes off the bench. "There's no room down here for us both to get dressed. I'm going on deck, it's still dark out so no one will see me."

"It wouldn't matter if it was broad daylight. Everyone's already seen you naked." He laughed again.

Tammy gave him a friendly slap across his shoulder before heading out to put on her clothes. Within minutes, she was fully clothed along with her slickers and rubber boots. "Are you dressed yet?" she hollered down to the cabin, throwing snacks and drinks into the ice chest on the little boat.

"Yes. I'm coming," he said with a giggle in his voice. "Damn, who needs an alarm clock when I have you?" Once on the deck, he grabbed his slickers and his boots and began putting them on. "What about coffee?" he asked while struggling with his boots.

"No time. I have orange juices and cereal bars on the dash of the *Little Boat*. We can eat those while on our way to our first trap."

Dwayne looked around the boat, checking to make sure they weren't forgetting anything. He had learnt to load the *Little Boat* with everything they would need the night before, which made the morning much easier. "Okay. I guess we're ready to go."

Not wanting to waste another minute, Tammy quickly jumped onto the *Little Boat* and began untying the lines while Dwayne fired up the motor.

"Let's go fishing!" Dwayne hollered as he pushed them off the *Baywitch*. Tammy beamed him a huge smile while scanning the harbor. All the deck lights shone brightly from the other boats and Tammy could see the crews preparing for their day. They were the first to leave the harbor, so she gave them a friendly wave as they drove by.

As they pulled out of the harbor, the waters were calm and the sun was just beginning to rise. "Nice day for fishing," Dwayne yelled from the wheel as Tammy stood close behind him with her gaff in hand, searching for the first buoy.

Within a few minutes, she spotted it. "There it is, at three o'clock." She pointed with her finger.

She grabbed it on the first try and wrapped the line around the puller. In turn, Dwayne worked the puller to bring the trap up to the boat. Peering into the clear water, Tammy squinted her eyes for a glimpse of the trap.

"Oh, the anticipation." She laughed while still looking. "I wonder if it has lobsters in it?" Suddenly, she jumped with excitement. "I see it. Here it comes." Within seconds, it was on the trap table, but to her dismay it was empty. "Not one bloody lobster," she moaned and looked at Dwayne with worry written across her face. "I hope they're not all like this."

While the boat was in idle, Dwayne pointed to the back. "Go ahead and bait it and stack it at the rear of the boat. We'll move it out deeper. There are obviously no lobsters here."

He waited until the trap was secured on the deck and Tammy had her hand on a rail before taking off toward the next one. The next two traps were identical to the first one, empty. Both traps were brought on the boat to be relocated, and Tammy and Dwayne rode in silence to the next one with looks of concern

It took a few minutes to reach it and with hesitation, they brought it onto the boat. Tammy squealed once it was on the table, as inside were a bunch of lobsters. "Yes! We got some."

"Halleluiah!" Dwayne cried while doing some sort of happy dance and reaching over to give Tammy a quick smooch.

Having never seen a lobster up close before, she opened the trap with caution.

"They look weird. They look like giant cockroaches."

"Hey! That's what we call them. We call them cockroaches of the ocean."

"I can see why." With the door of the trap now open, she leaned in to take a closer look. The bottom of the trap was covered with them. "Will they bite?" Then she noticed something. "I thought lobsters had claws and they pinch you. These don't have any claws."

"No, these are California spiny lobsters. They don't have claws; they have the long antenna instead, which they use as feelers. But see all the thorn-looking things on their back? If you get poked by one of those, it will sting for days. Always wear gloves when picking one up."

"I don't know if I want to," Tammy said with a hint of fear in her voice.

"It's easy once you know how. Here, I'll show you."

Tammy watched closely as Dwayne reached in and grabbed one with his gloved hand, touching only the shell part above the tail. As he slowly lifted it out of the trap, the lobster began flapping its tail, causing Tammy to jump back.

"That's another thing you've got to watch out for," Dwayne warned.

Once the lobster had calmed down, Tammy approached the trap again and watched as Dwayne reached over to the dash and grabbed some sort of metal gauge.

"What's that?" she asked.

"It's a measuring gauge. Every lobster must be measured, and I use this to make sure they are within the legal limit, which is three and a quarter inches. He moved in closer so Tammy could see what he was doing. Tammy watched as he placed the tool between the eyes and over its back, which was the shell part. He wriggled the gauge. "See this? There's movement. This is what we call a short. It goes back in the ocean." With one swift movement of his arm, Dwayne tossed it overboard.

"What?" Tammy protested. "You mean we can't keep all of these?"

"Nope," Dwayne said, picking up another lobster.

The second lobster was thrown back into the water too. "Okay, it's your turn. Try picking one up and handing it to me."

"Ugh. Really?" Tammy hesitated before reaching into the trap. "What if one pokes me?"

"Then you will be hurting for a few days."

After looking at the cluster of lobsters all piled on top of each other, she finally spotted one that she thought would be easy to pick up and slowly placed her fingers around the shell, like Dwayne had showed her. She was careful to avoid the needle-like thorns. "Here's one," she said softly while holding it loosely above the others, her arm still in the trap.

"Well, bring it out then," Dwayne said, chuckling at her nervousness.

In silence, her face scrunched and holding it far away from her body, she slowly raised it out of the trap. The lobster sensed the movement and began flapping its tail. Tammy screamed and held out her quivering arm. "Quick, take it! Before I drop it."

Dwayne laughed as he took the lobster and measured it. "Ahh, a keeper," he said as he tossed it into a barrel of circulating salt water.

"Finally!" Tammy sighed.

"Our first lobster," Dwayne said, wearing a huge grin. "Come on, hand me another one."

It didn't take Tammy long to figure out the correct way to pick up the lobsters or, as Dwayne kept calling them, *the bugs*. By the time they had emptied the trap, she was picking them up like a pro. Each time they got to keep one, she did a little dance across the deck, followed by a cheerful "Yes!" They counted thirty lobsters in the trap, out of which there were nine keepers. Dwayne said that was a good trap, but Tammy had expected there to be more.

Feeling pleased with the trap and their spirits now lifted, Dwayne decided to set the empties they had on the deck close by before heading off to the rest of the gear. As they drove to their next spot, Tammy noticed a sea lion following them. "Fuck," she said under her breath, secretly wondering if it was the same one that had paid them a visit on the boat. She took a quick glance at Dwayne to see if he'd seen it too, but he was facing the other way driving the boat. She waved with her arms and mouthed "Shoo!" at the seal. It didn't do any good, as the seal kept following the wake of the boat. Lost on what to do, she turned and simply ignored it in the hopes it would disappear by the time they reached the next trap. To her relief, it had.

Anxious to see what the rest of the traps held, they hustled all morning to get as many traps as they could pulled and rebaited by noon before taking a quick lunch break. They needed to get all one hundred fifty pulled by the end of the day. Leaving lobsters too long in the traps runs a high risk of other critters entering the traps and killing them. By midday, they had managed to pull sixty traps, just over a third of their gear, and they had close to three hundred lobsters. Dwayne was stoked.

"If we keep this up, we'll be out of the red in no time," he said while turning the motor off so they could drift and get a quick bite to eat.

"Sweet!" Tammy replied, now feeling more confident about this fishing adventure she was on. "You know, I've not heard anyone on the radio all morning," she said in between bites of her granola bar. "Every other day, it's been nothing but non-stop chatter all day. Today, nothing. Seems kind of odd, don't you think?"

"That's because the rest of the fleet, including us, have discovered their secret spots for lobsters. No one is going to come on the radio and ask how everyone is doing. Besides, fishermen never tell the truth and let you know how their catch is going. If they did, everyone would swarm their area." He let out a playful laugh. "We are all sworn to secrecy."

"Ha! That makes sense."

"Are you ready to pull more gear?" Dwayne asked after taking his last sip of Pepsi.

"You bet."

It took until sunset to pull the rest of the traps. Tammy and

Dwayne worked well together. Each knew their place on the boat and the tasks they had, making everything run smoothly. Dwayne held his position, driving the boat and working the hydraulics, while Tammy gaffed the line and wrapped it around the pulley. Once the trap was on board, it was up to Tammy to hand Dwayne lobsters to measure and then together, they rebaited the trap and threw it back overboard. Any empty traps, they'd stack until they found another fishing spot. After the last trap was pulled, even though Tammy was covered in fish goo and her feet ached from standing all day, she did her usual happy dance across the deck, which always amused Dwayne.

"Come here, beautiful," he said with his arms out. Tammy skipped over to him to meet his embrace. "You did great today," he told her before smothering her with kisses.

"Thanks. I had a really good time. But man, my body is sore. Please tell me we're done."

"Unfortunately not. Once we're back in the harbor, we have to clean the boat, cut bait for tomorrow and refuel the little boat using a hose. Oh, and we have to eat too."

"Well, looks like we'll be eating soup again tonight."

It was already dark by the time they were securely tied up next to the *Baywitch*, and they wasted no time getting back to work. Tammy noticed all the other boats were in and trailing behind their sterns were the lobster receivers, floating on the surface with their catch for the day. Tammy soon realized it would be a good way to see how much each boat had caught and grabbed the binoculars off the dash. She held them up to her eyes and counted the total number of receivers behind each boat. She saw Mitch on the *Sea-life* had the most with ten. "Damn, he did good," Tammy said while still checking out the other ones. Suddenly, she heard a commotion of flapping lobster tails and glanced over in Dwayne's direction. She saw he was putting their lobsters into receivers and making a train just like everyone else. "Need a hand?" she asked.

"Sure," Dwayne replied while struggling to get one of the

receivers overboard and into the water. In a snap, she returned the binoculars to the dash and rendered him some assistance. The count was good and Dwayne was thrilled. They had caught a total of five hundred lobsters and had eight receivers.

"How much is that worth?"

Dwayne gave her a big grin before answering. "Oh, about five thousand dollars."

"What! I don't make that much in a month, and we made that in one day? Yowza," she bellowed. "Now I really like this fishing thing." Stunned by the value of their catch, she couldn't believe how much these lobsters were worth. "Damn. And we have four more days of fishing before we head back in. This is un-fucking believable."

Dwayne stood before her and gave her a loving smile. He was thrilled to see her so happy. Not many women would have the stamina or enthusiasm that she constantly exuded. He truly admired her. "Well, we're off to a good start. But keep in mind we're about fifteen thousand in the red and we still need to make enough to get back out here. Let's hope the rest of the trip is just as good."

"Ugh. Damn. We still need to catch a bunch more lobsters. Well, you just burst my bubble. Come on, let's get our chores done. I want to cuddle up next to you and eat some soup."

"You got it. But first, give me a kiss, partner."

Tammy smiled and melted in his arms. She always felt safe with him, especially out here in the middle of nowhere. She admired his strength and his knowledge of boats and the ocean. She knew from experience that the seas could turn on you at any given moment, but she knew he wouldn't allow any harm to come to her.

As she sat close to Dwayne, finally in comfortable sweats and with a warm hearty bowl of soup nestled on her lap, she knew she was where she wanted to be. This would be her life from now on—Dwayne, boats and fishing. The only part of the equation that was missing was Matt. Being away from him tore at her heart. She thought of him in her sleep and kissed his picture good night before tucking it under her pillow. She couldn't be away from him for this amount of time again. Once he was home, he'd being staying home. Finding a way to come to the island and fish would be a challenge, but Tammy was confident they'd find a solution.

CHAPTER 35

*T*he intensity of the last few days was beginning to take its toll. Tammy and Dwayne were not the first to leave the harbor the next morning. They moved slow and were still tied up to the *Baywitch* an hour after the sun had risen. Tom, the captain of the *Lobster Fest* pulling up to their boat on his way out of the harbor, wearing a cocky grin and wasting ten minutes of their time, didn't help matters either.

"I see your woman is still standing," he said wearing a smirk. "How'd she do?" he asked Dwayne, who was busy making last-minute preparations on the *Little Boat*.

Tammy heard from the deck of the *Baywitch* and didn't like his sarcastic tone. "I did just fine, if you must know. I can't wait to get back out there." She placed her hands defiantly on her hips.

Tom looked surprised to see her and lowered his tone a notch. "Oh, I didn't see you there."

"Obviously," Tammy muttered under her breath.

"Well, I'm glad to see you're still with us. I'll have to check on you at the end of the week. Dwayne here might need help carrying you off the boat." He almost cackled.

"She's doing just fine. Stop giving her a hard time," Dwayne said with a hint of irritation to his voice.

Tammy marched to the rail of their boat, her hands still on her hips. "Why don't you go right ahead and do that?" She'd heard enough and waved him off before putting on her boots. "Have a good day," she added, her voice flat.

The rest of the morning couldn't have gone any better. Other than feeling somewhat fatigued, the fishing was going exceptionally well. They were catching just as many lobsters as the day before. That was until Dwayne suddenly yelled, "Fuck! I have no steering. My steering has gone!" He shut off the motor, feeling thankful they were not in shallow waters.

"What?" Tammy screeched, realizing they were dead in the water. "Now what?"

But Dwayne was already kneeling on the deck below the wheel to try and see if he could locate the problem. Tammy remained quiet and out of the way so he could concentrate. When he yelled the word "Fuck!" again, she knew he had found it.

"The steering cable is broken. We really are fucked!" He was clearly distraught.

Dwayne stood and looked out at the position of the boat, to make sure they weren't drifting too close to shore. He looked at Tammy, his face flushed with worry.

"Without steering, we can't pull the traps. I have to figure out a way to fix this. I don't have another cable, and we can't leave. We've not caught enough lobsters to get us out of debt and get back out here. What the fuck are we going to do?"

Tammy felt helpless. She knew nothing about the mechanics of a car, let alone a boat. "What about the *Baywitch*? Maybe we can get a tow from one on the other boats and use that to pull the gear."

"That's a great idea, except our traps are in too shallow for the *Baywitch*."

"Damn it!" Tammy said, now feeling the same frustrations and anxieties as Dwayne. She continued to think hard while Dwayne got on the radio and called Mitch to see if he had an extra cable, but he didn't. "Shit! We have to find a way to pull our gear in this boat," Dwayne said in a somewhat panicked state. He went to the back of the boat and sat on the hood of the motor, sliding his butt from side to side while pushing down hard at the same time.

"What are you doing?" Tammy asked with a puzzled look.

A smile appeared on his face, making Tammy feel a little more at ease. "I think I can steer the boat this way."

Tammy looked in the direction of the helm. "But the throttle and everything is up front. How can you work those from back there?"

Again, he smiled, but this time it suggested he had a plan. "I can't. But you can."

"Me?" she screamed, unable to hide her shock. "Now hold on a second. Let's talk about this."

"Come on. We can do this. In fact, we don't have a choice. I can sit back here and steer just like I showed you, and you can work the throttle, reverse and neutral from the helm."

Tammy began pacing the small deck. "That's the craziest thing I've ever heard. Driving across the ocean was easy. I didn't have to use reverse or neutral. But this is totally different. I have no idea what to do when we pull up to a trap."

"You don't have to. I will tell you from the back of the boat."

Tammy shook her head. "I don't know, Dwayne. I'm not sure if I can."

Eager to try his idea, he quickly stood and walked toward the helm. "Only one way to find out." He fired up the motor and motioned Tammy to come up to the wheel. "Come stand here and wait for my instructions."

Again, Tammy shook her head as she watched Dwayne take a seat on top of the motor again.

"Okay, put the boat in forward and go slow. You are my eyes. So when you see the next buoy, slow down some more and we will try and approach it. You are also going to have to gaff it and bring it on the boat. I'll come help once the trap is on board."

"Okay," Tammy groaned reluctantly. "I'll do my best." Once the boat was moving, Tammy scanned the ocean for their next buoy and spotted it within a few minutes. "I see it at two o'clock," Tammy yelled while pointing with her finger. Dwayne sat up as tall as he could and saw it too.

"Okay, slow the boat down and ease over there, and when I say reverse, don't hesitate. Just do it."

Tammy felt the palms of her hands beginning to sweat as she eased the boat towards the buoy, waiting for his command. When they were within a few feet of the buoy, Dwayne yelled, "Reverse!"

Tammy did it on cue while Dwayne steered the boat with his butt. It looked like a tough job to get it to move. The engine was heavy and bulky and he had to push down really hard while moving his hips in the direction he wanted the boat to go. By some sort of miracle, they were on the trap. "Okay! Neutral!" he yelled.

Again, she didn't waste a second and put the boat in neutral. She knew what to do next, and grabbed the gaff and hooked the line on the first try. Next, she worked the puller and brought it up on the boat. It was full of lobsters. "We did it!" she squealed, planting a big kiss on Dwayne's cheek as he approached the trap table.

"I knew we could! But I don't know about pulling like this all week. You'd have to do everything until I get to the trap table and my butt will be killing me by the end of the day."

"I'll be fine," Tammy said, handing him a lobster like she'd been doing it for years.

For the rest of the day, they had no choice but to pull the traps that way. It was slow going and they only managed to pull a hundred twenty traps. That meant whatever lobsters were left in the traps overnight were at risk of being killed by other critters. This was a concern. They could be losing money while they slept.

On the way back into the harbor with a good day's catch, Dwayne was quiet, deep in thought, trying to think of an alternative method. Mitch checked in over the radio, asking how it went and had a good laugh once Dwayne told him what they had to do.

Over dinner that night, consisting of Denny's Beef Stew, they thought hard about their dilemma. They wouldn't be able to get the boat fixed until they were back at the mainland, and there was no way they could cut their trip short.

"There has to be an easier way," Dwayne said, thinking out loud while deep in thought. Tammy didn't have a clue. Unfortunately, if there was another way, it was all up to Dwayne to figure it out. "The hardest part is moving the damn engine with my butt. If there was another way to steer it from the back, it'd be a lot easier." He turned to face Tammy. "You're doing fine on the throttle." Suddenly, his eyes lit up and he quickly rose from his chair. "I know. I have a long, thin piece of metal below the motor that acts as a kelp knife." He mulled over his plan in his head before continuing. "If I can somehow attach that to the base of the motor, I can use it like a tiller."

"A what?"

"A tiller. It's a long stick. You normally see them on dinghies and small boats with engines. The guy will sit at the back of the boat and steer the boat with the tiller."

"Oh, yeah. Now I understand," Tammy said, nodding.

Dwayne was excited with his idea and was anxious to try it out, so, for the next thirty minutes, he struggled with trying to get the kelp cutter off from the motor and finding a way to bolt it to the motor like a tiller. Next, he wrapped the whole length of the metal bar in duck-tape to protect his hands from getting cut. "That should do it," he said, feeling proud of himself. "I guess we'll find out in the morning."

～

Dwayne's idea worked brilliantly. They managed to pull all the traps every day for the rest of their trip. Tammy struggled at times with the extra workload at her end of the boat but, as always, she pulled through like a champ. They had become the talk of the fishery. Word soon spread about how they were having to pull their gear, and within a day they had earned the upmost respect from all the other boats for their perseverance and ingenuity.

Each night, all the boats stopped by to ask how they were doing and to see if they needed anything. Remarkably, they now looked at Tammy with admiration. Not once did they hear her complain or whine. She was always upbeat and wore a smile.

Tammy noticed the change in them and wanted to show her appreciation for accepting her into the fleet. She knew how to get to a man's heart—through his stomach. So, on their last day, knowing the guys would be stopping by on their way in, she surprised them each with a plate of grilled chicken, mashed potatoes and carrots. She knew none of these men had had a home-cooked meal all week, and it was worth the extra effort and hassle of cooking on the boat just to see their beaming smiles when she handed them the plate. In fact, it was also the first cooked meal Dwayne and Tammy had eaten. It made a nice change from a can of soup.

They left the next morning for the mainland, happy and content with over three thousand pounds of lobsters, worth about twenty-seven thousand dollars. When Dwayne told her the dollar amount, Tammy felt like she had just won the lottery. "Holy fuck!" she squealed. "I've never seen that much money at one time. That's more than I make in a friggin' year!"

Nothing could dampen their sprits. They'd pulled through and had a successful trip. They would soon be out of the red and catching lobsters for more profit. Tammy was excited about their future together. They would be back home for just a few days to fix the *Little Boat*, refuel, restock on bait and supplies and call their boys before heading out to do it all over again. Tammy couldn't wait.

CHAPTER 36

Over the next six weeks, Tammy and Dwayne fished hard, and it was grueling to the point of exhausting. It took a toll on Tammy, but she was determined to be successful and to prove not only to herself but to the rest of the fleet that she could do anything she set her mind to. Not only had it made her a stronger woman but it had also strengthened the relationship she had with Dwayne. They had built a foundation together. They were a team, having been put to the test so many times while living out at sea on a fishing boat for weeks at a time. In such a short time, she had embraced the life of commercial fishing, learning as much as she could about the industry while at the same time, falling deeply in love with Dwayne.

Since beginning this journey, she had noticed huge changes in herself, both physically and mentally. She found living and working on the ocean was a great therapy, especially when she had only recently decided to quit drinking. She no longer had the cravings for alcohol that had haunted her for such a long time. But she was also aware that the addiction would always be a part of her and could well be triggered at any given moment in her life. But, as

Dwayne had said numerous times while giving her words of encouragement to stay sober: *"As long as you don't pick up that first drink, you'll be okay. If you do, it's all downhill from there and you'll have to start all over again."*

Tammy was the fittest she'd ever been. Her arms and legs had defined muscle tone from hauling heavy gear daily, and her abs clearly showed a six pack. Being exposed to the intense rays of the sun while out on the ocean, her skin had become tougher and deeply tanned. Her hair was no longer a rich red color; the sun had bleached it to a natural strawberry blond.

But, unlike the rest of her body, there were some downsides to her newly acquired life. Her hair and hands had suffered the consequences of direct sunlight and being in salt water for days at a time. She couldn't remember the last time she'd styled her hair. It was dry and brittle and hung loosely around her face. And wearing make-up had become a distant memory. Her hands had constant sores and cuts, and blisters were a major problem, taking weeks to heal because of continually being around salt water and heavy equipment. Without fail, no matter how well she tried to protect it, the wound would somehow re-open while working. The skin on her hands was tough and chapped like a walrus. Her nails were no longer painted and manicured. All of them were short, broken or chipped, and feeling the pain of torn cuticles was a daily experience.

Solitude also came with her new lifestyle, which stirred some mixed emotions for her. Dwayne was the sole person she shared her life with. They were with each other twenty-four hours a day, doing everything together. She'd never had a relationship like that before. She no longer had to suppress her feelings behind alcohol, because she knew she could tell Dwayne anything. And the best part was, he'd listen.

While alone on the boat together, they had spent hours curled up in the berth or beneath the stars under a blanket talking about anything that came to mind. Tammy soon realized that being with a loved one, adrift at sea for many days at a time did wonders for a relationship. Tammy really felt like they knew each other.

But she also realized she had made many sacrifices and neglected those that used to be in her life. Being away from Matt troubled her the most. Even though he always sounded happy on the phone and couldn't wait to tell her about his week, the phone call always ended with Tammy having a huge sense of guilt and crying on Dwayne's shoulder for the next hour. She knew, once he was home, she'd never be separated from him again for such a long period of time.

Because her father and Joanne were taking care of Matt, they were still a part of her life too. When she called, she always talked to them first, giving them updates on their trips and any adventures that may have occurred. She could tell her dad enjoyed listening to her stories and she sensed the pride in his voice when he spoke. But she had failed to keep the rest of her family involved.

Each trip out to the island was done with such a quick turnaround that they only spent a few days on the mainland. Tammy would often let too much time pass before calling her sisters or mother, excusing it by telling herself she'd call them on the next trip in. But weeks would go by before that happened, and she felt the distance between them when she finally did call.

Her mother's sentences were short and cold and she often used harsh words. She expressed how sad she was that she couldn't watch her grandson grow up. *"I used to love getting pictures of him. Now I don't even get those anymore,"* she had said. She would also bring up Tammy's sister. *"When was the last time you three girls were in the same room together? It's been years, Tammy. Sisters shouldn't be that far apart from one another."*

Tammy felt the knife twist as her mother continued to fuel the guilt she was already feeling. She never contested her mother's words; Tammy knew she was right. She and her sisters had drifted apart and none of them were doing anything about it.

"When was the last time you saw Donna?" her mother had asked.

Tammy had calculated the time in her head and knew it had been months, but she didn't admit it to her mother. Before hanging up the phone, her mother had ended the call with an unusual request that stuck in Tammy's head. *"My last dying wish is to have all my three girls together in the same room. Is that too much to ask?"*

"No, Mom. It's not," Tammy had replied in a solemn voice.

She used to call her mother at least twice a week and send her pictures of her grandson in the mail every month. She hadn't called her in over two months and couldn't remember the last time she sent her photos. Her mother had every right to be upset with her.

It'd been almost three years since she last saw her. She had come over with the help of her dad for two weeks when Matt had just turned one, and she had stayed with Tammy and Judy at that house they had shared. Tammy had had good intentions of travelling to England with Matt the following year, but she had always struggled with money and with her finances, it just wasn't possible. Her mother refused to ask John for any more help and said she would somehow make it out on her own, but that hadn't happened yet either.

After receiving a reality check from her mother, Tammy spent some extra time at the phone booth and called Donna, only to receive another blow and have more feelings of guilt added to what she was already suffering.

Over the phone, Donna told her that she and Jason had eloped and had recently gotten married in Las Vegas. Tammy felt like she had been kicked in the stomach. *"I tried paging Dwayne to let you know. I was hoping you guys could join us and be at the chapel. But you were probably out on the boat again, as usual. I really hate not being able to call you,"* Donna had said. *"We use to call each other all the time."* Tammy listened with a heavy heart as she wiped away the tears of guilt that were beginning to roll down her cheeks. *"I miss my nephew too. I can't believe he's all the way in Florida,"* Donna had added.

Tammy had no words, just apologies. After everything they had been through together, she should have been present at her sister's wedding. She had missed both Donna's and Jenny's special days, a momentous time that all siblings should share.

Thoughts of Jenny had a clouded her mind as she listened to Donna's complaints. She hasn't seen Jenny in almost eight years. It saddened her to admit that she no longer knew her as a person. Neither one had made the effort to call. The cost of long distance calls was the main factor, and now that her only way to make any kind of call was via a phone booth, it was impossible to call England.

Sisters were supposed to know everything about each other. Tammy didn't even know what Jenny's favorite food was or what hobbies she had. She knew nothing about her husband or their two children. The only thing she had were a few photos that may as well have been the store-bought ones that come with new picture frames, filled with the faces of strangers.

Once she started thinking about her now distant relatives, not to mention her long-lost friends, she found herself adding to the list and right away, Judy came to mind. They had been best friends for years, raised each other's kids together and without fail they had always had each other's back. Tammy hadn't talked to her since she moved out of the house and decided she would try calling her after hanging up the phone with Donna.

She was surprised she still remembered the number. Then again, it used to be her number too. After several rings, a recording came on. *"The number you are trying to reach has been disconnected or is no longer in service."* Tammy hung up the phone with a knot in her stomach. Tammy wondered if Judy had moved. The only way to find out was to call the restaurant where they had both worked. Not giving it a second thought, Tammy picked up the handset of the phone, dug into her pockets for a few more quarters and tried calling the restaurant. A voice she didn't recognize answered the phone and after inquiring about Judy, she was informed she no longer worked there. Tammy was now numb. The one voice she was counting on for some sort of reconnection with her past had slipped away.

Tammy wondered how she could've allowed this to happen. How did she allow those closest to her to become so distant? And how was she going to fix it? It was impossible for her to drop everything and fly off to England for a visit. Even though she and Dwayne had had a good first six weeks, money was still tight after catching up with the mounds of bills, making unexpected repairs on the two boats and paying for fast turn-around trips.

The trips to the island were beginning to wind down. The catch was fewer and soon the ocean would become fierce with the winter storms, making it impossible to fish.

On the last two trips, they began bringing some of the gear home and setting it off the coast of Malibu where they would fish the rest of the season. The fishing wouldn't be as intense. They only needed to pull the gear every three days because, unlike the island, there wasn't a threat of other critters eating the catch. Another upside to fishing Malibu was it was only a thirty-minute boat ride from the dock, not nine hours, and they could be pulled with the *Little Boat* without lugging a week's worth of supplies in the *Baywitch*. This meant Tammy could stay on the *Baywitch* with Matt while Dwayne went fishing alone for three days a week. Of course, there was also the option of taking Matt with them.

She could also begin making crab traps while on the mainland. Lobster season would be ending in March, and for the first time, Dwayne was going to try and fish year-round by fishing for crabs off Malibu during the off-season of lobsters. But the fishing required a different trap, so Tammy eagerly volunteered her assistance in the building of them.

But there was a downside to fishing for lobsters off Malibu— the catch wasn't as plentiful as out at the island. Even though they would be letting the traps soak for three days between each pull, they wouldn't catch as much as a one day at San Clemente Island.

Tammy knew she needed to make some adjustments in her life, and that would begin with Matt when he was finally home in just a few days.

With the fishing winding down for the Thanksgiving holidays and Christmas and with most of the gear now in Malibu, Dwayne and Tammy were taking two weeks off and spending it with their sons.

Since being back on the mainland for the past few days, Tammy has spent most of her time scrubbing the *Baywitch* from top to bottom in preparation for Justin's visit and Matt's return home. Really, she was trying to keep busy to mask over the nagging guilt that haunted her. And the fact that she had spent far too much money on gifts for the two boys, from new bikes to skateboards and fishing rods.

Living by the beach in California had its advantages. They could pretty much camp anytime of the year and it was decided when the boys were home, that's what they'd do for a week. They needed to reconnect and be a family again.

CHAPTER 37

 hen the day finally arrived to pick Matt up from the airport, Tammy was beside herself with excitement. She wanted everything to be perfect for the boys. She bought new sheets for the area where they'd be sleeping, which was where the table was in the cabin. Amazingly, it folded down into a double bed. The little cupboard space they had and the fridge were filled with every kind of fun kid food imaginable. Rows of stuffed animals, which Dwayne had never seen on his boat before, lined the benches, and new clothes were squished and hung between theirs in the tiny closet. It would be cramped on the boat with all four of them, but Tammy and Dwayne didn't care—even though that was one of the reasons they decided to go camping. What mattered was they would be with their boys.

They took Tammy's car to the airport so the boys could ride in the back. They would be picking up Justin after they had collected Matt. When they pulled into the busy terminal, Tammy was reminded of the time she'd said goodbye to her mother after her last visit, and before that it was when she had reunited with her sister Donna after she had been missing for over five years.

Curled up next to Dwayne, with his arm hung over her shoulder, Tammy thought back to the emotional day of seeing Donna and how close they soon became, just like two sisters should be.

She thought back to saying goodbye to her mother and how much she took her for granted. She had no idea that three years and more would pass before she would see her again.

Tammy must have been reminiscing for some time because she hadn't realized the car was in idle, parked in their parking spot. "Hey, are you okay?" Dwayne asked, noticing her misty eyes.

Tammy dabbed at her face while sitting up and taking notice of their surroundings. "Yeah, I'm fine. This place just brings back memories of Donna and my mom."

Having talked for hours with Tammy about her reunions with her family members, Dwayne understood completely and pulled her back into his arms. "Oh, sweetheart, come here," he said, wiping a tear that had escaped. "You'll see them again soon."

"I know. It's just hard," Tammy said, fighting back her tears. Determined not to let her son see her upset, she shook her head to compose herself and wiped her face one more time before leaning in and giving Dwayne an affectionate kiss. "I love you. Now come on, let's go get Matt." Saying his name made her smile.

"I can't wait until both boys are riding in the back seat."

"Me neither," Tammy said while stepping out of the car.

Once inside the busy terminal, Tammy firmly holding hands with Dwayne, they checked the screen detailing all the flight information and saw Matt would be landing on time in about half an hour. Tammy glanced at her watch, synchronizing hers with the screen. "This is going to be the longest damn thirty minutes of my life," she whispered into Dwayne's ear as they made their way through the crowds and toward the arriving gate.

Unable to find two vacant seats, they stood arm-in-arm, mesmerized by the vast number of people around them and things one normally doesn't pay attention to unless standing idle for a stretch of time. They looked at the clothes people were wearing, their nationality, the language they were speaking and where they were going. Typical airport idle time.

Tammy lost count of how many times she checked her watch and each time only a few minutes had gone by, until finally, she heard the announcement of Matt's flight. Tammy squealed, "He's here!" and beamed Dwayne a radiant smile before giving him a big smooch.

Unable to stand still, she began tapping the ground with her feet as she anxiously waited for Matt to be escorted off the plane by one of the stewardesses. With her eyes pinned on the passengers walking through the gate, Tammy was once again reminded of the time she stood in the same airport waiting to be reunited with her sister.

After what seemed like an eternity passing by, Tammy finally saw her little boy being led by the hand of a middle-aged blond stewardess. Consumed with excitement and desperate to hold him, Tammy broke away from Dwayne's arms and squeezed her way through the people standing in front of her.

Waving her arms, she yelled, "Matt!"

But he was still too far away and her voice was lost in the crowd.

Dwayne finally reached her and used his louder masculine voice. "Matt!" he yelled while also waving his arms.

This time, Matt heard his name and began searching the mass of people before him.

Tammy waved her arms again. "Matt, over here."

Matt followed the direction of her voice and with a huge smile that melted Tammy's heart, he pointed in her direction while talking to his chaperone. Tammy hugged her chest as her eyes flooded with tears of joy. The stewardess saw her and Dwayne, smiled and waved and started walking towards them.

When there was ten feet between them, Tammy stopped and knelt, holding her arms out wide. Matt tore away from the stewardess's hand and raced towards Tammy, screaming at the top of his lungs, "Mommy!"

Tammy yelled back, "Matt! Come here, big boy."

Within seconds, he was in her arms. Tammy wrapped him tight, kissing him over and over across his face. "Oh, sweetie. I've missed you so much," Tammy cried, unable to control her tears. She couldn't help noticing how much older he looked. She held out his arms and smiled between her tears. "You've gotten so big. Look at you." And then she quickly pulled him back in. "Oh, I love you so much."

"I love you too, Mommy." And then he looked up at Dwayne. "Hi Dwayne."

Dwayne gave him a big smile before scooping him up in his arms. "Hey buddy. We've missed you. Have you got a high-five for me?"

Matt raised his hand and giggled before slapping Dwayne's palm.

While Matt was amused in Dwayne's arms, Tammy wiped her moist cheeks and shook the stewardess's hand. "Thank you for taking care of him."

"Oh, my pleasure. He's a very sweet boy. We enjoyed having him." She handed Tammy a piece of paper. "I just need to see your ID and have you sign this."

"Oh, sure," Tammy said, rooting through her purse for her wallet.

Once all the official business was done, Dwayne and Tammy thanked the stewardess again and Matt waved goodbye before all three of them headed to the car.

On the drive to pick up Justin, Tammy sat in the back seat with Matt, holding his hand tight while she listened to all his stories about his stay with Grandpa. His vocabulary was so much better, and he told her he was reading books too. In the few short months that he had been away, Tammy noticed how much he had grown up. Next year, he would be starting school. *Where has the time gone?*

Juggling fishing and having Matt in school was going to be a struggle, but she and Dwayne would somehow make it work.

As soon as they pulled up to Justin's house, they saw the front door open wide and Justin come running out yelling, "Daddy!"

Tammy leaned forward and squeezed Dwayne's shoulder. "There's your boy. Go get him. I'll wait in the car with Matt."

Dwayne turned his head and gave her a peck on the lips. His eyes misty, he whispered, "I'll be right back."

Tammy stepped out of the car, leaned against the hood with her arms folded and enjoyed the scene before her of Dwayne finally hugging his son. From inside the car, she heard Matt yell, "Justin!" It warmed Tammy's heart to know Matt remembered him and missed him too. Together, the four of them were a family. Matt looked up to Justin as his big brother, Dwayne treated Matt like his own son, and Tammy mothered them like they were both her own.

With her family now established, Tammy knew she needed to fulfill her mother's only wish. Those precious words entered her head again as Dwayne picked up Justin's backpack, took his hand and walked him back to the car.

"My only wish is to have all three of my girls together in the same room..."

ABOUT THE AUTHOR

ABOUT THE AUTHOR

Tina Hogan Grant loves to write stories with strong female characters that know what they want and aren't afraid to chase their dreams. She loves to write sexy and sometimes steamy romances with happy ever after endings.

She is living life to the fullest in a small mountain community in Southern California with her husband and two dogs. When she is not writing she is probably riding her ATV, kayaking or hiking with her best friend – her husband of twenty-five years.

www.tinahogangrant.com